SIREN

THE SIREN SERIES BOOK ONE

HANNAH WEST

Tethered Press

INFORMATION FOR READERS

This title was previously published in 2016. It has undergone an extensive rewrite and contains new content, though the story is the same.

ACKNOWLEDGMENTS

An enormous thank you to everyone who has helped with this
incarnation of *Siren*.
My husband for loving me fiercely.
Neil J Hart for the gorgeous cover art.
Katie and Shaun for their unwavering support.
Luke for his in-depth notes and knowledge of fantasy.
Beth for stepping out of her genre to read mine.
And Anne Loschuk for helping me so much with so many of my
manuscripts. Without your encouragement, most never would've
made it to publication.
And to every single one of my readers, for helping make this modest
dream a reality.

 Created with Vellum

For Darrell.

1

A nacho lands on the page I'm reading and I cut Helen a *look*. I eat the nacho and she smirks at my defiance.

'I've been calling your name for five minutes, Inara. Where the hell was that brain of yours?'

The nacho sticks in my throat and Helen's expression darkens. When I think of that night, my palms get sweaty.

'It wasn't your fault,' she says. 'He shouldn't have touched you.'

I look away, fingers curling around the hardback in my hands. 'Some people believe what he's been saying about me.'

'Being popular doesn't mean he has the right to touch you like that, Inara. Oliver got what he deserved and he knows it.'

I cut my gaze to hers. 'He deserved for me to break his hand?' I hadn't meant to do it but I was scared.

'I would've done worse to the pig.'

'I'm not like you, Helen.'

'You mean people expect that kind of reaction from me but not from you?'

'That isn't what I meant—'

'It's true, though. I'm an angry person and you aren't.'

'I don't regret what I did,' I admit. 'Maybe now he'll think twice about doing what he did to me, to somebody else. I just...hate the attention.'

'With a face like yours, you're *always* going to get attention, Inara. The fake glasses and ugly hats don't disguise your beauty. Just like hiding in the library at lunch doesn't make you invisible.'

'I don't go to the library to hide.'

'You love to read, I get it.'

'Do you?'

'No, I'll never understand your obsession with reading but I accept it's part of who you are, you ridiculous dork.'

'And I accept you for the angry little pixie you are,' I say.

She smiles. 'Exactly. You're my best friend and I'll always have your back.'

She throws another nacho and I snatch it from the air. 'Thanks.'

'Bloody cat-like reflexes,' she huffs.

'Thank you for coming tonight and for not telling my family about what happened, Helen.'

'Like I'd miss your birthday.'

'Do you think Oliver will go to the police about his hand?'

'And risk being reported for sexual assault? I heard he told his dad he injured it at rugby training.' She frowns. 'Are you sure you don't want to report him, Inara? He should be punished for what he's done.'

I shake my head. 'I heard he'll be lucky to regain proper function of his hand after it's healed. Some of his fingers might even remain deformed.' I look around my grandparents' snug for a change of subject and sigh, 'Pathetic way to spend my seventeenth birthday, isn't it?'

'Your grandma makes the best cakes I've ever eaten,' Helen scoffs, like it's nothing that she's my only friend at a quiet, family celebration.

'Did someone say cake?' Daniel asks poking his head through the doorway.

Helen blushes at the sight of my brother. She's been crushing on Daniel since she was thirteen but he sees her as a second little sister.

'Someone said cake!' Dad says following Daniel in.

Dad flicks off the lights and Mum hurries in with Grandma, carrying a cake. She puts it on the coffee table and everyone sings an out-of-tune rendition of *Happy Birthday*. I try not to laugh as I look around at the people I love.

Life has been crappy lately. Not just because Oliver got too touchy-feely and I crushed his hand, or that I've become a social pariah because of it. I've always been one but I'm okay with not fitting in. I'm always a bit *too* much of something to be accepted. Too beautiful. Too smart. Too quiet. Too weird. Nobody really wants me for a friend, though many have tried. Only Helen ever stuck around.

Lately, my life feels fragile, like it's made of thin glass and someone is throwing stones. I can't explain it, other than I'm waiting for everything to shatter.

'Make a wish,' Mum says.

I take a deep breath and blow out the candles.

2

Mum screams as the car swerves. I grip the cake box in my lap as the logo on the side of the lorry expands through the windscreen ahead.

I GROAN at the splintering pain in my head as I open my eyes to darkness. It smells like rust and diesel and I'm...compressed— caged; sharp edges poking at my bruised flesh.

'Hello?' I rasp, throat raw like I've been screaming.

There's the sound of hissing and of liquid dripping but no response to my call. Panic joins the painful haze in my head as I remember what happened. A lorry hit our car and I'm trapped in the wreckage. I remember Mum's scream and the crunch of metal. I rasp her name, wondering if she's hurt, if she's...

Heat, like the warmth from drinking hot tea, bleeds through my middle. I try to look at my chest in the cramped space but it's too dark to see. It burns hotter and grows concentrated, like a ball of fire in my ribcage. It gets steadily more uncomfortable then, turns suddenly searing. My insides start to blister and I scream.

The inferno eats a pathway through my flesh and I writhe and twist in white-hot agony. My spine tries to bend at an unnatural angle then releases a series of crunching pops. My screams soak the cramped space in response, until my voice is hoarse and the lava in my chest feels like it cracks open. I gag as blood surges up my throat, spraying my face and neck with copper. I gasp and cough between retches, until I'm too oxygen deprived to stay conscious.

Squealing metal wakes me and I sob in relief that the pain is gone. The wreckage rocks and it takes a few seconds for my aching brain to register that someone is out there, trying to save me.

'Here,' I rasp. 'I'm here!'

Eery quiet, follows my call for help like the emergency crew heard me and are listening for more. The metal around me rocks, keening and crunching under whatever device is being used to cut me free. Cool air hits my baking scalp, as a hole opens above. I grit my teeth against the pain of twisting and reach for freedom. A strong hand clasps my wrist then drags me free. My body, screams in protest of the rough exit and sharp edges scraping my skin.

My rescuer releases me the second I'm free and I crumple at the loss of support. I hit the tarmac, breathing the crisp night air, as glass and debris bite into my palms. Each inhale is icy, my lungs still fringed in the heat from before. I press a hand to my chest then stare at my palm when it comes back slick with blood. It's in my hair and painting my face, and fear that I'm dying bleeds through me.

Glass crunches in front of me and I look up. Instead of a first responder, I find a boy around my age. Ice-blue eyes, dark hair and... My gaze rakes over his odd attire, before catching sight of the wreckage behind him. The wreckage he just pulled me from.

I glance down at myself, confused at how I could fit inside that twisted lump of metal. I should be missing limbs or be a pile of mush. My gaze pans the road, looking for the rest of the car. Burning debris litters both carriageways, leading to the overturned lorry. There aren't any other chunks of metal or...bodies.

I push onto shaking legs and stumble over to the crushed remains of the car. 'Mum? Dad?' I touch the distorted metal. It's hard and jagged beneath my fingers and my voice turns reedy, 'Daniel?'

I stare at the puddle of blood and diesel, staining my trainers. It's too much blood to be from one person, and realisation sucks the air from my lungs. They're gone. My family are...gone.

The boy says something and I turn his way, heartbeat loud in my ears. I wipe tears from my vision then blink at the angry distain in his gaze. His startling eyes glare at me with so much hate, I physically recoil. He tracks my movements as I back away then appears right in front of me. I yelp in surprise because I never even saw him move.

'W-what do you want?' I rasp.

A glint of metal, catches my eye and I stare at the long, silver sword in his right hand.

A. Sword. A freaking *sword!*

My body convulses as if in response to that razor edge. Agony ripples across my shoulders and I drop onto my knees. I puke blood onto the tarmac by his feet, as my spine releases a series of crunching pops like before. Just like inside the wreckage, my vertebrae try to twist at an unnatural angle and I scream.

I pant on the ground when the pain ebbs and try to wipe blood from my chin. I'm painted in crimson, coppery liquid dripping from my skin. The boy glares down at me, disgust and fury, drenching his expression. He clips something vicious-sounding in a language I don't recognise then raises his sword in both hands above me.

I roll left and his sword whispers against my back. It strikes the ground where I'd been kneeling with a resounding crack. I glance over my shoulder and stare at the sight of him trying to yank it from the tarmac. Who the hell is this guy?

Sirens sound in the distance as I shove to my feet. I stagger away from the lunatic with the sword, limping towards the blinking blue lights. I pray they'll reach me before I'm impaled by some crazy nut with a medieval weapon. My spine cracks at the thought and I whimper as I force myself forward.

I make it around the overturned lorry before someone grips my hair. The ice in my middle rushes forward, sharp and focussed; like the night Oliver assaulted me and I crushed his hand. I ram my elbow backwards and a satisfying grunt sounds behind me. The boy releases my hair but grabs my wrist before I even make it a step.

My wrist snaps as I twist to face him and I scream. His gaze shifts from my face to the approaching emergency vehicles and he drags me to the fields lining the road. I glance from his unyielding grip, to the darkness of those fields and fresh fear blasts through me. I *know* if I let him drag me in there, I won't come out alive.

I lash out with my free hand, fingernails raking crimson grooves down his face. He has both my hands in a steely grip before I can blink and I hiss in renewed pain. His lips curve at the sound and I realise, he's enjoying this.

'Why are you doing this?' I sob.

He snarls in my face like an animal, before his gaze snaps from mine and a low, vicious growl sounds in his throat. I follow his glare to a man climbing from the cab of the lorry. The maniac releases his hold on me and is gone before I can fully turn back to him. I scan the road but he's nowhere, though I feel the weight of his gaze on my skin.

I back away from the fields then hurry to the lorry driver. I cradle my injured wrist to my chest as the dazed driver stares down at me. I stare back, as flashing lights fill the night around us.

3

Helen assesses me from the phone propped up on my dresser. Her hair is a coral colour this week, contrasting prettily with her rain-grey eyes. She looks like an anime character but she can carry it off.

'It's horrible,' she says.

I look down at the uniform in agreement. 'Aunt Gertrude says it hasn't changed since she went there.'

'What's with the socks?'

I tug at one of the woollen, knee-high socks. 'These are the winter socks. I can wear tights but they're woollen too and itchy.'

'Is your aunt there?'

'For you to shout at?'

'Someone needs to tell her.'

I smile at her outrage on my behalf. 'It's just a uniform, Helen. I'll live.'

'She isn't there, is she?'

My smile falters. 'She leaves for work early.'

'And gets home late.'

'She has a career and it isn't her fault she got dumped with me.'

'Don't say that, Inara.'

'It's true.'

'Has she said that to you?'

'Of course, not. Gertrude loves me. She stepped up when social care said Grandma and Grandad were too old to take me in.'

'Which is ridiculous! You're seventeen, not five.'

'Aunt Gertrude is kind but busy and I don't want to be a hindrance. In ten months, I'll have access to the insurance money and I'll be out of here.'

'Will you move back here?' Helen asks.

I look away. 'I don't know. It...it won't be the same.' *I'm* not the same and if I move back, Helen will find out.

'Helen, we're going to be late!' Amy shouts from somewhere off screen.

'I've got to go,' Helen says. 'Amy's dropping me at school. We'll chat tonight, okay?'

'Later,' I say.

'This conversation isn't over,' she adds then hangs up.

I grab my phone and head downstairs. Helen knows there's something going on with me but thinks it's just part of grieving. I spent the last hours of my birthday, sitting in the hospital while my family were being peeled from the remains of our car. The grief counsellor says my reactions are normal but she doesn't know everything that's been happening. Nobody does.

I glance at my left wrist, where the hand-shaped bruise used to mark my skin. It was the only injury I left the hospital with that night, even though I'd felt it snap in the crazy boy's grip. The doctor assured me it was just a sprain though and assumed the bruising was from a paramedic, pulling me from the wreckage. I didn't correct him because what would I say? A sword-wielding maniac tried to kill me? The doctor would've measured me for my straight jacket then and there.

I sigh as I make breakfast. Maybe I *am* going crazy. It all sounds so fantastical, so...unbelievable. I walked away from a car accident that killed my parents and brother. I've been in a daze since their funerals, going through the motions like I still care.

I rub the spot over my heart as the toaster pops, wondering if this agony will ever fade. My therapist says it will but how can it? I've lost everything that really matters and, as much as I know Gertrude loves me, her life would be easier if I'd just died that night too.

I eat my toast on the way to the bus stop. I hang back until the bus arrives then follow the line of students on. I tuck my hair behind my ears to make it obvious I'm wearing earphones as I find a seat. I sense the curiosity of the other students as I walk by. They want to know who I am. I push the glasses higher on my nose like they can shield me from the stares. They aren't prescription, just one of many pairs I brought to hide my face. I dig a woolly hat from my backpack and tug it over my hair then turn to face the window.

My reflection stares back from the dark glass: blonde hair, green eyes and smooth, creamy skin. I've got a small, narrow nose and pouty, cupid's bow lips, delicate jawline and high cheekbones. Even frowning, my beauty isn't marred. It's a curse, drawing the kind of attention that has made me a target for people like Oliver, my entire life. It's the reason Daniel taught me how to defend myself at age twelve, when boys really started to take notice.

People struggle to see past my appearance and the students at this school will be no different, so what's the point in trying to make friends? Nobody will live up to what I have with Helen anyway, which will crumble too when she realises, how broken I am. I'm not the same as before. There's a void in my middle now, a barren space where I hide my grief. Each day, it inches wider, consuming what's left of who I used to be. I didn't die in the accident but my spirit did. I'm just a shell now, with nothing left to give.

I look through my miserable reflection and meet the gaze of someone standing at the bus stop. He isn't wearing a school uniform, so it doesn't make sense that he's waiting at the school's designated stop. Dark jeans and a black shirt hug his tall frame. His broad shoulders are outlined by the tightness of his shirt and I frown at his lack of jacket. He must be crazy because it's freezing out.

Crazy...

I press closer to the glass to study him better. Piercing eyes glare back, like he doesn't care that I caught him staring. The breath jams in my throat as his features register. He's wearing different clothing and missing the sword but it's definitely him.

The hairs on my nape stand tall as we stare at each other. He doesn't look away, just watches with that fierce, unravelling gaze. I close my eyes, mentally count to three, then meet that electric glower once more. It's been nearly two months since the accident, since *he* saved me from the wreckage then tried to kill me. I'd started to think I'd imagined the whole thing.

A smirk tilts his lips and I narrow my eyes, feeding all of my grief into a glare of my own. I won't let him witness my fear, even as my heart pounds wildly in my chest. The bus doors close with a hiss and it pulls from the kerb. I refuse to break the stare-off and we glare at each other until he's out of sight.

I follow the other students into school, feeling like I've finally lost my mind. Am I hallucinating? Was there a boy at the bus stop? Nobody else seemed to notice him and, even without the armour and sword, he's noticeable. You'd have to be blind to miss how good looking he is, even with that wintry glare. He's like one of those marble carvings you see in museums.

I'm miles from where I used to live and it's been months since the accident. I was in shock that night and have been working through trauma since. This could be a manifestation of that trauma. My grief counsellor warned something like this could happen. Maybe if I tell her about the boy, she'll give me a way of working through it. Or admit me to a facility.

I go through registration then make my way to the back of my first class. The teachers are aware of what I've been through and have been really good in offering extra time to catch up. I haven't needed it. All that time I spent 'hiding' in the library has paid off, so I'm no longer behind on any of the work.

Chris smiles when I slide into my seat beside his. He's nice enough when he isn't openly staring at me and I actually like sitting with him. He's naturally built with muscle, which keeps the other boys away.

'Did you finish the assignment?' he asks.

I pull it from my bag. 'Ta-da.'

He flashes a wicked smile and taps the sheets of paper on the desk in front of him. 'Took me all night but your suggestions helped.'

'It might be easier to just do the assignments when they're set, instead of the night before they're due,' I say.

He shrugs. 'I work better under pressure. *I* can't believe you've done it when you've got the excuse of only having been here a few weeks. I heard Mr Bury say you didn't have to do this one.'

He did, but I have no life.

'I hope you all have this week's assignment,' says Mr Bury, sauntering between the aisles, holding out an expectant hand to each student.

'I was wondering,' Chris whispers and I eye his awkward expression. 'There's a party Friday night if you want to go?'

I bite my bottom lip to hide a grimace. Chris is nice to me but Oliver was nice to me and I can't risk being alone with another *nice* guy.

'I can't,' I lie. 'My aunt is really strict and doesn't let me go to parties.'

His hopeful expression falls. 'I understand.'

'Maybe some other time,' I say.

Some of the rejection eases from his face. 'Sure.'

I glimpse his profile as the lesson starts. He's got blond hair and warm brown eyes. His nose is slightly crooked but his smile has a mischievous edge that makes me want to respond in kind. I let myself wonder what it would be like to date him. What would happen if I actually opened myself to someone and they turned out to be what they seem?

I turn my gaze to the front in disgust and remind myself of each time I've been wrong. It's embarrassing how I can even contemplate trusting anyone, after all the times I've been betrayed. There's something about me that seems to...lure people in then strip them of their reserve. It always starts off so nice, like with Chris now. Then I end up somewhere alone with them and they suddenly don't understand the meaning of the word no.

The remains of my heart won't take any more hits. Daniel and Helen aren't here to run to and I'm not strong like either of them. *Daniel...* I used to go to him with my problems and it's difficult to accept I'll never hear his voice again. Grief wells in my chest, so I push him from my thoughts and concentrate on the lesson. I help Chris navigate some of the questions about the set text and the grief fades back to the periphery of my mind.

Halfway through the lesson, a familiar itch crawls across my shoulders. I flinch in recognition of what's coming then wince as the first sliver of pain licks my throat. Sweat beads my nape as tangy liquid floods my throat.

Chris glances my way when I gag. 'Are you okay?'

I slap a hand over my mouth and jerk to my feet. My chair topples backwards and Chris calls my name, as I bolt from the room. I've learned I can't stop what's about to happen, so need to be out of sight when it does.

The pain hits hard as I crash through the door of the girls' toilet block. My spine releases several loud cracks as I push into the nearest cubical and retch blood and breakfast into the toilet. The door opens behind me on my second heave. A girl I don't know gags then says she'll tell Mr Bury I'm being sick. She darts back into the hallway like her feet are on fire and I sag in relief.

I flush the toilet then sit on the floor to catch my breath. Another girl comes in a moment later and asks if I'm okay. I offer a weak smile then push to my feet and go wash my hands and face. She lingers behind me then hands me some paper towels. I thank her as I take them with shaking fingers then use them to dry my face. She hands me my backpack outside the school nurse's office.

'Thank you,' I murmur.

She smiles. 'I'd better get back to class.' She hesitates, like she wants to say more, then sighs, 'Feel better soon.'

I stare after her before pushing into the nurse's office. I hand her the slip from Mr Bury then tell her I've got cramps, so she won't automatically send me home. She offers to call my aunt but I tell her I feel much better. She makes me sit in the office for twenty minutes of monitoring then lets me leave.

Instead of going back to class, I head for the empty tennis courts. I slip through the gate then sink to the ground and sit out of sight behind the wooden panels along the bottom half of the fence. I hug my knees to my chest and think about what just happened. The attacks are getting more frequent and harder to hide. I know I should tell someone but part of me craves whatever's happening. I deserve to suffer like my family suffered, while I walked away with barely a bruise.

Footsteps disturb my musings and I turn my attention in their direction. They're getting closer, like someone knows I'm here. I hold my breath when the footsteps stop on the other side of the fence to me, wondering if someone saw me come in here. They're breathing heavy, like they've been running and my spine prickles with awareness. My lungs burn with the need to breathe but a niggling thought in the back of my mind warns me against it.

'Dammit,' a male growls after a moment longer and the footsteps hurry away.

I push to my knees and peer through the wire mesh topping the wooden fence panels. A tall, dark-haired figure is jogging away, towards the science block. I'm still squinting in his direction when he suddenly stops and spins back to my hiding place. I duck back behind the fence and glance around for an escape route, heart racing. Even from this distance, I recognise the cut features of the boy from the bus stop.

His footsteps grow loud again, until he's right back on the other side of the fence. I press my spine to the panelling and hold my breath. Long, tanned fingers appear above me, gripping the meshing until the knuckles bleach. He inhales a deep breath, like he's trying to scent something. I close my eyes at the thought, heart beating such a wild tattoo I'm afraid he'll hear it. My shoulders start to cramp and I bite back a whimper, praying that my back doesn't crack.

The boy growls something that sounds suspiciously like a curse then the whole fence shudders, as if he's slammed something against it. Wood splinters rain over me and I fight the need to cry. The breath shudders out of me the moment his retreating steps fade. I sag against the fence then stare up at the fist-sized hole in the wooden panel above my head.

I catch my breath then sprint to my next class. A few people from my English lesson ask how I'm feeling and I pretend I'm not three kinds of terrified at officially having a stalker. One who can punch holes in fences and has an affinity for medieval weaponry.

I stick with the crowds for the rest of the day, pretending to like the attention it gains me so I don't find myself alone again. I'd rather pretend to be someone I'm not and fit in than risk meeting the pointy end of that sword again.

I spend the last lesson of the day pondering why a maniac is stalking me. I don't remember meeting him before the night of the accident and can't think of anything I did that night to offend him so much. Does he think I caused the accident somehow? Was there another car on the road and he lost someone too? I can't think of any other reason why he'd have tracked me down. It's all just too, ludicrous.

My spine prickles and I look around at the sensation. I'm learning to trust the instinct and it proves right once more, when my gaze lands on a familiar figure outside. He's sitting on the wall that borders the science block. His broad back is to me but I don't need to see that glacial gaze to recognise who it is.

Fear threatens to choke me at the sight of him. I think of him trying to skewer me to the asphalt and my insides liquify. He wants me dead, enough to track me across the country and it's terrifying.

The bell startles me and I look around at the other students packing away. When I look back through the window, the boy is gone. I snatch my things from the desk and stuff them into my bag, making sure I'm within the thick flow of students rushing to leave.

I'm just shy of the main gates when I see *him* there, waiting. I duck out of view before he can spot me and turn in the opposite direction. My back and shoulders throb as I hurry for the gate on the opposite side of campus. I swallow against a sudden rawness in my throat then grit my teeth against it. Before the accident, I never once suffered from a sore throat and now they're a daily ailment.

I reach the bus stop in time to watch my bus sail by. My heart sinks and I stare at the empty bus stop, contemplating waiting for the later bus. An image of my stalker flashes through my mind and I turn away to start the long walk home. I'd rather walk than sit here, waiting for him to find me.

I left my coat at school in the rush to leave, so tuck my hands under my armpits and hunker into my blazer for warmth. I keep glancing over my shoulder to make sure my stalker isn't there. It isn't until I turn onto Aunt Gertrude's road, that I let myself relax.

The street is deserted, except for a single runner in the far distance. The big houses look empty in the twilight, making me shiver in my blazer and pick up the pace. All I want is to get inside and lock the door behind me. I focus ahead but falter when I notice the runner is so much closer than before. I stare at him for a long second. His gait is fast-paced like he's sprinting.

Bright eyes come into focus and I shake my head in denial. It dawns on me that he knows where I live and I whimper. I try to calculate the diminishing distance between Aunt Gertrude's house and my murderous stalker and decide there's no way I'll makes it before he does. I back up a step then spin and run in the opposite direction.

He shouts in a thickly accented voice for me to stop but I push on faster. His pounding footsteps echo behind me, sounding out the closing distance between us. I round the corner at the end of the street, backpack sliding from my shoulder. I leave it where it falls, hoping he'll trip on it and break his pretty neck.

A hard body crashes into my back, knocking the air from my lungs as it slams me to the ground. Hot pain lances my skull when my head hits the pavement. Warmth trickles from my forehead as the boy crushes me against the concrete, pinning me in place with his heavy frame.

'Get off!' I pant.

Hissing fills the air, followed by heavy thudding like someone's chopping wood. Gravel scrapes my face as I'm shoved tighter against the pavement. It's a struggle to breathe, until the weight suddenly leaves me and I'm jerked onto my feet. I blink through dark spots in my vision then try to run but familiar vice-like fingers shackle my wrist.

'Don't make me break it again,' the boy growls down at me.

I twist in his grip despite his words. 'Let go!'

He yanks me close, pinning me against him with one strong arm then grips my chin in a bruising hold. He forces my face to the right, to the fence bordering the nearest house and snarls, 'Those were meant for you and I just saved your life.'

I stare at the thick, wooden poles jutting from the fence. They look like arrows but are the size of javelins, sharp points buried in the fence.

I jerk my face from his hold and glare up at him. 'What the hell are you talking about?'

Instead of answering, his gaze snaps to the fields across the road. His eyes narrow, expression darkening. He turns that glower on me and seems to assess me. He stops at my shoes then grumbles something in the same exotic language he used the night of the accident. Any doubts about him being the same guy, evaporate and I find myself assessing him back. More specifically, looking for a certain deadly weapon.

More hissing fills the air and the boy spins me to the left. Three more javelin-sized arrows thud into the fence behind where I'd been standing and I stare at them in shock.

'Oh my god,' I rasp.

'Come on,' he growls and jerks me into a run so fast it feels like I get whiplash.

I try to keep up but he's too fast. He doesn't stop or alter his pace to match mine, just grips my wrist tighter and drags me along for the ride. The image of those arrows buried in the fence, stop me from complaining about his rough treatment. Maybe he still wants me dead but, for now, he seems adamant about keeping me alive.

'W-why, is, this, happening?' I pant.

'Shut up and run,' he snarls.

Wants me alive but obviously still hates me.

Pain explodes through my right thigh, as my body is catapulted forward. I scream as my leg buckles but my face never meets the ground. The boy scoops me up without ever breaking stride, rips something from my leg and carries me bridal-style against his chest. His heart thuds against my ear as searing pain erupts through my thigh. Excruciating fire floods my body in its wake and I whimper at what's about to come. It's the same incendiary heat from the night of the accident: same phantom lava that's burned through me at least once a week ever since. It burns until I feel like I'm turning to ash and praying for it to just happen. Black spots invade my vision and I thank God for the encroaching darkness.

The boy jostles me back into awareness and snarls, 'Fight it!'

Our gazes meet and I'm surprised to find something other than distain. His eyes are alight with something that looks like regret.

'I don't want to fight it. I don't deserve to live.'

His surprise is the last thing I see before I pass out.

4

S tars and branches come into focus when I blink awake. I frown, wondering why I'm outside on the ground. My face is cold from the night air, each exhale fogging before my face, while my body is toasty warm. I'm wrapped in something and I run my fingers over the soft fabric. Not fabric, *fur*. I cringe at the thought and fight a gag as I try to get my bearings.

I'm on a woodland floor, wrapped in a fur blanket. A small fire is crackling not far from my right, casting eerie shadows along the tree trunks. My right leg is throbbing something fierce and my head feels fuzzy.

I push into a sitting position then cry out as severe pain shoots through my right thigh. I pant through gritted teeth until the pain ebbs enough to focus. My fingers shake as I try to pull the fur back to get a look at my thigh.

The boy materialises from the shadows, grips my shoulders and forces me onto my back. 'Don't move until morning,' he growls in thickly accented English.

'W-who are you? Where are you f-from?'

He fixes me with his signature glare, then huffs and stalks away. He goes to the fire, glares at me again then pulls a small blade from a sheath on his ankle and sits down. I stare at him in disbelief because, who the hell walks around with an arsenal of swords and daggers? He picks up a fuzzy lump from the ground and pushes the blade into it. The sound of tearing flesh comes a second later and I snap my gaze away in realisation.

Bile snakes up my throat as the sounds continue. Saliva pools in my mouth and I gag, before rolling onto my side to vomit. Fresh pain radiates through my thigh and tears bead my lashes.

As soon as I stop retching, a hand grips my shoulder and tries to force me to lie flat again. I turn to glare at the boy but notice the glossy wetness coating his hand. The rusty aroma registers a second later and I recoil from his touch. His hands are covered in the blood of whatever poor animal he was butchering and now it's on me.

'D-don't touch—oh god, the blood,' I turn away and retch onto the soil again.

The boy is staring at me intently when I finally slump onto my back, exhausted. He's looking at me funny, like I just confused the hell out of him.

'I told you not to move,' he says. 'Do you want your leg to heal, or would you rather be in pain?'

I look from him to my throbbing thigh and tug at the blanket again. 'What happened?'

His hands cover mine, stopping my efforts. Undiluted rage rolls through me when his skin touches mine. Somehow, I *know* the emotion belongs to him, I just don't know *how* or *why* I know it. This boy hates me with an intensity that steals my breath and fills me with paralysing fear. I'm frozen with it as he realigns my body. The stars and branches come back into view above and I try not to cry.

'You were hit,' he says once he's satisfied that I'm back where he wants me. 'Lucky for you, I got the arrow out but it shattered bone and now we must wait for you to heal.'

My mind blanks when I realise, he means I got hit with one of those javelin arrows. My shock dissolves into anger at his annoyed tone. He sounds so inconvenienced that I got shot, like it's my fault somehow.

'If I got shot, shouldn't I be in a hospital?'

'Remain still and you'll heal by morning.'

I baulk at his insane answer before remembering he's certifiable. Bones don't heal overnight. Desperation bleeds through me that I'm at his mercy and I try thinking of a way to escape. I need to get away before he turns that knife on me and it's *my* blood painting his hands.

'I'll be still if you go do that somewhere else,' I say. I look pointedly at the little mound of fur by the fire. 'Unless you want me to throw up again.'

Surprise then amusement light his face, like it's both shocking and hilarious that skinning an animal would turn my stomach. 'Fine.' He stalks to the fire and scoops up his kill, before disappearing into the darkness.

I hold my breath and listen for a long time, until I'm sure he isn't sitting just out of view, watching. I pull the blanket off and roll onto my side as a test, pretending to vomit. When he doesn't come running, I sit up and stare down at my injured leg. A homemade bandage covers my right thigh. There's a reddish starburst staining the fabric halfway up. I lean closer to get a better look and my eyes widen at the crusted texture of dried blood. The arrow must've gone right through.

It was real. All of this is...real?

But if I really was impaled by a javelin-sized arrow, shouldn't I be rolling around in agony, or passed out? Wouldn't I need at least some kind of medication to cope with the pain? I scrutinise my surroundings, contemplating whether any of this is actually happening. Maybe I'm in a coma and this is all just a nightmare. Either way, I still need to escape. I can't just sit here and wait for him to carve me up.

It takes a while to ease onto my feet then take an experimental step. I bite my fist against the scream that bubbles up my throat and my vision turns wobbly with tears. I cling to the nearest tree and pant through the pain, until it's tolerable enough to try again. I hop over to a long, thick stick and test it as a crutch. It alleviates the weight from my right leg enough for me to hobble and I take my chance to get away.

I limp through the trees, panting and shoeless, with no idea of where I'm going. It's dark and freezing and painfully slow progress. Within minutes, something warm and wet is snaking down my right leg. It soaks into my sock and I press my fingers to the bandage to find it drenched with blood.

My head spins and I lean against the nearest tree for balance, leg throbbing so much I want to curl up and cry. I wipe sweat and tears from my face and try to think of a better plan because this isn't working.

'Inara!' the boy yells from somewhere in the forest, enraged voice echoing and making it difficult to pinpoint.

I shove from the tree and stumble the way I'd been heading. I make it a few steps before my right thigh gives out with an audible snap. I hit the dirt, hard and bite back a scream, refusing to give away my location. I claw at the dirt instead, scoring deep groves into the forest floor.

My back gives a painful shudder then cracks, like it's trying to bend unnaturally again. My throat starts to burn, filling with something acidic. *Not again, not here.* Blood gushes up my throat and into my mouth. I cough against it, trying to breathe as it sprays my front. I suck in a breath, just as my spine jerks violently and I can't hold back the screams any longer. I don't know why this keeps happening, I'm just surprised I'm not already dead.

The boy appears like an apparition and stands over me, watching me suffer at his feet. He waits for me to stop convulsing, then scoops me from the ground. I wince, still tender from the attack despite the worst of it being over. It's the worst one yet and I'm miserable that it didn't just kill me.

I use the sleeve of my blazer to wipe my chin then try to speak. No sound comes out though, which isn't surprising. My throat is always raw after an attack, swollen and burning like I've been eating glass. I press tentative fingers to it, mind going to how easily the boy can murder me now and I won't even be able to scream.

My shoulders slump in defeat, pain and fear fading behind a wave of hopelessness. The boy is watching me and I turn my face from his probing gaze. Might as well let him kill me. It would be preferable to this hell I'm living.

Instead of laying me on the blanket, he puts me down beside the fire and drops the blanket over my shivering shoulders. I stare at him in confusion but he doesn't pay me any heed, as he comes to kneel beside my right leg. He probes it with surprisingly gentle fingers. It's strangely numb now but I still flinch when he uses a dagger to cut the soaked bandage free. My thigh has a kink in it, just above the knee and a deep gash where the arrow obviously pierced it.

'I'm going to realign the bone,' he says. 'It will hurt.'

Ten points for stating the obvious.

I nod, wondering why he wants to fix my leg when he intends to kill me. He puts his hands on my thigh, either side of the kink. I take a deep breath before pain jolts through me. It's electric and fizzing and I black out.

5

I cough as I wake, mouth tasting like pennies and lungs burning. Each inhale feels like I'm breathing brimstone and I roll onto my knees to pant through it. The sensation gradually fades and I sag in relief. I wipe blood from my chin then look at my hands. I'm covered in it, both fresh and old, the coppery scent mingling with the stench of body odour. I can't even remember the last time I showered or slept in a bed. From the smell of me, it's been a while.

I look around, squinting through the darkness, to find myself on a concrete floor. I'm in some kind of shack, with boarded-up windows. Daylight slices through thin gaps between the wooden panels of the structure, filtering in enough light for me to make out stacks of deckchairs and windbreakers lining one wall. It's a beach hut, I realise, like the one my grandparents own, except this looks like it's used for storage.

I push onto my feet and realise the pain in my leg is gone. I move to a shaft of light to examine my thigh. There's a faint, puckered scar where the arrow hit but that's it.

'It's really real,' I whisper.

I look around again, wondering where the boy is. Has he dumped me in a random shack and left? I go to the door, try the handle but find it locked. I push against it but it won't budge.

Movement on the other side blocks some of the light and the lock clicks. I back away from the door, pressing myself against the opposite wall as it swings open. Daylight momentarily blinds me, before a silhouette steps into the doorway. The boy steps inside and shuts the door behind him. He looks unsurprised to find me awake, before his gaze zeros in on my right thigh.

'W-why have you brought me here?' I demand then gasp and press my fingers to my throat. My voice is different: melodic and... What the hell is going on?

The boy ignores my question and offers a pile of folded clothes. 'Put these on.'

I glance at the clothes. 'No.'

He scowls. 'Put them on, or I'll do it for you.'

I glance between his face and clothes again, before snatching them from him. He folds his arms across his chest and waits.

'Are you going to turn around, or am I supposed to strip for you?' I snap.

Sarcasm sounds peculiar in my new voice—like listening to an angel swear. My voice is ethereal now, like a wind-chime or harp. I press a hand to my throat again and the boy's expression turns wary.

He backs up to the door. 'You have two minutes,' he growls then slips outside and locks me in. I don't know what his problem is. He'd seemed almost kind in the moments before he reset my leg but he's back to being a dick.

I strip from my dirty clothes then shiver as I pull on the clean ones. They're a little damp, like they've been plucked from a washing line. But they're my size and clean so I'm not complaining, even if it *is* slightly creepy. I'm pulling my shoes back on, when the door opens and the boy's glare meets mine.

'You look like one of them again,' he says stepping up to me. He picks up a length of my dirty hair and rubs it between his fingers. 'We need to remove the blood from your hair though. It will draw too much attention.'

I snatch it from his fingers. 'What do you want from me?'

His laughter is harsh. 'I want nothing from you, Noisemaker. In case you hadn't noticed, I'm trying to keep you alive.' He sneers at me. 'I thought you'd be more grateful.'

Noisemaker? At least I know now he's no longer trying to kill me. Images of javelin-sized arrows flash in my mind, a reminder that someone else still wants me dead.

'I'm grateful you saved me,' I say knowing he's the reason I'm still breathing. 'I just don't understand why any of this is happening. Why is somebody trying to...k-kill me?'

His eyebrows knit together. 'You really don't know?'

Frustration rakes through me. 'Would I ask if I did?'

He studies me for a long moment before saying, 'My father sent me to...find you. I'm taking you to Anthemusa.'

Something feels off about his answer. 'Who's Anthemusa?'

He snorts. 'It's not a person, it's a place.'

His amusement grates at my frayed emotions. I don't know why he finds my distress so funny. I don't know him and he doesn't know me, yet he seems to be judging me for something I've done.

'My parents are dead.'

He smirks. 'Your parents aren't dead, Inara. Immortals aren't so easily killed.'

I blink at his ludicrous declaration, anger rising. 'Is this a joke to you?' My parents died when our car collided with a lorry. You should know, you were there.'

He starts laughing. 'You thought those humans were your parents?' He throws his head back and laughs harder.

The icy rage in my middle flares bright at his reaction. My family are dead and he thinks it's funny? I slam into him, surprising him enough that we crash to the floor. I land on top of him but he flips us easily then grins down at me like he's having buckets of fun. I snarl a vicious sound before my fist connects with his nose. Just like Daniel taught me. The cartilage crunches under my knuckles, filling me with sick satisfaction, as his blood sprays my face. My hand hurts like hell but the look on his face is worth it.

He grabs my wrists in one hand and pins them to the concrete above my head, shifting his weight to pin the rest of my body. I thrash beneath him, trying to buck him off but he's bloody heavy.

He brings his face close to mine when I slump in defeat. 'Are you finished?' A bead of blood drips from his nose, adding to the crimson painting his lips.

'You have no right,' I growl, eyes stinging with tears. I thought I'd never feel as helpless as the day of the funerals but he's determined to keep proving me wrong.

'You punched me in the face, so I have every right to restrain you.'

'I meant my family, you callous monster!' I twist in his grip to no avail then snarl, 'It isn't funny that they're dead! They were good, beautiful people and I...I loved...' I look away, my pretty new voice breaking.

I close my eyes as the first tears fall. A keening sob bursts free and I hate it. Hate that he's witnessing my grief. I bite my bottom lip to keep the next sob inside but can't stop my body from shaking with it.

His weight leaves me and I roll away, curling on my side with my back to him. His footsteps are silent as he leaves, the only indication he's gone the sound of the door locking behind him.

I stay in a ball on the floor, lost in my grief for a long time. When I finally uncurl from my foetal pose, the temperature has dropped and the light filtering from outside has dimmed. The boy has been gone for hours and I'm starting to feel antsy without him. Did he leave me here to be found by the person with the huge arrows?

I get up and rattle the door but the boy doesn't appear like last time. I consider calling out for him but don't know his name. My stomach knots at the idea that he's left me to fend for myself. It wouldn't surprise me after I broke his nose.

I retreat to the wall opposite the door and slide down to sit on the concrete. My stomach growls as I tuck my knees to my chest and stare into space. I think about what the boy said about my parents not being my parents, and that my real ones are immortal. He's crazier than I'd thought. But then I think of my strange new voice and the painful fits I've been having. I can't explain any of it.

My head jerks up from my bent knees when the lock clicks hours later. I've been sitting in complete darkness for a long time, so it takes a moment to adjust to the torchlight sweeping inside the hut. I hold my hand up to block the glare when it rests on me.

The boy comes over and places the torch on the floor, illuminating his features as he kneels in front of me. He holds his hand out, offering something and I eye him warily. I consider refusing but don't want to fight again. I need him to answer some of my questions. I sigh and hold out my hand, so he can place his offering in my palm. It's warm and greasy and I flinch at the unexpected sensation.

'What is it?' I ask.

'Food. It isn't poisonous,' he adds when I continue to stare down at it. 'I'm trying to keep you alive, remember?'

My gaze moves from whatever food is in my palm to him because it's the first time he's really spoken to me without a growl in his voice. 'What kind of food?'

My stomach growls at the prospect of being filled and he smirks. 'Rabbit.'

My stomach lurches at his answer and I shove my hand at him. 'No, thank you,' I rasp. The greasiness of it is suddenly all I can feel. It's thick and congealed in my palm, the thought of cooked animal flesh making me gag. 'P-please take it back.'

He does but holds it right in front of me, confusion painting his face. 'You're hungry and need to eat.'

'I can't eat *that*,' I say, wiping the grease from my palm on my newly-acquired jeans. It's a sacrifice I'm willing to make.

'Why not?' he demands. 'It isn't raw, I cooked it myself.'

I bet he did. 'I'm vegetarian.'

He blinks at me. 'Vege...what?'

I blink back, unsure if he's being serious. 'I don't eat meat.'

His face goes slack with shock, before he throws his head back and roars with laughter. It isn't the sarcastic, mean laughter from before. This is real, honest amusement but I don't get the joke.

'You have to eat and this is all there is,' he finally says, still chuckling.

'I'm not hungry.' My stomach growls on cue, disputing my words.

His laughter fades. 'You haven't eaten for two days. If you don't eat, you'll get weak and it will slow us down.'

The last time I ate was at school, the day he kidnapped me. 'Two days?' I glance down at my thigh in disbelief.

'Would've been one if you'd stayed still like I'd told you.'

'Broken bones take weeks, not days to heal.'

'Not for us. Now: eat and we'll both stand a chance of staying alive.'

I stare at him and he stares back, his blue eyes seeming to glow in the darkness. I'm reaching my limit of the bull crap he's spewing, without much in the way of true explanation. I need facts to back up what he's saying, if he wants me to believe him. I can't just trust a random, walking arsenal who's tried to off me on several occasions.

'What you said before, about my family,' I say. 'I need to know what you meant.'

He sighs, 'About what exactly? It's difficult to remember specifics, after you punched me.'

'About my parents. You said my parents weren't really my parents.'

'The Thompsons weren't your family, Inara. They were surrogates, a family chosen to integrate you into human culture, to better hide you.'

'My mother gave birth to me,' I argue. 'I've seen pictures of her holding me in the hospital.'

'That human woman wasn't your mother, she adopted you.'

'They would've told me—'

'Didn't you ever notice how different you looked from them? Did you never wonder where that pretty blonde hair and green eyes come from?'

'I had an aunt—'

'You're supposed to be intelligent,' he snaps.

'You seem to be the expert on what I am and how I'm supposed to feel,' I snap back. 'Try losing everyone you love on your birthday then being stalked by a couple of killers, before being told you're not who you thought you were. Go on, expert, how am I feeling? Maybe you should just start laughing again, huh? You seem to find my pain amusing.'

He stares at me after I've finished ranting, the sound of my angry breathing the only sound between us. He looks away, throat dipping with a swallow, before he turns those eerily-luminous eyes back to me.

'I didn't realise you'd be so...attached to them,' he says. 'It isn't normal for someone like you.'

Someone like me? 'I wasn't *attached*,' I scoff, offended beyond belief. 'I loved them, something it seems you don't have the capacity to understand.' I look at my hands. 'Please just...leave me alone, okay? I'm not... I don't want to talk to you anymore.'

He hesitates for a moment but gets up. He leaves the torch by my feet and stops at the door. 'I'm sorry I laughed,' he says before locking the door between us.

I wait for the sound of his footsteps to fade then go to the door and press my ear to the wood. I stand there for a long time, listening to the sound of wind and ocean, until I'm sure he isn't lurking outside. I snatch up the torch and investigate the stacked deckchairs and windbreakers.

'I thought you'd be more intelligent,' I mock in my best imitation of his stupid accent. I'll show him intelligent. I might be a coward but I'm far from stupid.

I tug a wooden pole from its fabric slot on one of the canvas windbreakers. One end of the pole is sharpened to a point and I jam it into the gap between the door and its frame, where the thickest shaft of daylight streamed inside earlier. I take a deep breath, then push on the pole, using my body weight to create a lever. The doorframe creaks then, splinters. The wood around the lock bursts apart and the door pops open.

I drop the pole and peer outside. Salty air brushes my skin as I stare out at the dark ocean, black and enchanting before me. The tide is in, licking the edge of the promenade and the boy is nowhere in sight. I glance around one last time then start running.

Night air cuts against my face as I run, cooling my heated skin. It feels good to be out here, stretching my aching muscles despite the fatigue. The night is cold and quiet and I run for ten minutes, before a string of lights appear on the horizon. I push faster at the sight of civilisation. Lights mean people and people mean safety. Houses come into view, windows lit and inviting and I almost sob in relief. My relief grows when I see another person, jogging down the steps leading from the houses, onto the promenade. They turn in my direction and step under one of the lampposts lighting the way.

I stop in my tracks at the sight of the boy. He sees me in the same moment and stops too. We stare at each other for a stretched moment, frustration raking through me that I ran towards the one person I was trying to flee.

Before I can think of anything to say, his gaze ices over and he drops the bundle in his arms. A shard of light erupts from his back and it takes a second to process that he's just drawn his sword. Moonlight glints from the blade, projecting pale light over his angular features as he runs at me.

My insides liquify at the sheer rage on his face. This is it; he's finally going to kill me and I don't even know his name. His muscles bunch as he reaches me, arms coiling as he lifts his sword to deliver the final blow. Pain cramps my shoulders and ripples down my spine but I'm too frozen with fear to even flinch. I shut my eyes and wait for death.

His sword strikes with a resounding clash and I snap my eyes open, as I whirl towards to the sound. The boy is hanging from the hilt of his sword, its blade buried in the shoulder of an enormous... man? The boy wedges his feet against the giant's torso then yanks his blade free. The giant roars as the blade sucks from his flesh, leaving a gaping wound in its wake, a yawning mouth in his greasy shoulder.

He stumbles on his bare feet, long, oily hair falling like ink over a pitted face. A quiver of javelin-sized arrows rests on his shoulder, the same as those buried in the fence three days ago—the ones meant for me. But the arrows pale against the sight of the giant, with a singular eye in the centre of his forehead.

He looks to me then twists at the waist and backhands the boy in one, brutal swing of his arm. The boy is thrown over the metal railing and disappears into the dark water.

That single, orange-ringed eye pans back to me and I stare back, transfixed. He's a Cyclops. An honest-to-God, Cyclops. I pinch myself to make sure I'm not dreaming and his thick lips pull into a grin, displaying rows of jagged, yellow teeth.

'Noisemaker,' he says, voice rumbling with the same accent as the boy. He moves closer but I counter his steps. 'Don't worry, my pretty. I'll make it quick, no more than a second.'

'W-why are you doing this?' I rasp.

'It's my job to kill you,' he says.

'But I've done nothing wrong!'

'Your kind aren't allowed to roam free from the Flowery Isle,' he says.

'The Flowery Isle...?'

'Anthemusa, realm of the Sirens,' he says like it's obvious.

Anthemusa—the place the boy claimed he would take me. I stop retreating and let the Cyclops advance, deciding to at least learn some answers before I die. The giant grins and bends to cup my face, his huge, calloused hand engulfing the side of my skull. I flinch under the gaze of that one eye and try not to gag at the stench of his rancid breath.

'It's a shame to end such a beautiful thing,' he murmurs. 'If you weren't to grow into something so deadly, I'd keep you for myself.'

'I'm not deadly.'

'Not until you come into your voice,' he agrees.

I frown in confusion, thinking of my altered voice. 'How do you know I haven't already?'

'If you had, Aaron would've killed you.'

'Aaron?'

He chuckles. 'He's been coveting you but hasn't even told you, his name?'

I look at the ocean realising, he means the boy. I turn back to the cyclops and sigh, 'Please make it quick, like you promised.' This is what I've wanted since my family died, isn't it? Now I'll get to be with them and end my suffering.

He releases my face and steps back to retrieve his bow from his shoulder. He slides a long, thick arrow from the quiver into place and draws it back. His muscles bunch as he brings the tip of that enormous arrow, level with my racing heart. It isn't until I'm staring down at the razor barb, that I realise I want to live. His fingers loosen, single eye focussed along the shaft...

A tanned arm locks around his throat and pulls tight, cutting off his air. The bowstring slackens, arrow clattering to the concrete, as he reaches to pull on the arm around his throat. I jerk back as his bow joins the arrow on the ground. His abdominals flex then he jerks forward, flinging Aaron over his mountainous frame. Aaron crashes onto the concrete then rolls and regains his feet in a series of fluid movements.

He spins back to the Cyclops, sword drawn and glinting. 'Yield,' he snarls as he positions himself in front of me.

'You know what she is,' the giant snarls back. 'She needs to die. Let me finish this before she comes into her voice.'

'She's innocent.'

'We both know it's a matter of time. She'll kill. They all do. Move away, so I can complete the mission.'

Aaron sighs, 'I cannot, Bedros.'

'Then why are you here?' Bedros growls. 'You should understand the most, why she needs to die.'

'I don't kill innocents,' Aaron says.

Bedros lunges, slashing at Aaron's throat with a dagger pulled from seemingly nowhere. Aaron jerks back, a crimson line creeping across his cheekbone. He dabs at the wound then examines the blood glossing the back of his hand.

'Cheap shot,' he says then moves in a blur of motion.

Aaron's attack reminds me of a grotesque dance, movements elegant, his sword a streak of silver in the moonlight. It kisses Bedros over and over, until the giant is laced in cuts. Black liquid oozes from the wounds, painting the giant until he's a distorted version of his previous self.

He falls to his knees, still taller than Aaron yet obviously less of a threat. Other than the cut from Bedros' 'cheap shot', Aaron doesn't have a mark on him. Even with the giant on his knees, he doesn't stop his attack. He keeps cutting, until the Bedros slumps onto his front and tries to crawl away.

I watch on in abstract horror, as Aaron climbs onto Bedros' back and grips the hilt of his sword in both hands. He raises it above his head, just like he did the night of the accident. This time his blade meets its target, plunging deep between Bedros' shoulder blades. The giant's back arches before he slumps against the concrete, unmoving.

A black puddle grows beneath his motionless body. It seems to reach for me and I back against the railing. Aaron jumps from Bedros' back, plastered in the black ooze I've now figured out is Bedros' blood. He wipes his sword on his jeans, then returns it to the sheath on his back. His movements are precise and business-like, as if he hasn't just killed someone. His gaze meets mine: stark blue, like sapphires amid the ebony blood painting his face.

6

I slide my way along the railing, away from Aaron. He watches calmly, like he won't chase me when I run, even though we both know different. He told Bedros he hadn't killed me because I'm an innocent but innocent of what? What is the line I'd have to cross before he changes his mind?

I flinch when something crunches beneath my right foot and look down to find a crushed biscuit under my shoe. I stare down at it, before noticing fruit, cheese and bread scattered across the promenade. They must be what Aaron was carrying before he dropped them to fight Bedros. It dawns on me that none of the items are meat, which means he got them for me.

I meet his gaze then take a deep breath and kneel on the concrete. Aaron appears by my side and ignores my flinch as he helps gather the food. We stuff it into the bag it has rolled from then he picks it up and waits for me to stand. I push to my feet and he starts walking in the direction of the beach hut. I stumble after him, glancing at Bedros as we pass.

'Sh-shouldn't we hide him?' I croak.

Aaron tosses a small, golden coin at the body without looking back. 'He's the Ferryman's problem now.'

The coin lands in the dark puddle and a skeletal hand reaches up from beneath to collect it. The bony digits grasp the gold disk and pull it under. The hand returns to grip Bedros with fleshless fingers. It drags him into the abyss and the puddle bursts into dark flames. It burns for a few seconds before the flames dissipate, leaving no trace of Bedros behind.

I scream when a hand grasps my shoulder. Aaron catches my fist when I swing around to defend myself.

'*Now* you're willing to fight,' he scoffs.

Static sparks between us and I jerk away from his stinging touch. 'What the hell was that?' I practically yell in his face, clutching my still tingling hand to my chest. 'Where did that...that thing take his body?'

'Bedros was a bounty hunter,' Aaron answers, 'He's on his way to Hades, the same place you'd be if I hadn't killed him for you. Standing around looking pretty is a fast way to get killed, Inara.'

'We don't all walk around with an arsenal of weapons, *Aaron*.'

'Your voice is your weapon,' he says not reacting to my use of his name.

There it is again, another mention of my voice. 'What am I supposed to do, talk people to death?'

'Not what I meant but in your case, it might just work.'

'You're crazy,' I hiss as I walk away. 'The whole damn world is suddenly crazy!'

Aaron is at my side before I've made three steps. 'Where do you think you're going?'

'The bad guy is dead, so I'm going home.'

He grabs my arm. 'You don't get it, do you? I'm *taking* you home.'

'Anthemusa, isn't my home.'

'It's the only place you'll ever be safe,' he argues. 'Do you honestly think Bedros was the first assassin to find you? Do you think he'll be the last?'

'T-there'll be more?'

'As long as you're outside of the Flowery Isle, the assassins will keep hunting you.'

'Why? Why do they even want me dead?'

He stares at me with those burning, blue eyes. 'Because you're a Siren: a bringer of death, wrapped in the guise of a beautiful female.'

'O-kay... What?'

'You're a predator, Inara. You're designed to lure prey in.' He gestures to my being. 'Your beauty, your voice. Even your smell is alluring. Your species are designed to entice others close enough for you to strike.'

'A Siren,' I scoff. 'As in, Greek mythology. Beautiful women, singing to lure sailors into crashing ships on the shore?'

He nods. 'You know the fundamentals at least.'

'I sound like a dying cat when I sing,' I say pulling my arm from his hold. 'What you're peddling is myth, Aaron. Sirens aren't real. They don't exist.

'And what of the Cyclops I just killed? Is that not part of the same so-called mythology?'

He has a point and I don't like it. These are the facts I thought I needed earlier but the more I hear, the more I don't want to listen.

'If I'm really a Siren, why am I only just finding out about it then? Why haven't I been drowning sailors, or making millions from this melodic voice all my life?'

'What was special about the day of the accident?' he asks. 'Why were you travelling that night?'

'We were coming back from my grandparents—'

'Why?'

I hesitate. I've blamed myself for the accident since the night it happened. We were on the way back from my lame birthday party at my grandparents' house, when the lorry hit our car. The only reason Helen wasn't in the car with us, was because she had to be up for a dance exam the next morning, so her dad picked her up an hour earlier.

'Why, Inara?'

'You know why,' I rasp not wanting to say it. If I say it aloud, it makes it real.

'Sirens are harmless until they reach seventeen,' he says. 'When they transition, their voices turn lethal and their bloodlust grows uncontrollable. They're confined to Anthemusa to keep the rest of us safe.'

'Transition?' I whisper, pressing fingertips to my throat. 'That... It's why I've been vomiting blood?'

He nods. 'Your voice is *already* lethal.'

I swallow. 'But Bedros said you'd have killed me if it was.'

He looks away. 'I don't kill innocents.'

Everything he's saying makes sense. The physical changes are there but, it's the part about luring others in that really sticks out. It's been happening all my life. Others are drawn to me. They want to get close and I've never been able to explain why.

'If all Sirens are confined then why aren't I?'

'It's complicated.'

'Complicated,' I drawl glaring at him.

He glares back. 'Sirens reproduce with the men that survive drowning and make it to their beaches. Once they get what they want from them, the men are killed. All offspring are born within the confines of the Flowery Isle, Inara. They're born, trapped by the curse of the island and cannot leave.'

'I'm not confined to an island I've never even heard of and don't have an overwhelming need to kill, Aaron.'

'You're an exception to the rule.'

'Why?'

'It's complicated.'

'Uncomplicate it!' I huff, frustrated by this whole, cryptic conversation.

'Because you're different!' he growls, sounding just as frustrated. 'You're not like the rest of them. You were born on Anthemusa but had help escaping when you were just a babe.'

'Right,' I scoff. 'And why would anyone help me escape such a safe haven for Sirens, if all it meant, was for me to be hunted as soon as I turned seventeen?'

He rakes his fingers through his dark hair. 'All you need to understand is, it isn't safe for you off the Flowery Isle anymore. If you don't go back there, you'll be hunted until someone succeeds in doing what Bedros just failed to do.'

Aaron looks away, gaze searching the night. I *feel* the anger rolling off him, like prickles against my skin, adding merit to everything he's saying. I'm different from what I used to be and like it or not, he's been right about a lot of things. Like the transition stuff. All those bouts of pain and vomiting blood make a sick sort of sense now. I've been transforming into something else. Something supposedly deadly, even if I still don't fully believe it. But myths do hold some grains of truth, right? All legends have to start from somewhere.

'Why didn't you kill me when you had the chance?' I ask. His gaze meets mine, angry and intense but I force myself to hold it. 'The night of the crash, you tried and failed but you've had plenty of chances since. You were just like Bedros then. You wanted me dead—I felt it.'

He turns back to the ocean and curls long fingers around the railing. 'If it weren't for the human witness that night, you'd be dead.'

My heart thuds against my ribcage at his admission. 'You mean the lorry driver?'

He nods. 'I tracked you after, waiting for my chance but you were always surrounded.' My blood chills at the confession. 'And when you were finally alone, I broke into your dwelling.'

'You were in my house?'

'Your aunt's house,' he says. 'You were sitting at the kitchen table, talking to someone on the phone. Your back was to me and you were so oblivious to my presence. You didn't even sense me there, sword raised to finish the job.'

I swallow around the revulsion to ask, 'What stopped you?'

'You were crying,' he says, a wistful edge to his voice. 'I watched the tears drip from your chin and splash the table.'

'Why would that stop you from killing me?'

He turns his gaze back to me. 'Sirens are monsters, Inara. They can't cry, even if they wanted to because they can't generate the emotion required for it.'

I stare at him, wondering how *he* can call anyone a monster. He just admitted to trying to kill me more than once and I just watched him butcher a Cyclops. Aaron has this...rage inside of him that's terrifying to behold. And, he's trying to claim *I'm* the monster.

'I backed away, thinking you must be the wrong girl,' he goes on. 'I'd been so sure, though. The way you look and your scent... I followed you the next day but you seemed so fragile, so...human. And you were kind.' He shakes his head like he can't comprehend it.

'I'm not a monster.'

'But I kept watching,' he says like I haven't spoken. 'Witnessed your transition. Witnessed how you tried to fight it, even though there was no way to stop it.'

I think of how he stood over me that night in the woods, while I writhed in pain on the ground. The cold look in his eyes as he stared down at me, disgust creasing his features, despite everything he just admitted. He says he witnessed my kindness yet he still claims I'm a monster.

'You aren't what you're supposed to be,' he says. 'You don't deserve to die but not everyone will care.'

'You mean, they don't all share your moral compass,' I drawl.

'You're angry I didn't kill you?'

'I'm angry that you ever thought you had the right to decide if I should live or die,' I say. 'I'm *angry* anyone wants to kill me because of *what* and not *who* I am. We don't get to choose what we are, Aaron. I don't want anything to do with whatever this is. I'm not the monster everyone thinks I am. I'm not evil or hungry for blood. I just want—'

'They don't care what you want, Inara. I know it isn't fair but life isn't fair. You don't have the choice to become something other than what you were born to be, but I'm giving to you back the option of choosing to live, if you want it. Let me take you to Anthemusa or stay here and die.'

We glare at each other for a tense moment then I push from the railing and start walking back towards the beach hut. Aaron falls into step beside me. I hug my torso and refuse to look at him. I'm actually doing this. I'm letting a killer take me to an island of murderous monsters because I'm terrified of the alternative. I'm not a fighter, I'm a coward. I wouldn't last five minutes against an assassin. But is the alternative much better? It's a decision I still need to make.

7

The sun peeks above the horizon, sparkling over the silver ocean and burning away morning mist. I inch closer to the fire on the sand, attempting to warm up while not getting too close to whatever animal Aaron is cooking in the metal bucket. *Ugh.* Steam billows from the top in ominous ribbons.

I shift my gaze to where Aaron is standing in the surf, blood-stained jeans rolled up so the waves lap his shins. His dark hair sticks up in all directions from the dried blood in it. I didn't see him sleep last night but he definitely has bedhead.

His bright gaze pans to me and I snap mine back to the fire. He sloshes from the surf then uses the bottom of his shirt to lift the bucket. My eyes round when he grabs the hem of his shirt and pulls it off his body.

'What are you doing?' I demand.

'What does it look like I'm doing?'

I choke on nothing then say, 'Like you're taking your clothes off.'

I stare at his bare torso. Blood has stencilled the outline of his shirt on his skin, which would be hilarious if my eyes weren't drawn to a diagonal scar on his body. It starts at his left shoulder then travels down over his chest, ending just below his right ribs. My fingers go automatically to my right thigh, where the puckered scar marks my skin. I feel the indentation through the denim of my jeans.

'You'll attract too much attention covered in so much blood,' he says.

My face heats at being caught staring. I comb self-conscious fingers through my tangled hair and wince at the knots of dried blood. At least it's mine and not the stinking, black stuff covering him. I push to my feet and peer into the steaming bucket, the salty aroma prickling my nose. The water is clear and I realise, he's been heating it for washing, not cooking.

'You first,' he tells me. He smirks when I glance his way. 'It will be filthy when I'm done.'

Right. I eye his encrusted skin but refrain from telling him he'll need way more than one bucket of water. He laughs and my gaze snaps back to his because I didn't know he could make such a warm sound.

'What's so funny?'

'You look more horrified than when I told you you're a Siren!'

The warmth fades from hearing his laughter and I look away. How can he even joke about it? He laughs even harder at my surly reaction and my anger spikes. I scoop a handful of warm water from the bucket and throw it at him. His laughter cuts off and he stares at me with wide, blue eyes. Warm water splashes my face in the next moment and I stare up at him, startled. Is this actually happening?

'Eat brine,' I say, snatching up the bucket and throwing the contents over him.

I screech and drop the searing metal onto the sand then look from my blistering palms to Aaron. A sob dies in my throat, laughter bubbling out instead at the state of him. The water has streaked the black blood and he looks like a drowned zebra.

I squeal when he suddenly tackles me, fear spiking that he's changed his mind about my being innocent. The air punches out of me as my stomach lands on his hard shoulder. I stare down at the back of his legs, then up at the retreating fire on the sand.

'Wait!' I squeal when I realise he's running to the ocean. I slap my blistered palms against his bare back. 'Aaron, no! I'm sorry, okay? Put me down!'

He splashes into the surf until the water laps his chest then throws me off his shoulder. I hit the freezing water with a painful slap and glimpse his grinning face before I sink. Blind panic grips me as salt stings my eyes and nose. I reach my arms out and flail but the tide grips me and drags me under. My lungs start to ache with the need to breathe...

'*Reach with your arms and kick your legs,*' Daniel says, voice warm in my mind.

'*I'll drown,*' I whine back.

'*If you learn to swim it won't happen again,*' my brother promises.

I try to do what he says but the ache in my lungs is making it difficult to concentrate. My limbs grow heavy and slow and relief blooms through me when Daniel's arms wrap around my middle. I cling to him, practically coughing up a lung when he pulls me from the frigid water.

'Daniel,' I rasp, burying my face in his shoulder.

He lowers me to the sand and I tighten my grip, like if I let go, he'll disappear. He brushes hair from my face, breath real and hot on my skin. But it isn't right, isn't real. I open my stinging eyes to meet Aaron's bright gaze, instead of the warm, chocolate I really want.

Aaron's dark brows knit together, saltwater clinging to his lashes. 'You can't swim,' he says, disbelief staining his tone.

I let my arms fall from his neck, devastation that he isn't Daniel, threatening to choke me. My brother is gone. I'll never see him again.

Aaron moves us closer to the fire and drapes a fur blanket around me. It smells like him and I tuck it against me, oddly comforted by the smell. It makes me feel safe.

He paces in front of me for half a minute, then asks, 'Who's Daniel?'

I stare at the sand. 'My brother.'

Aaron hesitates then says, 'You'll go back to the beach hut.'

My gaze snaps to his. 'I thought we were leaving?'

'You need dry clothes,' he says then picks up the bucket and stalks down to the ocean. He dunks it in the water then uses it to douse the fire. It hisses into submission, sending a string of black smoke into the silver sky.

I stand up. 'I'm coming with you.'

'You look half drowned,' he argues.

'And you don't?'

'I'll lock you in the hut if I have to,' he warns.

'Because that worked so well last time,' I say.

His eyes flash icy blue before he huffs and starts gathering our things. 'Don't become a liability.'

'If your aim is to keep me alive, like you claim it is, then I'm already a liability,' I say. 'We both know I won't stand a chance if another assassin finds me while you're not there.'

He considers my candid honesty then nods. 'Good point.'

SOUVENIR SHOPS LINE the pavements and the scent of fresh coffee fills the air. The apple I ate for breakfast feels inadequate against the multiple windows filled with baked goods. I eye the fresh pastries on display and bite back a groan. I'd kill for a Portuguese tart right now.

Kids in school uniform hurry past, weaving around those dressed for work. Everyone seems to be going somewhere, not sparing mine or Aaron's appearance a second glance.

He startles me when he suddenly takes my hand and pulls me into a mini-market. I grit my teeth against his stinging touch and frown at the back of his head as he pulls me forward. I used to think he just gathered a lot of static from carrying all those blades around but touching Aaron sometimes hurts. I think it's connected to his emotions because it didn't hurt when he held me on the beach. He's tense right now though and annoyed that I'm here.

Despite his dark mood, he smiles at the girl with sandy hair behind the counter. She blushes at the rare smile from him and I narrow my eyes. It isn't like I want him to smile at me like that, I just wish he wasn't so obvious about how much of an inconvenience I am. I didn't ask for any of this, yet he makes it seem like it's all my fault.

He grabs a basket and starts filling it with food, stopping at the boxes of hair dye to look at me. 'You'd be harder to recognise if we change your hair.'

'Doesn't work on me,' I say. 'I've tried it with Helen several times but it always comes out the same shade of blonde.'

He grunts and I hiss when his hand practically electrocutes me. I snatch it from his hold and he frowns at where I'm cradling it against my chest. Something like regret flits across his face but it's gone before I can be sure it was ever there.

I follow him around the shop then to the checkout. He smiles at the girl from before while she scans our items. She gives him a shy smile back and I fight an eye roll.

I go rigid when Aaron's lips brush my ear, breath hot against my skin. 'Time to shine, Siren,' he breathes. 'I'll be back in one minute. Don't sing, just hum.' He's walks away before I can respond and I stare after him in utter shock.

'Fourteen sixty-nine,' the girl behind the counter says.

I turn back to meet her expectant gaze. I don't have any money to pay her and don't want to use my voice like Aaron wants. If I'm really a Siren and they're the monsters he claims, what will it mean for the girl on the checkout, if I use my voice on her? I bite my lip and look around for another option. My shoulders cramp with the need to leave. I can't do it, can't risk—

'Sometime today would be nice,' she huffs.

I frown, reluctance melting at her rudeness. The wintry rage I keep locked in my middle, flares bright—more easily than it ever has before and a chime-like sound, reverberates from me. Everything stops, the girl's expression blanking at the sound of my humming. Her eyes glaze over and a tiny smile curls her lips. She sighs and stares at me dreamily like a dazed mannequin.

The cold sensation grows, uncurling through my insides like icy smoke. It likes what I'm doing, craves for me to lean forward and...

Something hits the floor and scatters around my feet. I glance over my shoulder and suck in a breath at the unseeing eyes behind me. I back up against the checkout, horrified by the three young boys staring at me, packets of sweets in their hands. They must've been waiting behind me to pay. I glance at the girl behind the counter, remembering the cold need to...

'Have you finished humming?' Aaron yells from the doorway, fingers jammed in his ears.

I remove my heart from my throat at his abrupt entrance and nod. He pulls his fingers from his ears and joins me at the counter.

'Proof enough that you're not human, Noisemaker?' he asks. There's an edge to his voice as he stares at the young boys with their gazes transfixed on me.

My mouth works but nothing comes out. I am what he claims. A monster, a bringer of death.

The girl behind the counter doesn't even blink when Aaron waves a hand in front of her face. Satisfied, he grabs the bag of groceries and walks away like what I've done is nothing.

He turns back when he reaches the exit. 'Are you coming?'

I stare at him then at the spaced-out children. Monster... Bringer of death. Aaron sighs and comes back to me. He takes my hand, making my palm sting. It snaps me out of my pending panic attack and I meet his gaze.

'I... I didn't—'

'They'll wake in a few minutes with no recollection of ever seeing you,' he says, something like regret in his tone.

I look at the children again then nod. Aaron guides me past them. Dead gazes, track me out and I shudder. Just as we make it outside, I hear the checkout girl shouting at the boys for spilling sweats all over the floor.

'Satisfied?' Aaron asks.

I rip my hand from his. 'You really hate me, don't you?' I say then turn and storm away.

I don't care about his protection anymore. It's true. All of it. I'm not human. I've seen some pretty fantastical stuff and even suffered through a lot of horrific pain but... I never truly believed it until now.

I hug myself, feeling sick, as I think of those children in the mini-market. Of how my actions seemed to feed that wintry sensation in my middle. If I did all that by just humming, what will happen if I actually sing?

Aaron grabs my arm. 'Inara, stop.'

I whirl on him. 'How could you do that to me? What if I'd killed them?'

He seems surprised by my outburst. 'You didn't.'

I turn away and stare at the pavement. No, I'm not a killer, not yet. But how long before that changes and the...urges I felt back in the shop overwhelm me? I swallow around the thickness in my throat and force back tears. Bedros said it was only a matter of time before I became a killer and I think he could be right.

'I'm a monster,' I rasp, 'capable of killing.'

'Everyone is *capable* of killing, Inara. You just have to choose not to.' I meet his gaze and it's filled with a warmth I've never witnessed from him. A ray of sunshine breaks through the clouds and he looks to the sky; eyes turning sapphire in the golden light. 'They're watching.'

I glance up. 'Who?'

'The gods.'

I drop my gaze back to his, ready to argue but hesitate. If Sirens and Cyclops are real then why not the gods?

'They want me dead.'

'Not everyone wants that, though,' he says.

I push around him and keep walking. 'Feels that way.'

Aaron's fingers catch mine, warm and stinging but not painful. He steers me across the road, touch gentle like I'm made of glass. I feel fragile enough to shatter, so I let him guide me.

8

Hot water is a bliss I'd forgotten. It pelts my frigid skin, banishing the cold that's been seeping its way to my bones for days. I use complimentary body wash to scrub away the sea salt, before rinsing conditioner from my hair. The water stopped running red ten minutes ago but I'm in no rush to relinquish this heaven.

I wrap myself in a towel when I'm done then use one of the toothbrushes I stole from the mini-market. Aaron assured me our little escapade wouldn't be on any of the CCTV footage. God knows how he managed to mess with their security but I'm not complaining.

Steam billows into the hotel room as I leave the bathroom. A pile of neatly-folded clothes await me on the end of the bed. I pick up the underwear, a little freaked out that Aaron not only attained it but knows my size. My face heats at the thought and I quickly pull them on before he gets back.

I glance at the door as I pull on the clothing. Emerald top, blue jeans. Brown, calf-high boots and a winter coat. I don't know where he got them but I'm grateful that they're dry and warm.

I eye the door again, wondering where he is. The hotel staff don't know we're here. We broke in through the fire door over an hour ago and into this room. I take a deep, calming breath at the prospect of being discovered. I've found there are much scarier things in the world to being arrested.

I slump onto the bed and turn on the TV. I'm flicking through the channels, bored and antsy, when Aaron bursts into the room. I drop the remote, heart stuttering in fear. He chuckles at my reaction and I throw a pillow at his head. The jerk catches it with a grin and throws it back. Of course, it smacks me in the face and he laughs once more.

'Isn't it too warm in here to be wearing that?' he asks eyeing my coat. He drops two rucksacks on the floor by the bed. 'It's like a sauna in here.'

I unzip my coat and wriggle free. 'I was making sure it fits,' I lie. 'What took you so long?'

'Miss me?' he asks as he walks past the bed, yanking his shirt off on the way to the bathroom. 'How's the shower?'

'Beats a bucket of lukewarm seawater,' I answer, averting my gaze from his tanned, muscled flesh.

His laughter is warm as he shuts the bathroom door behind him. I scowl at the closed door, wondering why I'm acting so strange around him. I don't stare at boys, ever. I think it's the allure of being around someone who actually wants nothing to do with me. It's a novelty I've never experienced and, despite everything that's happened, it makes me more relaxed around him.

My gaze drifts to the rucksacks on the floor and curiosity gets the best of me. I slip off the bed to investigate, the navy carpet soft beneath my knees when I kneel beside the bags. My eyes widen at the contents of the first one and I let go. It topples on the carpet with a muffled thud and some of the weapons slide free.

I touch one of the shiny blades, cold and smooth beneath my fingers then snap my hand back with a hiss, stuffing a bleeding digit into my mouth. Ice spreads through my core when I wonder which of these Aaron planned to use on me, before he changed his mind and decided not to kill me. Probably the one he never takes off, even in the shower, apparently.

My gaze turns to the TV at the sound of my name. 'Please just come home, Inara.'

I push to my feet, gaze fixed on the screen. The morning news is reviewing the day's stories and my image is plastered across the screen. The picture is a year old, the grey and burgundy collar of my old school uniform visible along the bottom edge. The image disappears to a view of the news room.

'The search for missing teenager, Inara Thompson continues. The seventeen-year-old was last seen leaving Saint Augustine's Community School at three p.m. on October twenty-eighth. Her school bag was found close to her home, where it's reported there were signs of a struggle,' the female presenter says. 'She disappears just weeks after surviving the tragic accident that killed her parents and brother. Police are concerned for her wellbeing and urge anyone who has information on her whereabouts to come forward.'

I wait for her to mention the javelin-sized arrows in the fence but she doesn't. Aunt Gertrude appears on the screen, behind a bunch of microphones. She blinks against a bombardment of camera flashes, looking pale and distraught. Her hair isn't perfect and her hair is *always* perfect.

'Please, Inara...' she swallows, eyes glassy with tears, 'please, if you see this, come home. If you left of your own volition, I'm not angry. I just... Come home. I love you.' She looks to her left. 'Helen, loves you.'

The camera pans left and Helen comes into view. Her hair is an unusual shade of natural brown, pale grey eyes red and puffy. Her thin shoulders shake as she steps up to the microphone. It's so out of character for my angry bestie. I've never seen her look so...fragile. A look of determination slides over her face, steeling her features and relief bleeds through me. That's the Helen I know and love.

'Inara, I want you to know that I love you. I miss you and hope you're safe,' she says. She licks her lips and takes a breath. 'I want you to come back, so you can see the bacon tree at my house.'

I stop breathing at the coded message she just blurted on national television. Her tear-stained gaze seems to meet mine through the screen, sad and frightened but so ridiculously brave. I know her better than I know myself. Her warning about the bacon tree is a play on words: bacon tree—ham bush—ambush! She's warning me not to go home because there's an ambush waiting for me.

I press my hand against the screen like I can touch her and tell her I'm okay. My fingers curl against the glass when her image disappears, replaced by the presenter in the newsroom.

'An emotional plea from Inara's aunt and best friend,' the presenter says, before moving on to the next story.

Images of flooding in southern England fill the screen but my thoughts are with Helen. She knows something, something about what's happening to me. The warning about an ambush sends a shiver down my spine. Is there a monster in her house? A monster like Bedros?

I glance at the phone on the nightstand but can't risk using it and alerting the hotel staff of our presence. I look from the phone to the bathroom door, chewing on my lip as I weigh my options. I don't even have to ask to know Aaron isn't going to let me call her. It's a stupid thing to do but...I need to check on my friend.

I snatch my coat from the bed and pluck a knife from those spilled on the carpet. I slide the dagger gingerly into the sleeve of my coat and hurry from the room. There's a payphone on the corner near the hotel's front entrance. If I hurry, I can be back before Aaron knows I'm gone.

I push into the phone box, relief blasting through me when I find an actual phone that hasn't been replaced by a defibrillator or a community library. I lift the receiver and reverse the charges, hoping Helen will accept the call.

'Hello?' she says, answering the call.

'Helen, it's me,' I rasp, nearly sobbing in relief.

'Sorry, Julie, there's no news yet,' she says, voice tight.

I hesitate. 'Is someone there, with you?'

'Yes.'

I swallow against my terror. 'Are you okay? Have they hurt you?'

'Not yet.'

'I'm coming to get you,' I say.

'No!' she shouts surprising me so much I almost drop the phone. Her voice calms. 'There's no need to come here, Julie. I told you I'd let you know if there was any news and I will.'

I grip the phone so hard the plastic creaks in my hand. 'I can't let them hurt you.'

'I'm fine,' she lies then sighs, 'I love you too.'

The line goes dead and I look at the black, plastic receiver in my hand, dread snaking through me. Impudent frustration flashes in a slicing wave of angry ice through my middle. I slam the receiver against the interior of the phone box and a crack forms in the thick glass. I blink at the damage then hang up the phone.

Tears blur my vision as I push from the phone box and look around. I need to figure out which seaside town I'm in, so I know which way to go in order to get home. I'll likely die when I get there but I can't leave Helen to deal with whatever is there with her. She wouldn't leave me if our roles were reversed.

I clutch my right arm to my chest, the cold metal of the hidden blade pressing to my skin. It's my only defence against whatever has Helen. Except for my voice, which I can't risk using around her in case I hurt her too. I scoff at the irony of it. I'm being hunted because I'm a deadly creature but can't even use my *deadly* powers to help my friend. All I have is a stolen dagger that I have no idea how to wield.

Aaron appears at the end of the road before I've found a sign telling me our location. I duck behind the phone box and flatten myself against the wall. My shoulders cramp at the anger creasing his features and I arch my spine in an attempt to stretch it out.

Sunshine glints from a shop window on the opposite side of the road, smacking me in the eyes. I squint at the source, to find a gorgeous blond man watching me from behind the pane of glass. His green-gold eyes twinkle when our gazes meet, a smile curving his carved, beautiful lips. A feeling of familiarity shoots through me, like I know him from somewhere but can't remember where.

He points to the ground in front of me and I follow where he's pointing, to see a gilded instrument by my feet. It's shaped like an open-ended heart with strings spanning the gap between the two sides.

'*Take the lyre*,' a smooth, masculine voice breathes inside my mind. I jerk at the sound, looking around for the source but there isn't anybody here. I look across the street, to the man in the window but he's gone.

I pick up the lyre and it fizzes to life like there's a current running through it. I study it, turning it over in my hands, before I remember the angry Aaron storming in my direction. I tuck the lyre into my coat and zip it to my neck, as I spy him through the warped panes of the phone box.

He steps in front of me a few moments later, dressed in clean, black jeans and a dark hoodie. I push to my feet, an apology on my lips but my words cut off, when he pins me against the wall.

'Give it to me,' he growls.

The lyre suddenly feels like it's burning inside my coat. My shoulders itch and a ripple of pain slides the length of my spine. I don't know why that keeps happening. Aaron said my transition was over but it's like I get a visceral twitch each time I feel nervous or trapped.

'G-give you what?'

He growls again, the sound so animalistic, the hairs on my nape stand tall. 'The dagger, Inara; give me the dagger you stole.'

Oh right, the dagger. I pull it from my sleeve and offer it to him. It's gone in a flash and I inspect my hand to make sure I still have all my fingers.

'I only *borrowed* it in case I was attacked,' I say.

'Like you'd know how to use it,' he scoffs then, 'Why in Hades are you out here, alone?'

'Because they have Helen.'

He arcs one dark eyebrow. 'Who's Helen?'

'My best friend!' The words burst out of me in a panicked rush. 'There was a report on the TV while you were taking a shower and Helen did a press conference with my aunt. She said not to go home because there's a bacon tree—'

'Calm down,' he says. 'Your accent is difficult to decipher when you rush and English isn't my first language.'

'It isn't my accent, you heard right! Helen was speaking in code. She was trying to tell me there's an ambush waiting for me if I go home.'

'Then it's good you aren't going there,' he says.

'We have to help her! I could tell she was scared and I can't leave her to suffer because of me.'

'No,' he answers.

My eyebrows reach for my hairline. 'No?'

'No,' he repeats.

I try shoving him off. 'You don't have to come. I'll go alone and—'

'Get yourself killed,' he finishes. His tone softens, 'They want you, not your friend. If you turn up it will make things worse for her.'

Tears drip from my lashes. 'How can I just leave her?'

Aaron wipes at my tears with electric fingers. It doesn't hurt and his expression has lost its usual, hard lines. 'Trust me, Inara.'

Trust the boy who tried to kill me? I swallow hard against the foreign warmth his request ignites. Do I trust Aaron? I'm trusting him with my life, so why not with this? I don't see what choice I have anyway.

My shoulders sag. 'Okay.'

The tenseness leaves him and he releases me from the cage of his body. He takes my hand, the sting gone from his skin when he curls his fingers around mine.

I stay in my coat when we get back to the hotel room. It's boiling inside the room but I haven't told Aaron about the lyre and I'm reluctant to ruin the rare, happy mood he's in. He's been gentle with me since finding me at the phone box and, frankly, it's freaking me out. I chew my lip as I watch him reorganise and pack his buffet of weapons into the rucksacks.

I slide from the bed thinking he's distracted but his attention snaps to me. 'Where are you going?'

I point to the bathroom door. 'To wash my face.'

He regards me, then the windowless bathroom and nods. Aaron wants me to trust him but doesn't trust *me* not to bolt. He's right to do so. I'd do anything to save Helen. He goes back to checking his knife collection as I close the bathroom door between us.

I unzip my coat and pull out the lyre. It glitters under the spotlights when I turn it in my hands, inspecting it for... something. It glows and vibrates in my grip but it seems like nothing more than a pretty piece of metal.

I sigh and strum the glittering strings then drop the lyre when, instead of music, a pulse of invisible energy ripples out of it. The atmosphere shivers and distorts, quivering like heatwaves rising from hot tarmac. The sound of the lyre clattering against the tile, sends its own ripples through the air and I realise, I can *see* sound.

Aaron knocks on the door, sending more ripples through the air towards me. 'Are you okay?'

His voice adds more rumples to the air, making it reverberate and ripple in my direction. The sound presses against my skin, like a soft caress. I shiver at the sensation and release a sigh.

The door rattles. 'Open the door, Inara.'

I take a step towards the door but hesitate, when a familiar voice sounds behind me. I turn to face it, disbelief striking through me.

'Helen?'

'Open the door, Inara!' Aaron growls, voice lapping against my back.

I glance over my shoulder, see the hotel bathroom melting away. Helen's bedroom faces me, the hotel bathroom a distorted mirage at my back.

'What the hell is that?' Helen asks, staring at the shivering image of the hotel bathroom.

'It's—'

A loud crash cuts me off, image shaking as the bathroom door burst open. Aaron falls inside, burning blue eyes meeting mine. A heavy feeling grips my chest at the desperate look on his face. I hadn't actually meant to leave. I reach for him but whatever doorway I opened is closing.

'Where are you?' he shouts but it's too late. His gaze flicks to Helen before the doorway shuts between us.

9

The doorway closes and something like grief rakes through me. Aaron might have wanted to kill me but he's saved my life and shown me kindness since. He let me see a gentler side of him and I liked it. I'll probably die before I get to see him again and it makes me ache. I think of the beautiful blond who gifted me the lyre and wonder if this was his plan. I'm a sitting duck without Aaron to protect me.

I turn to meet Helen's wide, rainy gaze. She's shaking as she looks at me.

'Helen—'

She slaps a hand over my mouth and whisper-hisses, 'Quiet!'

'What's going on up there?' her sister Amy calls from somewhere downstairs.

'Crap,' Helen mutters.

She shoves me into the closet then hurries out and pushes the door to. I fall against a rack of clothes, stumbling over the mountain of shoes covering the floor. I steady myself then go peek through the gap between the door and frame, as Amy stalks into Helen's bedroom beyond. Her raven hair rests in a long braid over one shoulder, grey eyes sharp and assessing. She's two years older than Helen and has always been funny and kind. But there's something almost...ancient about the cold look in the eyes now. And the way she's moving is odd.

'I heard a loud noise,' she says.

'I fell out of bed,' Helen answers. 'Did Mum and Dad phone?'

Amy's eyes narrow. 'Mum wanted to cut their trip short when I told her about the press conference, but I told her you begged for them not to. You wouldn't want to ruin it for them, would you? That would be selfish and you aren't selfish, are you, Helen?'

'I try not to be,' she says meekly.

Amy strokes the crown of Helen's head. 'You miss Inara, don't you?'

I frown at the unnatural way Amy is speaking, as Helen glares up at her and says, 'She's my best friend.'

'You'd tell me if she contacted you, would you not?'

Helen drops her gaze to the carpet, body rigid. 'I tell my sister everything.'

A creepy smile curls over Amy's face before she steps back. 'Good girl. I will return downstairs for when you need me.'

Helen shuts the door behind her sister then hurries over to the closet and yanks the door open. She grabs my hand and pulls me out.

'What the hell happened to your sister?' I whisper.

'That...*thing*, isn't my sister,' she says then glares at me. 'Didn't you understand my message? I told you not to come!'

'What is it?' I ask ignoring her anger, since Helen's always angry.

She glances at the bedroom door, fear painting her expression. 'I don't know. She was acting strange for a few days then...two nights ago I went downstairs for a glass of water and Amy was in the kitchen. She—she...'

'What?'

'Her eyes were bleeding,' she whispers.

I blink, horrified. 'What?'

'It was like she was crying; only the tears were blood.' She frowns at me. 'What happened to your voice?'

I press a hand to my throat. 'There was this thing that happened...'

'This *thing*?' she drawls. 'You just materialised out of thin air, Inara. What the bloody hell is going on? Are you an alien? You're an alien, aren't you?'

I snort at how ridiculous she sounds then frown when I realise, it sounds more plausible than the truth. Before I can respond, the bedroom door bursts open, shards of the wooden frame spraying the purple carpet.

Amy steps into the room, eyes fixing on me. 'You've been keeping secrets, Helen.'

I step in front of Helen as crimson brims in Amy's eyes. Her pupils elongate into slits as the braid resting on her shoulder uncoils into three, writhing ropes. Hissing fills the air and I realise they're not ropes but snakes.

'Holy crap,' Helen rasps behind me.

A raspy laugh rumbles from Amy. 'I've been waiting for you, Noisemaker,' she says flashing sharp teeth. 'I smelt you the moment you stepped foot inside this dwelling.'

Blood tracks from her eyes down her face and drips from her chin. It soaks her shirt and moulds it to her skin. I search my brain to figure out what the hell she is but come up blank.

'I've done nothing wrong,' I say trying to sound brave for Helen's sake. 'You don't have to do this. You can choose not to.'

She curls her lip in disgust. 'Even if you were the saintliest creature to roam beyond your island, your existence is breaking several laws and I'm here to restore balance.'

Claws extend from her fingertips and she uses them to slice the sodden shirt from her body. It drops to the floor, revealing a bronze breastplate hugging her torso beneath. Twin, metal serpents coil her upper arms, matching vambraces around her wrists. Her skin grows paler as we watch, bleaching white and gaining a peculiar sheen. Blood from her chin paints her chest in seconds, highlighting a pattern formed by insipid scales.

I look from her snake-like skin to her serpent stare, my insides turning to liquid fear. 'What have you done with Amy?'

'The human girl is not your concern,' she hisses then wriggles her shoulders until two, leathery wings open behind her, knocking things from Helen's desk. 'You should have let Bedros kill you. I will not make it quick.'

Her snake hair grows agitated, hissing louder and snapping needle-sharp teeth around her frame. They seem to grow longer as they coil and thrash against her.

'Medusa,' Helen breathes.

'I am no Gorgon, child,' the creatures snarls. 'We Furies have a noble purpose. My sisters and I dole out justice, punishing those who dare break the law.' She lifts her arm and a flash of black light bursts from her palm. It delivers a heavy-looking weapon into her waiting hand, the long-handled axe curved and sharp.

'I haven't broken any laws!' I insist, fear threatening to choke me.

'You are the product of a law broken by your parents,' she says.

Parents, which parents? Her answer differs to Aaron's claim. He said I'm being hunted because of what I am yet the Fury is saying it's because of something my parents did?

'I'm being punished for something my parents did? That isn't fair!'

The Fury regards me then says, 'I agree.' My relief fades when she adds, 'As recompense, I will make it a quick death.'

Helen whimpers behind me and my shoulders cramp at the sound. The urge to grab her and run is overwhelming but there's nowhere to go. The Fury is blocking the exit and I left the lyre on the floor of the hotel bathroom. I look over my shoulder to see Helen shaking. I can't risk using my voice and don't have a weapon. I glance at Helen's hockey stick by the door but I'd still have to get past the Fury to reach it.

I sigh and meet the Fury's gaze. 'I'll surrender, if you let Helen leave before you kill me.'

'I'm no fool,' the Fury warns, slitted eyes wary at my easy surrender. 'Your voice cannot affect me, Noisemaker.' She points to her left ear. 'Deafness was a price I chose to help end you.' If she's deaf then how is she hearing my words?

'I'm not asking for her to leave so I can use my voice on you,' I counter, suddenly noticing how she concentrates on my mouth when I speak. 'I just don't want her to see me die. She doesn't need to go through that.'

The Fury considers Helen then hisses, 'She may wait downstairs.'

'How do I know you won't hurt her when I'm gone?'

She bares her teeth, sharp and painted with the blood. 'You dare question my intent, vile abomination?'

I bristle at her insult, sick of the monsters I meet claiming *I'm* the threat. 'Last I checked my kill count was zero. *You're* the murderer here.'

'I uphold the laws,' she snarls before her slitted eyes rest on Helen. 'If she is a good girl, I will let her drink of the Lethe,' she says gesturing to a small vial hanging from a chain around her neck.

'The River of Forgetfulness,' I say staring at the glowing liquid inside the vial, then frown wondering how I know what she's talking about.

'Her life will be as it should: like you never existed,' the Fury says. 'Order will be restored and my job complete. Helen will live a long and happy life without you, Noisemaker.'

I meet Helen's gaze over my shoulder. Can she really forget me so easily? The thought hurts but it's a sacrifice I'm willing to make.

'Okay,' I rasp stepping aside to let Helen pass.

'No!' she cries, grabbing my arm.

I prise her fingers away and meet her gaze. 'It's the only way, Helen. *Please.*'

She stares at me, eyes wet with tears before taking a shaky step back. The Fury moves to let her through and Helen watches me from the doorway, before running away.

The Fury blocks my escape when she's gone. Blood paints her face from the eyes down, dripping onto her chest and snaking down her torso. She steps in my direction, clawed fingers tight around the axe handle.

My heart stutters when she lifts the weapon above her head. Once again, my life is about to end and I don't know how to feel about it. It doesn't get any less terrifying but it does get easier to accept this as my fate. Maybe I'm supposed to die. I don't want to but I don't want to live this way either.

I stumble when the Fury grunts and jump back in time for her axe to slam into the carpet at my feet, barely missing my toes. She spins, blood spilling from a wound in the back of her head. Helen stands in the doorway, gripping her hockey sick like a baseball bat.

Oh crap.

The Fury snarls something in the same-sounding language Aaron uses then pins Helen to the doorframe by her throat. Something snaps and Helen goes limp, hockey stick thudding to the floor.

'NO!'

I launch myself at the Fury and land on her back, fingernails digging into scaly flesh. Helen drops to the carpet, grey eyes wide and unseeing, as the Fury whips around trying to throw me off. Take it back! Please, God, take it back!

Snake hair hisses and snaps and sinks needle teeth through my coat and into the skin beneath. Each bite burns like acid but my grip tightens. The glacial well in my middle bubbles over, dark and desperate for vengeance. I lock my arms around the Fury's throat and she thrashes beneath me. We leave the floor and my back slams against the ceiling. I gasp at the crunch of several ribs breaking, tears blurring my vision, but cling on.

The more the snakes bite, the more feeling I lose in my arms, until I lose my grip on the Fury's neck and land beside where her axe is buried in the carpet. I shove to my feet and grasp the handle in both hands. I manage to yank it free, even as my fingers start to tingle with whatever poison is numbing my arms.

I stumble under its weight, wondering how the Fury lifts it so effortlessly. She shrieks and swoops at me and I scream, blindly swinging the axe at her. She screeches and hot wetness, sprays my face. The axe slips from my grip and I blink through Fury blood to watch her writhe on the carpet, right wing slashed in two.

An elongated snarl vibrates from her, bleeding eyes zeroing on me. She hits me a second later, throwing me into the mirror across the room. Glass rains over me as I thud to the carpet, gasping for air as pain radiates through my right arm. I look down at the bone protruding from my ripped coat sleeve and gag.

The Fury chuckles drawing my focus and I look up to see her swinging her axe, inches from my face. She drops a coin on the carpet at my side and grins. 'Payment for Charon. Give Hades my regards.'

I shiver at the thought of the Ferryman's bony fingers clutching my remains and her smile turns triumphant. Her throaty laughter presses against my flesh, making my skin crawl and I frown at the wrinkling air around us. Familiar ringing slices the air and the Fury jerks; axe slipping from her fingers, before her head topples from her shoulders. The twitching, headless body slumps sideways onto the carpet.

Aaron stands in her wake, sword drawn and dripping with blood. The relief of seeing him is so potent it's painful and I blow out a grateful sob. He's here. I'm safe. I bite back a whimper when he scoops me from the carpet and carries me to the bed. He sits me on the edge, brow furrowed as he carefully examines my broken arm.

'You don't have to do that,' he says.

'Do...what?' I pant.

'Pretend it doesn't hurt. I've broken enough bones to know different.'

'I've spent so long hiding my pain, I don't know if I can stop.'

His bright gaze meets mine. 'Inara—' He looks away at a noise somewhere in the house then goes to the door. 'Wait here while I check the rest of the house.'

He darts from the room and I let my gaze drift to Helen, prone on the floor. Aaron was right in saying I shouldn't come here. He said it would make things worse for Helen and now she's dead.

I go kneel by her side and use my left hand to brush hair from her face then close her eyes. I take her hand and rest it in my lap, so I can finger the band of coloured fabric on her wrist. It matches the friendship bracelet circling my left wrist and I start to cry. This is my fault. She's dead because of me, just like my family.

Aaron squeezes my shoulder. 'We need to go.' I stare up at him through my tears to find his gaze filled with pity.

A chill sweeps the room and the dead Fury bursts into flames. Charon's skeletal hand reaches up through the blood-stained carpet, bony digits retrieving the coin the Fury gifted me for my passage to the Underworld. The payment disappears into the abyss and the flames wane, the body gone with them.

Aaron takes a coin from his pocket and places it in Helen's mouth. Charon's fleshless fingers rise once more and wrap around her ankle.

'No!' I hiss, ignoring the agony in my broken arm to pull her against me. She isn't going with the Ferryman. His bony fingers can't have her!

'What are you doing?' Aaron demands. 'She's gone, let her rest.'

'He can't have her!' I snarl but Charon has the strength of eternity behind him and my grip is failing. I sob as I press my cheek to the top of Helen's head and pray for the first time since my family died. I'm not even sure the god I'm praying to exists but it's all I've got. 'You. Can't. Have. Her!' I scream.

My flesh grows blisteringly hot and light explodes through the room. I squint against the dazzling glow, fire searing my insides as I clutch Helen closer. Then it fades, taking the fire inside with it and Charon releases Helen. His hand sinks into the carpet and I look from the coin in her mouth to Aaron's shocked expression.

'Why didn't he take her?' he whispers.

I open my mouth then close it, not knowing what to say. All I know is that I feel like I've been roasted alive. Helen coughs and sits up, startling a scream out of me. She spits the coin from her mouth then frowns from me to Aaron.

'Who the hell are you?' She asks him.

'It's a miracle,' I breathe.

'How did you do that?' Aaron asks.

'Do what?' I say, vision blurring. I feel shaky and weak, like I've been sapped of energy. Fighting a Fury then being broiled alive will do that to a person though.

'The thing you just did with the light,' he says.

He thinks the light was my doing. 'That wasn't me, Aaron.'

'It was,' he insists. 'Your skin lit up and the light from it filled the room. Charon refused to take Helen because she's no longer dead, Inara. You did that. You brought her back.'

'I swear, I didn't—'

'He's right,' Helen says. 'I was in a dark place and there were people crying. Some were begging to go back but none of us could remember where we'd been. Then you turned up, shining like a star in the night sky. You held out your hand and when I took it, you brought me back.'

I look between them. 'I don't know what to tell you. I remember feeling hot and light filling the room but...' I shrug.

I try to stand but only have use of my left arm and my legs are too weak to hold me. My broken arm is throbbing and it's difficult to think through a similar ache in my skull. If it weren't for Helen being alive I'd be miserable. Aaron lifts me from the carpet and puts me gently back on the bed. He cups my face and searches my gaze.

'Are you okay?'

'Tired,' I slur.

He releases me when Helen comes to sit beside me. 'You saved my life, Inara.'

'And you saved mine with your badass hockey moves.'

'That wasn't a hockey move.,' she scoffs then throws her arms around me, making me cry out in pain. 'Oh crap, sorry!'

'I'm fine,' I lie.

Helen looks around her wrecked room. 'What was that thing and where did it go?'

I wince.

'There's a human female in a room down the upstairs hallway,' Aaron says. 'She's been fed Milk of Morpheus to make her sleep but without further doses, it will wear off in a few hours.'

'Amy,' Helen whispers then jumps up and shoves past him. She runs from the room then comes back half a minute later. 'It's her. It's Amy,' she says then bursts into tears. 'She's okay.'

'I'm glad she's okay,' I say blinking against dark spots in my vision.

Helen's face falls and she looks at my arm. 'We need to get you to the hospital.'

'No hospitals,' Aaron says putting himself between us.

She looks at him in disbelief. 'Her arm is broken.'

Aaron turns his back on her then kneels at my feet to examine my arm. 'She'll be fine.'

Helen frowns and I ready myself for the ensuing rage blackout. 'Fine? Fine!' Here it comes. 'Do you not see the bone sticking out of her arm?'

Aaron gives her a dismissive look. 'If you want to help, do something useful. Bring water and something to wrap her arm in.'

I cut off Helen's retort before she can voice it. 'Please?'

I watch the argument die on her lips. 'Fine,' she huffs and storms away.

A door slams somewhere in the house a moment later and I cringe. It bothers me that she doesn't seem to like Aaron. I'm not his biggest fan either. At least, I didn't used to be. I frown at the direction of my thoughts. I don't know what changed but things are...different between us. He's gentle and kind and protective now.

I watch him probe my broken arm with careful fingers. 'I didn't mean to leave,' I say.

'I know,' he says not looking up from my arm. 'If you'd known what the lyre was, you wouldn't have left it on the bathroom floor.'

'What is it, exactly?'

'An Apollyon key.'

'Apollyon—You mean Apollo? Young guy, blond hair and green eyes?'

His gaze snaps to mine. 'You've met?'

'He was across the road when the lyre appeared at my feet.'

'Why didn't you tell me?'

'I didn't know he was a god,' I defend. 'I thought he'd look older, like gods do in films.'

'I meant the lyre,' he says. 'Why didn't you tell me you had it?'

I consider lying then blow out a tired breath. 'I didn't want to ruin it.'

He frowns. 'Ruin what?'

'Your mood.'

He stares at me in confusion. 'My...mood?'

'Once the anger at my *borrowing* your knife faded, you were kind and caring and...sort of happy, organising your weapons.' I chew my lip at the intense look on his face. 'You asked me to trust you and I realised, I do. I trust you.' I shrug then fight a wince when it sends pain cascading down my broken arm. 'I didn't want to ruin that.'

Aaron huffs then smiles at my answer and it steals my breath. 'You haven't ruined anything, Inara.'

I stare at him, heart giving an unsteady flutter. 'Why would Apollo give me his key?'

His smile fades and I regret the question. 'I don't know.'

My stomach cramps at his answer and somehow, I *know* he's lying. I don't know how I know, I just do. Aaron just looked me in the eyes and lied.

I look away. 'My arm hurts.'

'I'll set it for you.'

I nod, unable to look at him as he takes my arm in both hands. The lie hurts more than every ache in my body right now. I thought we'd been forming a bond but he owes me nothing. He's like everyone else I've been stupid enough to trust in my life. Pain bolts through my arm and my gaze swings back to his. His eyes flare electric blue, as the darkness claims me.

SAND SIFTS between my toes as I pad toward the sound of the ocean. The air is humid and heavy, making the white dress stick to my skin with sweat. I've been searching for Aaron for what feels like hours but he's nowhere in sight. I stand in the surf to cool off, letting the waves lap my aching feet.

I head inland again, where black rock rises from the powdery, white sand. I pass between a crevice in the rock then climb and follow its path, as it moves around the shoreline. I keep climbing as it rises taller, ignoring the pain of scraping skin from my bare knees. I scramble to the highest peak until I can see the vista of the ocean.

The dark mass of a distant island rises on the horizon, hazy in the dying light of day.

Movement catches my eye below and I look down to a woman standing on the beach below. Her feet are bare like mine, the high tide lapping her ankles as she stares out at the ocean. She hugs her swollen belly, gaze fixed on the burning orange of the setting sun. It slips behind the distant island and her dark eyes fill with pain. She doesn't move as the stars come out, just stands there, midnight hair swirling around her hips in the breeze.

She stiffens when a golden shimmer appears on the dark waves. A stream of light glitters down from the heavens, dancing over the water before a man appears in its wake. Apollo's blond hair and green eyes are instantly familiar and I start scrambling down the rocks in an attempt to get closer. He walks across the water until he's nearly at the beach and I'm forced to stop, unable to descend more without risking a sudden drop.

'Did he agree to help?' the woman asks when Apollo stops shy of touching distance.

I blink at the sound of her beautiful voice. It's a vocal caress, despite the sorrow drenching her tone. Apollo closes the distance between them at the sound, pulling her close and kissing her softly. He splays his hand over her pregnant belly.

'He agreed to free our daughter from the curse but not you.'

Devastation crumples her features. 'She will not know me, Apollo.'

'We knew this was a possibility. Callista. She will be free of the curse and safe from the others.'

She closes her eyes. 'I know.'

'Poseidon meets us at the barrier tomorrow night to collect her.'

She clutches her belly. 'So soon?'

'This is the only way to protect her. I will hide her like we discussed. Nobody will find her; she will be safe.'

'But if she transitions—'

'I'll watch over her,' he promises, stroking her ebony mane like he's fascinated by the texture.

'There's no way he'll change his mind about releasing me from the island?'

My breath stalls at her question and I look around. A beautiful woman with an ethereal voice, trapped on an island... Is this Anthemusa? Did Aaron bring me here while I was passed out and leave me to rot? Betrayal stabs through me and I blink against the threat of tears. I refuse to cry, though. He did what he promised and I don't know why it hurts so much.

'Have you decided on what you will name her?' Apollo asks.

Callista cradles her bump. 'I want to name her after you,' she says, 'a name meaning ray of light, heaven-sent.'

Apollo's smile is radiant. 'I'd like that.'

Her smile turns coy. 'Of course, you would.' She strokes her baby bump, smile turning wistful. 'I will name her Inara.'

10

I jerk awake, heart racing against my ribcage. The dream was so vivid, so real. I push hair from my sweaty face and look around. I'm hot all over like I really was just on a humid island. I swing my legs off Helen's bed and palm my face, wondering why I'd dream that Apollo is my father.

I blow out a shaky breath and look around. Someone has tried to clear away the evidence of my fight with the Fury but blood still stains the carpet. *My blood.* I look at my right arm, which is no longer broken. I hold it out and flex my fingers. It feels perfect, like the bone wasn't snapped before I passed out. I prod at the skin through a hole in my coat sleeve, fingers brushing the ridge of a new scar.

I sigh and push from the bed, heading towards the door and the angry voices beyond. Aaron stands just outside, his back to me, facing off with Helen.

'I swear to God, if you don't let me in there, I'll—'

'What?' he scoffs.

'If you've hurt her—'

'I told you, she'll be fine,' Aaron says. 'She just needs to sleep it off.'

'You don't sleep off a broken arm!' Helen snarls and tries to push around him. She squeals and jerks back as static snaps between them. 'Stop shocking me, you bloody electrified moron.' She sucks on her hand. 'Anyone would think you've been doing that on purpose.'

'Who says I'm not?'

I huff at his answer, drawing his focus. I assumed his static shocks were involuntary but I guess that's something else I have wrong. I feel like a fool for ever trusting him because the truth is, I have no idea who Aaron really is. Yes, he's shown me kindness but he's tried to kill me more than once and I was *still* stupid enough to trust him.

'You're awake!' Helen says shoving past him. She falters when she sees me, eyes going wide. 'Your arm... How?'

Aaron pushes past her and takes my arm, sliding my sleeve up to inspect it. Satisfied with what he finds, his cerulean gaze meets mine, a smile gracing his handsome face. My insides tumble in response, before I remember the trust is dead and tug my arm from his hold.

He snags my hand when I move to step around him. 'Where are you going?'

'To the bathroom,' I answer, tugging free once more.

Helen follows me across the landing. 'What's wrong?' she demands.

I stop outside the bathroom door and pull her into a hug. 'Thank you for being my friend, Helen.'

Her arms come around me, hugging me back. 'I'll always have your back, remember?'

'Even if I'm a monster?'

She goes rigid but doesn't let go. 'What do you mean?'

'I'm a monster, Helen. I'm adopted and it turns out, not even human. The thing that I am... It's evil, so I've got a lot of things trying to kill me.'

Her arms tighten around me like she can keep me safe. 'I don't care what you are.'

'My family died because of me and today I watched the same thing happen to you.' I let her go and meet her gaze. 'Aaron's the reason I'm alive right now, so try to tolerate him for me, okay?'

Her eyebrows flatten. 'I make no promises.'

I huff a watery laugh. 'I love you. I just need a few minutes to piece my head back together.'

She sighs, 'What can I do?'

'You haven't asked what I am.'

She shrugs. 'Does it matter?'

Some of the tightness eases from my chest. 'I don't deserve you.'

'Yeah, you do,' she argues and pushes me into the bathroom. 'Take a shower while you're in there. You're getting sand all over the carpet.'

She shuts the door between us and I look down in confusion. Muted arguing erupts on the other side of the door but I ignore it as I stare at my feet. I wriggle my toes and, sure enough, they're covered in a fine dusting of powdery, white sand. I stumble backwards in realisation, until my back meets the sink. It isn't real. The dream wasn't real.

Apollo, isn't my father. He can't be. He... I look up, meeting my panicked gaze in the mirror and I realise, it's been smacking me in the face all along. His green eyes and blond hair have always seemed so familiar because I stare at them each time, I glimpse my reflection.

I shove my jeans down to my ankles, revealing skinned knees from climbing the black rock of Anthemusa. I don't know how it's possible to graze my knees in a dream but here I am. I sink onto the edge of the bathtub, mind bending around what it all means.

The dream was a real, tangible thing. I'm dusted in pearly sand and have scraped knees to prove it. Which means Apollo is my father. I grit my teeth and close my eyes, guessing Aaron is aware. It's the lie I sensed from him earlier, when he claimed not to know why Apollo would gift me his key. Makes me wonder what else Aaron's lied about. That woman–Callista, is a Siren but didn't seem evil, like he claimed all Sirens are. She seemed...sad and desperate over giving me up and, even that, was to save me from the curse of the island. A curse Aaron wants to take me back to.

A sob crawls up my throat, threatening to choke me. I'm an idiot for ever trusting the guy who tried to murder me the night we met. He's been stringing me along this whole time and I fell for his lies.

I wash my face and try to calm down. Whatever Aaron has planned for me, can't be good. I need to get away but have to be clever about it. I think about Apollo and the promise he made to my mother that I'd be safe. If I can find him, maybe I stand a chance of surviving.

Knowing I'm his daughter, actually explains some of the things that have happened. He's the god of the sun and *I* apparently caused that sunlight earlier. He's the god of healing and both Helen and Aaron claim I brought her back from the dead. He's the god of music, which is probably why his key is a lyre. And he's the god of truth, explaining how I sensed Aaron's outright lie. The fact I know any of these things about him, has to mean something. It's like I've been preparing my whole life to meet my real father, I just didn't know it.

I stare at my face in the mirror, recognising the features belonging to my father and those belonging to Callista. Despite everything, there's something...settling about knowing the truth of my parentage. Aaron asked in the beach hut if I'd ever noticed how different I looked from my family growing up. Of course, I'd noticed. How could I not? They were all dark haired and featured, while I'm blonde with green eyes. I believed my father when he told me I resembled distant cousins but I won't lie and say it never bothered me.

I loved my family and I always will. They gave me a wonderful seventeen years and I'll never regret being blessed enough to have had them. But when I think of Callista's distraught look at knowing she needed to give me up, or the smile on Apollo's face when he gifted me the lyre... I can't help wanting to meet them. Part of me hopes they can fill some of the void in my middle.

I dry my face, braid my hair then look at the bathroom door. The arguing has stopped but I can still hear them, moving around. I turn on the shower, filling the bathroom with sound and steam, as I carefully clear the windowsill and ease the window open. I climb up to sit on the sill, stomach dipping as I peer at the garden below. If this doesn't work, the worst that will happen is I'll have more bones to set.

I blow out a breath and shove from the window, letting gravity do its thing. My feet thud into the flowerbeds below, the impact shuddering through my frame. I open my eyes and uncurl slowly from my landing crouch. I huff a breath at finding everything intact and look up at the steam billowing from the window above. Hopefully it will take a while for Aaron to realise I'm gone.

I round the house and start running, bare feet slapping the pavement. I woke sans footwear and couldn't risk alerting Aaron by going back to fetch any. I ignore my sore feet and climb the fence bordering the estate. I land on the opposite side, frost crunching under my soles and wade through the tall grass of the field beyond. It's secluded here, fields spread out before me like a patchwork quilt.

I reach the middle of the field and look at the starry sky. 'Apollo!' My breath fogs the frigid air. 'I need to talk to you. Did you give me the lyre because I'm your daughter?' It's quiet and cold for a long time and my tone is desperate when I shout, 'What do you want from me?'

After a while the silence turns suffocating and I drop onto my knees in the tall grass. I curl my fingers against the frozen earth, feeling stupid and alone.

'*You're not alone,*' a smooth, male voice I recognise from before breathes into my mind.

I stand and search the darkness. 'Apollo?'

'I'm here,' he answers voice clear in the night air this time.

I spin in a circle, trying to spot him. 'Why didn't you tell me? I needed you.'

'I've always been with you, Sunbeam.'

'Liar,' I accuse even though I sense no lie. For all I know, I can't sense lies from gods.

'They loved you like you were their own,' he says, 'held you when I could not but I was always there, Inara.'

'I was alone when they died. You could've come then.'

'It was my hope that you wouldn't inherit Callista's...abilities,' he sighs. 'When they started manifesting, the whole of Olympus felt the change. They discovered my secret and I could no longer protect you from the rest of the gods.'

'Your secret,' I whisper, hope of him wanting to help fading. After the dream I'd thought I meant something to him but it's obvious I was wrong. I was a secret, a mistake he's been trying to hide.

'Are my family happy?' I ask.

He hesitates then, 'What?'

'You're a god. I want to know if my human family are happy, wherever they are.'

'I had Makaria take them to the Isle of the Blessed.'

'I don't know what that means.'

'It means they are happy.'

That's all I need to know. Nothing else really matters. 'Tell, the assassins to stop hunting me. I won't hurt anyone.'

'I cannot.'

'You're a god, aren't you?' I yell, angry for too many reasons. It calls to that dark, cold place in my middle. 'You know what, forget it.' I make my way further away from the fence, knowing I'm on my own. 'When I'm dead, which will likely be soon, I hope you feel guilty for the lie you told my mother.'

Light floods the field before I make it another step, turning night into day. Warm bands of light swirl around then weave together in front of me, forming the outline of a man. When the light ebbs, Apollo is standing in its wake. His skin glows as he places hot hands on my shoulders, feeling near-scalding even through my tattered coat. He looks more like an older brother than an eons-old god. His tanned skin and messy hair give him a carefree-surfer look, even dressed in gold armour like he is now.

'I'm forbidden to intervene,' he says. 'Your only hope of survival is to let the boy take you to Anthemusa, Inara.'

'Where I'll be trapped for life.'

'Once you pass through the barrier, your Siren blood will seal you inside and the other gods will no longer deem you a threat. They will call off their hunters.'

'Why would the other gods fear me, though? I didn't even know they existed until they sent their monsters to kill me.'

Apollo's gaze snaps towards the sky, like he hears something. 'I must go.'

'But—' He shackles my wrists in his hands. Searing light flares bright under his palms and I scream at the blistering agony. He releases me moments later and I stagger away from him, tears streaking my face. 'What the hell did you just do to me?'

'I've gifted you a weapon,' he says reaching for my throbbing wrists. I jerk away from his touch and he drops his hands, expression sad.

I follow his gaze to the carved, metal bands circling my wrists. The one on my left is silver and decorated with a crescent moon. The one on my right is gold and embossed with a design of the rising sun. They don't look like a weapon.

'Does Aaron know about any of this? About the curse and that you're my father?' I ask.

'Aaron knows everything but you can trust him to get you to Anthemusa, Inara. I don't understand why he's chosen to help you but he's a skilled warrior.'

Trust Aaron? I can't trust anyone. Apollo cups my face and wipes a traitorous tear from my cheek. I close my eyes against his penetrating stare and when I open them again, he's gone.

I stare into the night, cold creeping in now my father's heat is gone. I didn't get the answers I wanted and it's dawning on me that this is my life now. I either let the hunters kill me or allow Aaron to take me to an island of murderous women. Either way, I'll never go to university. Never travel the world, fall in love or get married. I'll never have children or a cat. I always wanted a cat or a dog but Daniel was allergic. I suddenly understand Callista's desperation to get me off that island, even if it meant I only got to experience freedom for a little while. Part of me wishes she hadn't bothered because at least then, I wouldn't know all the things I'll miss.

I trace the bracelets on my wrists, wondering how they could possibly be a weapon. They're warm and fused against my skin like Apollo burned them into place. No wonder it hurt so much when he put them on me.

I drop my hands and start walking away from the fence leading back to Helen's house. I can't risk putting her in danger and can't go to Anthemusa with Aaron. I'm a monster being hunted by monsters and maybe it's best that one of them finds me. I've made my decision to fight, knowing it will mean my death and I feel...okay with it. There really is nothing left for me and I feel ready to die.

11

I stumble, feet so cold they're numb. It was stupid to do this barefoot because apparently being a monster doesn't make feet more durable. Mine are sore and bleeding, so I stop to sit on the floor and rest against a dry-stone wall. I've spent most of the night jogging to put as much distance between Aaron and me as possible. It kept me warm but as dawn broke my energy levels dropped and I'm thirsty.

I don't have anything to drink and as I sit panting at the edge of some unknown field, the cold seeps in. My coat suddenly feels paper thin and I hug my knees to my chest. Mist sits low in the fields and a flock of crows erupt from somewhere beneath, scattering into the brightening sky as I catch my breath.

Silent minutes stretch out, the mist settling around me and I feel insulated from the world. I'm wrapped in a cocoon where nothing can reach me and some of the tension leaves my shoulders. The day emerges, illuminating the mist and transforming it into an ethereal blanket of light and water. I'm sitting in a dream, except dreams don't ache this much.

I pray Aaron thinks I'm dead so he'll go back to wherever he came from. The more I think about him, the angrier I get. He knows everything and still thinks it's okay to trap me on Anthemusa? He should have just killed me.

Maybe I don't have to die. Maybe if I stay hidden long enough, his gods will think I'm dead. If Apollo can hide me amid humans for seventeen years, why can't I do the same? All I need to do is wait it out until they think I'm dead then integrate back into human society. I might not *be* human but it's all I know.

Footfall snaps me from my musings and I go rigid with fear. I'm too far from the trails for it to be ramblers and it's too early for someone to be wandering alone. The pounding of my heart threatens to give me away, as a stone shifts on the wall close by. Bleeding eyes and leathery wings, flash to the fore of my mind and I shut my eyes at the thought. I don't have a weapon or the strength to fight another Fury. If it weren't for Aaron, I would've lost against the last one.

Droplets start to form on my skin and I stare at the water beading my coat. I realise the mist is lifting and I'll soon be visible to whatever is out there, waiting to kill me. I roll onto my front and crawl as quietly as I can into the field. Rocks and twigs dig into my front but if I get up, I'll be dead. Even if I knew how to fight, I'm too much of a coward to try. I'm supposed to be a badass monster but I couldn't even save my best friend.

My fingers brush the gnarled root of a tree, twisting up through the dirt. I drag myself towards it then slowly circle the trunk. I push from the dissipating mist and plaster myself against the bark, waiting to be spotted. A cloud of birds, shivers into the air from the opposite side, signalling the location of the hunter.

My shoulders itch as I look around for an escape but the only way is up. I scramble up the rough bark and into the branches. My aching body screams for rest but I don't stop until I'm hidden within the dense curtain of autumn leaves. I slump against a thick branch, black dots invading my vision. I blink them away, fighting my body's need to curl up and sleep.

A sleek figure steps into view below, the girl's dark skin like polished oak. Her petite form is covered in only the essential places, despite the cold. She lacks any feminine curves and when she looks up, I see why. She's a child, no older than nine or ten. Kitten-blue eyes shine like jewels from her dark face, as her gaze scours the auburn leaves. I stare from her pretty face to the sharp spear in her right hand.

She trots the circumference of the tree while I lock my muscles tight and pray she doesn't see me. If I've learned anything from my time with Aaron, it's that appearances are deceiving. This girl is just a child but I don't doubt she'd kill me easily.

Her gaze snaps away, whipping a dark braid around her shoulders as she lifts her left hand. A raven lands on it a moment later and squarks, as if telling her something. The raven flaps its wings, flying away and she looks back into the canopy. Her gaze seems to clash with mine before she darts after the raven.

A sigh lodges in my throat at the sound of Helen's voice. 'You can't just kill her!'

My eyes widen as she comes into view below with Aaron. He stops and drops to one knee, fingers tracing indentations in the ground.

'If I don't kill her, she'll kill us,' he says, distracted. 'She might appear innocent and defenceless but she's a vicious killer.'

I try and fail to swallow against the pebble of fear in my throat at his words. Not only has he tracked me down, he's brought Helen with him and they're casually discussing my death.

'It's barbaric,' she says.

He stands and turns to her. 'You need to be brave, like we discussed. Ending her is the only option.'

'There has to be another way,' she says.

'I shouldn't have allowed you to come,' he growls.

'Then why did you?' she fires back.

'Because Inara said you're her best friend. I thought she'd come to you.'

He brought Helen as bait?

'Maybe you brought us the wrong way,' she says.

Aaron jerks his sword from the sheath on his back in response and smirks at Helen's horrified expression. 'I'll find her.'

She glances between him and his blade but holds her ground. 'Fine, go kill her if you must but I won't watch.'

'You speak like I'd let you,' he sneers then stalks away.

Helen huffs a frustrated growl and kicks at a protruding root, before slumping against the tree. She rubs her face looking exhausted. I'd feel sorry for her, if I hadn't just witnessed her agreeing with Aaron that I should die. The shock of it is still burning through me.

She sinks to the ground, back against the tree and pulls her knees to her chest. She yawns then closes her eyes and rests her chin on her bent knees. It only takes a few minutes for soft snoring to reach my hiding place and I fight a snort because the girl can sleep anywhere.

I take my chance and climb down. Defrosting earth depresses beneath my feet as I run, adrenaline and fear driving me forward. I falter three fields from the tree at the sound of my name. I spin to find Aaron silhouetted against the backdrop of the tree I hid in. Helen pushes to her feet and waves at me. I give her a one-fingered salute and she drops her arm in shock. Even from here, I feel the burn of Aaron's gaze on my skin. An electric charge builds in the air between us then snaps when he explodes into a run.

I sprint at the next wall, throwing myself over it into the next field. Tall stalks of whatever plant is growing, snag at my arms and legs but I scramble forward. It's slow going but Aaron doesn't seem to be having my problem. I glance back to watch him vault over the wall into my field. He's cleared three fields in the same time it's taken for me to get across this one.

I reach the next wall and drag myself over. One field remains between me and acres of woodland. If I can get there, maybe I'll be able to lose him in the trees.

'Inara,' he shouts, making the hairs on my nape rise at how close he sounds.

I keep running, making it to the last wall, when his hand clamps on my shoulder. I stumble and slam into the hard stones of the wall. It crumbles beneath me as white pain flashes behind my eyes. Aaron curses as he crashes against me. He growls a string of words in his language then rolls off me. I slide fingers over the blood streaking my left cheek then shove onto my feet and scramble over the new hole in the wall.

Aaron grabs my hand. 'Ina—'

My fist glances off his cheek and he drops my hand, shock painting his face. I back away, trying to shake the pain from my hand, then turn and bolt into the woods. Leaves carpet the ground, making it impossible to move quietly. Aaron doesn't get the memo though. He steps from behind the next tree as I'm glancing behind me and I smack into him. Strong arms band my body as I struggle to get free.

'Get off!' I scream, thrashing against him.

He shoves me against the nearest tree and pins me with his body. The more I struggle, the tighter his snare grows. He presses me into the bark, spicy scent growing potent around me. It's a heady, exotic aroma that saps the fight from me and I sag in defeat. I go still, Aaron so close, his jaw eclipses my vision. I stare at it, then his lips. He's panting, bathing me with blasts of warm breath.

'Let me go, Aaron.'

He backs up enough to look down at me. 'I cannot.'

I see the regret in his sapphire eyes and look away. 'Just make it quick, okay?'

He's quiet for a stretched moment then, 'You mean, kill you?'

I stare at his swollen cheek where I punched him and nod.

His response is whisper-soft: 'Close your eyes.'

I lick my dry lips and close my eyes. This is it. This is the moment I'm finally going to die. His fingers graze my neck and I swallow, waiting for the hard edge of his blade to slice me there. The strange, electric burn of his fingers makes me shiver and my heart pounds. His fingers pause at my pulse-point and I brace for pain.

His lips meet mine and dizzying confusion pours through me. My spine goes rigid, his scent and electricity flooding my senses. His tongue licks mine and I taste the spicy, delicious aroma that coats his skin. I moan, heat and electricity warming my insides.

His kiss is gentle and caressing and I lose myself to the sensation. Sharp joy strikes through me at my first real kiss. I didn't realise I wanted this from Aaron but it's kind of perfect. The taste, the softness of his lips on mine. I want it to last forever but it can't. He's here to kill me and I clench my fists that he's torturing me with such sweetness before he takes my life.

I shove at his chest. 'Stop!'

He drops his head to my shoulder, voice like gravel. 'I don't want to.'

'Stop torturing me and get on with it,' I rasp.

'I didn't spend the night tracking you to kill you, Inara.'

I pull his face up to meet my gaze then press a hand to his mouth when he tries to kiss me again. He sighs and takes a small step back. I slip from between him and the tree and put some space between us.

'I heard what you said to Helen. I might look innocent but I'm a vicious killer, remember?'

'I was talking about the Daughter of Okeanos that's been following you.'

'What?'

'They're perpetual children but deadlier than the most experienced of hunters.'

The girl with kitten-blue eyes and dark skin flashes into my mind. 'Oh.'

He frowns. 'How did you hear Helen and I talking?'

'I was hiding in the tree you were arguing under,' I say then take a step back when he moves closer. 'I'm not going to Anthemusa with you, Aaron. I don't care if it's where everyone thinks I'll be safe. I'd rather die than get trapped there for the rest of my life.' I turn and stalk away. 'You can leave now. I don't need your idea of keeping me safe.'

He catches up to me. 'I could've taken you to Anthemusa last night, while you were unconscious but chose not to, Inara.'

I stop. 'Why? Why not just do what you came to do and get on with your life?'

He takes my hand, hold firm but gentle. 'I don't want to kill you, or take you to Anthemusa anymore.'

'Then what?'

'I want to keep you.'

My heart flutters before I remember the situation. He can't just decide to keep me. There isn't a happily ever after for us, when every monster the gods can muster is hunting me. Aaron will want to protect me but what will happen when he loses to one of the monsters? The thought of Charon's fleshless fingers gripping his lifeless body...

I rip my hand from his. 'I won't let you do this.'

He catches my arm. 'Listen to me—'

'Go home, Aaron. There is no *us*,' I hiss with as much vitriol I can muster.

'You'll die if I leave you!'

'I've accepted the inevitability of that. What I can't accept, is you or anybody else I love getting hurt because of me. I won't let what happened to my family and Helen, happen to you.'

'You love me?'

Oh crap. 'I didn't say—'

He cuts me off with a kiss and I melt against the warm electricity of him. This kiss is fierce and I curl my fingers in his hair. I startle at the soft texture, such a contrast to what I expected.

He jerks his mouth from mine, gaze intense. 'I won't let you throw your life away under some misguided idea that it will protect me.'

'You don't get to decide that for me.'

He blurs and my stomach lands on his shoulder a moment later. I stare down at the back of his legs in shock as he starts walking, then my brain reboots and I slap at his back.

'Put me down!'

He just keeps walking, grip firm on the back of my thighs. Sunlight warms my back as we leave the woods and I squirm. Hitting him is having no effect, so I try a different tactic.

'I'm going to get you killed, Aaron.' He ignores me and my frustration boils over. 'Put me down you bloody fool!' His shoulders bob and I stare at his back, incredulous. 'Are you laughing?'

'You're cute when you're angry.'

'Oh my god, shut up!'

I slap his back again then fume in silence, thinking of ways to escape as he carries me across the fields. I can't believe I blurted that I love him. I do feel some kind of way for him; warm and... It can't be love. Falling for a guy who tried to kill me would be the stupidest thing I've ever done.

'What happened? Helen asks when we reach the tree. She steps around Aaron so she can meet my angry gaze and I frown at her dishevelled appearance. I reach to pluck a leaf from her hair and cringe at the icy feel of her skin.

'You're freezing,' I murmur then slap Aaron's back. 'Put me down, Spartacus.'

Helen's eyes narrow into angry slits. I stare at her, something seeming...off about my friend. She marches around to face Aaron.

'Put her down!'

Aaron tenses at her demand. 'No.'

'What's the plan, carry her all the way back to my house?' Helen scoffs.

'If it keeps her alive.'

'It didn't kill her to walk out here.'

'She didn't have a death wish when she left your house,' he says. 'If I put her down, she'll try to escape under some stupid idea that it will protect you and I from the assassins hunting her.'

It goes quiet and I mentally curse Aaron out, until Helen comes back to face me. There's a storm brewing in her gaze and the tiny hairs on my body jerk upright in response. My back cramps in that way it does when I feel trapped and I squirm on Aaron's shoulder. Helen is an angry person. It's part of her personality, part of her charm but this is different. *She* is different.

'Helen—'

'Don't you dare ask me to stand back and watch while you give in,' she hisses. 'I'm the only family you have left and nothing...' She narrows her eyes at Aaron, 'can come between us. Not a host of monsters. Not *him*. Not even Olympus.'

My frown deepens at how much she knows. She's spent one night with Aaron but did he really tell her so much already? It took me days to get this much from him.

'I won't risk your life, Helen.'

'That isn't your decision to make.'

'What do you expect me to do?' I huff. 'Being around me requires an insurance policy, Helen. When you died...' I slap Aaron's back again. 'For God's sake put me down! I promise not to run. I just want to talk with Helen, without looking like road kill.'

He slides me down his front onto my feet, then tucks wayward hair behind my ear. 'I'll catch you if you run, Inara.'

'Fine,' I say then scowl at how breathy my voice sounds.

He cups my jaw, strokes his thumb over my lips then steps back. I watch him walk away and sit on the wall bordering the field. I touch my lips, still tingling from the pleasant sting of his thumb. Why does he affect me so much?

Helen snatches my hand, snapping my focus from Aaron to her. She drags me to the other side of the tree until he's out of sight then glares up at me. I pull from her frigid grip and rub at my bruised fingers.

'What's wrong with you?' I huff.

She glances in Aaron's direction. 'We should make a run for it, while his back is turned.'

'What?'

She snatches hold of my hand again. 'Hurry,' she insists, dragging me away from him.

'Helen, no.' I break free and frown at the indentations her nails have left on my skin. A pearly membrane blinks vertically over her eyes and I recoil.

'You lust after the warrior,' she hisses, voice different.

I stumble back. 'What's going on? What the hell are you?'

'He'll kill you,' she snarls.

'And you won't?' I scoff sick of this scenario repeating itself. 'Where the hell is my friend? Where's Helen?'

Aaron appears at my side and zeros in on my wrist with the indentations. He examines the crescent-shaped markings then pulls me behind him and snarls at Helen. Honest-to-God, snarls. He leans into a fighting stance and Helen smirks, revealing razor teeth.

'I will kill you first then, Son of—'

Aaron has her pinned against the ground by her throat before she can finish. She claws at his fingers, throaty laughter rumbling out, even as she wheezes for air.

'Where is she?' he growls.

Fake Helen laughs harder, then spits a string of foreign words at him. Aaron looks left then growls something foreign back. She snarls and he tightens his grip on her throat. Her body convulses and her pupils elongate. Blood overflows from her eyes and streaks her temples, skin turning scaly.

'Go help Helen,' Aaron grunts as he wrestles the Fury. He jerks his chin to the left. 'Over there, in the next field.'

I run to the wall then vault over into the next field, skidding to a halt at the sight of Helen's nearly naked body. I hurry to her prone form and kneel to press an ear to her chest. Relief slams through me at the sound of her heart, a relieved sob choking from me. Her neck is peppered with bites, like the ones on my arms after I fought the Fury in her room.

Her brow creases and she blinks up at me. 'Inara?'

'You scared the crap out of me,' I huff, helping her sit.

She tries to stand but her knees buckle. 'I can't feel my legs,' she says. 'That thing bit me and stole my face.'

'I know,' I say looping her arm over my shoulders. I push from the ground and help her stand.

'It stole from me,' she growls.

My gaze drops to her underwear. 'I noticed.'

'Not just my clothes, my memories! The snake-hair numbed me and when I couldn't move, it morphed into me and stole from my brain. I thought...I thought it was going to kill you.'

'I'm sorry I came back. None of this would've happened if it wasn't for me.'

'This became my fight the second your life was threatened, Inara.

These things can't mess with my family and expect to get away with it.'

We look to the tree when an unholy scream rents the air. Aaron is battling with a black-winged Fury, its axe deflecting his blows as it hovers in the air above him. It circles him, hissing hair flailing. He blocks returning blows, metal clashing. I tilt my head, wondering why his sword is in his left hand. He twists, following the Fury's flight and I stare at his right arm, crimson with blood.

Helen grips my arm when I lower her to the ground. 'No,' she begs, desperation drenching her tone.

'I have to help him.'

'It wants to kill you, Inara!'

'And it will succeed, if it takes Aaron out,' I say tugging free.

I ignore her pleas to come back and run towards Aaron and the Fury. They're circling each other, seeking the best opportunity to strike. Sparks fly with each clash of their weapons, the air feeling charged with electricity.

A pair of jagged, leathery wings rise behind Aaron as I jump the wall. The second Fury is white, like the one I fought in Helen's room. Decorative, bronze serpents coil its upper arms, matching the shining breastplate wrapping its torso. It's wearing a leather skirt and its snake-hair is red. An axe flashes into its hand and it raises it above its head. Aaron's facing away, distracted by the other Fury.

Something instinctual cascades through me and my right arm snaps up, stretched out and level with my ear. The bracelet on my wrist glows bright with gold light and a blinding flare of sunshine delivers something warm and solid into my palm. The enormous bow arcs from my clenched fist like a butterfly wing. The top reaches over my head, while the bottom brushes my knees. It's featherlight in my grip, like I'm holding air.

I follow the need to bring up my left hand, the silver bracelet shining with light as I curl my index and middle fingers around an invisible bowstring. Another bright flash delivers a shimmering arrow between my curled fingers as the bowstring pulls tight, razor barb aimed at the red-snaked Fury.

I've never fired a bow, never even held one but I *know* this, like I've been doing it my whole life. My eyes narrow, world disappearing beyond my target, as I ease out a breath and release.

My arrow leaves a streak of silver fire in its wake, the scent of burnt ozone stinging my nostrils. It thuds into the Fury about to bury an axe in Aaron's back and she screams. Her axe swings past Aaron and embeds itself in the earth to his left. He spins in time to watch her disintegrate into nothing, the silvery outline of her body visible for a few seconds after she's gone.

The remaining Fury turns her gaze to me and screeches. Aaron doesn't waste the distraction, ploughing his sword through her chest. She bucks on his blade, sinking to the hilt, coiling snakes flailing around her like black ribbon in the breeze.

She slumps against Aaron and he shoves her away, his sword making a wet sound as he yanks it free. He throws a coin at her body then turns his bright gaze to me. Charon's hand reaches up to collect the remains as Aaron makes his way to where I'm standing. I watch, frozen in place as what I just did catches up with me.

I've taken a life.

Blood-slicked fingers curl around mine and I blink at Aaron in surprise. I look from him to my fingers, so tight around the bow my knuckles are bleached. He prises my fingers free and the bow disappears in a flash of gold light.

'I killed it,' I whisper.

'You are a natural,' he agrees.

'No,' I say backing away. 'I'm not a killer.' I look around for an escape but know if I run, he'll catch me. I choke on a sob and Aaron sighs, pulling me into a hug.

'You saved my life, Inara.'

'I hate that I had to, I hate all of this!' I turn my face into his chest and close my eyes. 'I'm not a killer, Aaron.'

'I'm still grateful that you did it.'

I crane my neck to meet his gaze. He stares down at me, eyes warm and filled with something that resembles respect.

'I guess you know how I feel most of the time now,' I say.

His lips form a new kind of smile; one I haven't witnessed before. He holds me close, blood spatter staining his face and I remember his injured arm. I pull from his hold to examine the bloody limb. A cut runs the length of his forearm, so deep I can see the white of his bone. Another instinct rises from deep inside, growing overwhelming until heat pools in my palms. I look down at my hands then reach out and press them palm-down against his wound.

'It's okay,' he grunts trying to pull free.

'Stop,' I order, fingers locking into place.

Heat rises through my centre and my palms ignite with gold light. I gasp in agony, sunlight pouring from my hands into Aaron. He snarls something fierce, as lava sears through my veins. I breathe deep enough to voice a scream, arching into the sound as the fire blisters through me. It feels like I will burn to ash, before finally ebbing into manageable warmth.

I choke on a sob as it retreats, drawing back to a deep place inside. I yank my hands from Aaron as soon as I can and stumble back. He stares at me then down at his healed arm and I stare back, before the ground rushes up to meet me.

12

White flashes through the dark room followed by a furious boom that shakes the house. I scream and dive under the covers, yanking them around my head. Flashes permeate the sheets and I hold my hands over my ears against the following thunder. The covers rip back and I scream at the dark figure looming over my bed. More lightning illuminates Daniel's features and my scream tapers to a whimper. He climbs into bed with me and pulls the sheets over us, forming a makeshift tent.

'You scared me,' I huff.

'You didn't come to my room when the storm started,' he says taking my cold hands in his warm ones. Another flash burns a snapshot of his silhouette into my vision.

'I'm twelve now, Daniel. I'm not a baby anymore.'

Helen doesn't run to Amy's room when there's a storm and I have to start being brave like her. Another boom sends cold terror through me and I shuffle closer to Daniel. He tugs me into a hug and I relax, knowing my brother will protect me.

'It's just cold air meeting hot air in the atmosphere,' he says.

I've heard it all before and it never makes it any less scary. What about the energy that builds in the air, until it feels like my nose will bleed? What about the thick rage prickling my skin? Everyone just dismisses it, like it isn't there but I can't ignore the raw anger of a storm.

I yawn. 'Daniel?'

'Yes, Nara?'

I frown at his use of my nickname. I asked him and my parents to stop using it, now I've started senior school. I don't want another reason to stand out.

'Don't tell Helen I was scared of the storm, okay?'

'I won't,' he promises.

'And stop calling me Nara.'

His responding laughter melts into the next rumble of thunder.

A THOUGHT WRIGGLES at the periphery of my mind. I'm warm, the haze of sleep rising despite my attempt to pull it back around me. I bask in the floaty place between sleep and waking, knowing Daniel will drag me out of bed in time for school. He tugs me closer, spicy scent wrapping around me...

My eyes pop open and I stare at a wall of olive skin in front of my face. I carefully peel myself from Aaron's warm skin and stare up at his relaxed features. He looks younger in sleep, dark lashes two crescents against high cheekbones. He's beautiful.

I wonder what it would be like if he was just a boy and I was a normal, human girl. Him in a school uniform, playing sports instead of killing monsters. I can't picture him with brushed hair and no weapons. I comb my fingers through his dark tresses, remembering the softness then find myself on my back. His weight presses me into the mattress, distain painting his features. Something cold and sharp rests against my throat and I squeak in fear.

His gaze seems to clear and he jerks back, pressing gentle fingers to my throat in place of his dagger. They come back glossed in blood and he rolls from me. He pulls me to sit on the edge of the bed and kneels on the floor between my thighs. He tilts my head to get a better look at my stinging throat.

'I'm used to sleeping alone,' he says.

'Then why weren't you?' I snap.

'*You* climbed into bed with me,' he defends.

I drop my gaze to his. 'I did not.'

'Just before dawn, you scrambled into my bed mumbling something about not telling Helen you were scared of the storm,' he says. 'You curled up next to me like a lost kitten and I didn't have the heart to kick you out of my bed.'

'A lost kitten,' I scoff then look away, disgusted. My gaze falls on a bed on the opposite side of the room, sheets tangled and lending truth to Aaron's claim. 'Where are we?' He doesn't answer and I look back to find him grinning at me. 'What?'

'Why shouldn't I call you Nara?' My mouth drops open and he says, 'You talk in your sleep.'

'That's *not* my name, Aaron.'

'I don't know, I think it suits you.'

I slap his hand from my throat and shove from the bed, crossing the room to see outside. I gawk at the view; blue ocean under a brilliant sun and white waves frothing against the dark sand. An eagle rides the thermals like a talisman in the cloudless sky. We're high up, like we're on a cliff, the edge not far from the front of whatever building we're in.

'Where are we?' I ask again pressing my palms to the uneven glass of the window.

'The Guardian Isle—my home,' Aaron answers, coming to stand beside me.

'It's warm.' Frost hardens the ground at home, meaning we must be somewhere far way. I glance at the lyre on the nightstand. 'Is that how we got here?'

He nods. 'You were unconscious for a while after you healed my arm, so I had no choice.'

I grab said arm, panic striking through me. 'I left Helen in that field to help you!'

'Helen's fine,' he says.

'Is she here?'

He shakes his head. 'Humans aren't allowed on the Guardian Isle.'

I stare at him in confusion. 'But...I thought you were human.'

He barks a laugh at my admission but sobers quickly at the scathing look on my face. 'Only half.'

'And the other half...?'

'Let's just say, I have issue with my father and don't like to talk about them,' he answers cryptically, gaze shifting to the eagle still circling outside.

'Talking about fathers, thanks for the warning about Apollo. He told me you know everything, so start talking.'

His gaze goes to the bracelets on my wrists, which apparently turn into a wicked bow. 'What would you have me say? Does knowing nearly every god on Olympus wants you dead, make you feel better?'

'You lied to me, Aaron. It's why I left you at Helen's house.'

'I kept it from you to keep you safe.'

'That's bull and you know it.'

He cups my face. 'I'm sorry for lying to you.'

I stare into his sincere gaze, waiting for that strange feeling to clench my insides again but it doesn't. I blow out a breath, the fight leaving me.

'Don't do it again.'

He nods then takes my wrists, thumbs stroking over the carved metal bands circling them. 'You met your father.'

'I did.'

An envious gleam fills his gaze as he examines the bracelets. 'He gave you a bow fashioned by Hephaestus.'

Daniel used that tone when he talked about Ryan Fishbourne's dad's new sports car. Hearing it from Aaron sends instant prickles up my spine. Only a top-of-the-range weapon could impress Aaron like this and I study the delicate bracelets with new appreciation.

My stomach rumbles and he grins. 'Hungry?'

'You mean you heard that?' I ask.

'I think the whole of the Guardian Isle heard that,' he teases. 'I'll have to go out to get food for you, though. Vegetarians aren't really a thing here.'

'You're leaving me?'

He retrieves a canvas bag from the other side of the room and hands it to me. 'You need to fit in. Put these on.'

I fish a mass of brown hair from the bag and raise an eyebrow. 'Are you serious?'

'It was Helen's idea,' he says. 'Everyone will be looking for a girl with blonde hair. Since we can't dye yours, this is the best option.'

I stare at the chestnut wig Helen wore for Halloween and sigh, 'It's a good idea.'

Aaron smiles at my capitulation and leads me from the room. The hallway beyond is light and airy, the rustic walls painted white with dark wood flooring. I finger the wig in my hands, trying to ignore the knot in my stomach. I'm somewhere foreign, somewhere I won't be able to find my way back from if Aaron doesn't return from fetching food. He stops in front of the next door along the hallway and pushes it open. The room beyond is tiled in beige stone.

'I trust you don't have any bathroom-related excursions planned,' he teases.

I smirk as I step into the bathroom but it fades, as I fish the rest of the things from the bag. 'Erm, what kind of clothing is this?' I ask, dangling a strip of brown leather from my fingers.

'Many of the inhabitants of the Guardian Isle have never been to the Human Realm. They won't recognise human clothing and it will make you stand out.' He gestures to the bag. 'These will help you blend in.'

'Right,' I agree absently, pulling out another strip of leather that I think buckles to the first piece.

'If the Olympians can't find you, they can't kill you,' he says at my frown then turns. 'I'll be back with food soon.'

The canvas bag hits the floor as I grab his hand. 'Maybe I should just change and come with you.'

He cups my jaw, lips meeting mine in a dizzying press of electric heat. I sigh at the first touch of his tongue, his unique and delicious taste infusing my senses. Plenty of boys and even some girls have tried to kiss me but it's never been like this. I've never wanted to reciprocate.

'It's safer for you here for now,' he breathes against my lips. He presses another, soft kiss to the corner of my mouth then leaves.

I trace my still-tingling lips as he strides away. How did we get from Aaron trying to kill me, to my craving his touch? It seems unreal but then, none of this feels real. Half of me still expects to wake up and part of me still wants it.

I go back into the bathroom and shut the door. Sun streams in through a stained-glass window on the far wall, painting pretty patterns on the stone floor. It's huge for a bathroom, steam billowing from the far corner, where a continual stream of water pours from an outlet high on the wall. It fills a sunken pool in the floor, which never seems to overflow, despite no obvious drainage. I don't try to make sense of anything, since nothing seems to follow what I've been taught about the world since meeting Aaron.

I peel off my clothes and go stand in front of the ornate mirror on the wall. I look like I've been sleeping on a park bench after rolling in mud. A faint line marks my throat from Aaron's accidental attack and I pray it won't scar like my leg and arm.

I groan when I step under the warm water and it hits my aching muscles. I use a block of lemon soap to scrub the crusted mud and blood from my skin. The pool clouds with grime but clears in minutes, some kind of hidden filtration cleaning the water—I think. I'm obsessed with discovering what makes everything here work, like I'm trying to prove that I'm not dreaming.

I soak in the pool, pretending I'm in a themed spa. It's, rustic compared to the gleaming whites and greys of home but somehow magical. If it weren't for the constant tick of fear over being discovered, I think I'd actually enjoy myself.

I pause when I reach for a towel and stare down at my naked body. My skin and hair are dry, like I haven't just stepped from a pool of water. I turn in a slow circle, wondering if I've missed some kind of magical drying device, then meet my surprised gaze in the mirror. There have to be worse things than instant drying powers but...I'm not sure I want to discover anything *new* about myself. I'm clinging to the hope that one day I'll be able to go home and that means fitting in with humans. I never fit before but it's better than what I've seen of Aaron's world and it's what I know.

I tuck stray hairs under the wig after I've pulled it into place. Chestnut curls bounce around my shoulders, making my eyes seem a darker shade of green. I grin when I wonder what Helen would think if she saw me now but it fades, when I pull the rest of the outfit from the bag. I study the bits of leather, wondering if it's the whole outfit or if maybe parts of it are missing. My gaze goes back to my filthy, discarded clothing and I sigh before turning back to the leather.

I trace the design of an open-winged dove, decorating the dark leather hugging my torso. The tiny skirt barely covers my backside and the halter-neck leaves my back bare. The whole outfit—if anyone could call it that—is ridiculous. My midriff is bare, for God's sake. I sit on the floor, stone cold against my exposed derriere and pull on the leather sandals. Matching shin-guards go on next, offering a little more coverage to my legs.

I stuff my old clothes into the bag and take them back to the bedroom. Aaron is nowhere in sight, so I decide to explore. My fingertips skim the white walls as I descend the stairs and stop at the bottom. Warm sunlight floods in from a skylight above, painting a patch of light on the wooden floor. I breathe the scent of warmed wood and catch something delicious in the air. I follow my nose down another hallway and through a door at the end. Like the bathroom, this room is tiled in beige stone except, this is obviously a kitchen. It's got a farmhouse vibe and the first thing I notice is a distinct lack of electrical hardware.

Aaron is across the room, back to me, flames licking the bottom of the pan in his hand. I stare at his leather-clad body, mesmerised by the play of defined muscle in his arms and legs. It's like he's been hewn from stone then made flesh.

I remember why I'm here and stalk across the kitchen to him. 'I can't wear this.'

His goes rigid then moves the pan from the heat and turns to face me. A boy who definitely *isn't* Aaron, studies me with a dark, intense gaze. He's got the same high cheekbones, straight nose and strong jaw as Aaron. He even has the same messy dark hair and lean, muscular build; but his eyes are lightless pools of night.

A lopsided grin parts his plush lips as his gaze rakes my form from head to toe. 'You can always take them off.'

I take a step back, some sort of internal danger meter blaring inside me. 'Sorry, I thought you were Aaron.'

A dark chuckle leaves him. 'Aaron's been busy,' he says countering my step. He sniffs the air as he gets close then tilts his head. 'Let me guess your origins.' He captures a curl of my fake hair between his fingers. 'A pretty thing like you has to be a Daughter of Aphrodite.'

I tug the hair from his grasp and put some more space between us. Can he really smell that I'm half god? What if he gets close enough to smell that I'm also part Siren?

'How did you know?' I ask feigning innocence.

'All Aphrodite's children inherit her beauty,' he says then runs a hungry gaze over me again. 'I can tell, you're new here. Why don't I show you around?'

'She's only here for the Games, Logan,' Aaron says stepping into the kitchen, 'so back off.'

Aaron comes to stand behind me and rests a possessive hand on my hip. Logan smirks and steps up to my front, sandwiching me between them as they face off. Two, distinct, dominant personas press against my skin, threatening to choke me.

'Word is, you failed to kill the Siren,' Logan says then tuts, 'I thought you'd be able to kill a little girl, Aaron.'

'I said, back off, Logan.'

Logan laughs. 'Did you make time to go visit your whore of a mother while you were gone?' His gaze drops to me. 'Or were you too busy cavorting with pretty, little demigods?'

'*Our* mother isn't a whore,' Aaron snarls.

I look between them. They're brothers?

Logan scoffs then bends to bring his gaze level with mine. 'Let me know when you decide to train with someone worth their salt.'

He laughs when Aaron growls in warning and saunters from the kitchen, pausing only to wink at me on his way out. The second he's gone Aaron spins me to face him. For the first time I realise, he's dressed like Logan, except they have different emblems painted on the leather. Logan's was a helmet design, whereas Aaron's is an eagle.

'What did you tell him?' Aaron demands.

'N-nothing,' I answer, surprised by the sharp edge to his tone. 'He could smell I was demigod but guessed I was a Daughter of Aphrodite and I let him believe it. What was I supposed to do? You didn't tell me he was here, or I would've stayed upstairs.'

'He shouldn't be here today,' he sighs and rubs his face.

'You don't get on?' I hedge, stating the obvious.

He snorts. 'We share a mother but that's where the connection ends. You can't trust Logan, Inara. Promise me you'll stay away from him during the Games.'

'I thought I was here to hide, not play games.'

'Thousands of demigods flock here each year to participate in the Guardian Isle Games,' he says.

'Aaand...you want me to compete?'

'What better way to hide you than in plain sight?' he answers. 'Nobody will expect the hunted Siren to do such a thing.'

'What sport will I be competing in, exactly?'

'Not sport, war games. Weaponry, strategy and combat.'

I start laughing until I realise, he's serious. 'Oh my god, have you not seen me in a fight? I'm a coward, Aaron. I can't fight—'

'Would a coward have faced-off with a Fury?'

'That was one time,' I argue.

'Two,' he corrects.

'Both were to save someone else,' I cry. 'I'm not a fighter.' I fold my arms across my chest. 'I'm not doing it.'

'It's a good plan. Be reasonable—'

'Reasonable! What the hell am I supposed to do in bloody war games, Aaron? I can't use a sword or a knife and can't exactly stroll in and use my voice.'

'You nearly killed a Fury in Helen's dwelling with your bare hands, Inara. You're not just a Siren, you're half god. If you can do everything I just said without training, imagine what you can do *with* it.' He takes my hand and squeezes my fingers. 'Train with me. Let me teach you how to fight.'

'Fighting to save someone I love is different. I have something driving me to win.' I look away and confess, 'I stopped caring about my life a long time ago, Aaron.'

'I care about your life,' he says. 'If you won't fight for yourself, then fight for me.'

I stare into his fierce eyes and see the fear behind them. The fear I've felt since the night of the accident; a fear that's never gone away. Of losing someone you care about and never being the same again.

'Do you really care about me that much?' I ask in disbelief.

His gaze softens. 'Like you cared about me enough to take on a Fury?'

I blink at his answer. I do care about him. It's too soon to be anything likened to love but it *is* warm and wanting. I want to be near him and want him to want me back. It's enough that I don't want him to ever suffer the loss I felt that night, when the accident stole three people I loved.

'Okay.'

His eyes widen like he can't believe my answer. 'You'll fight?'

I sigh, 'I'll fight.' My stomach grumbles and we both look down at the sound.

'Let's feed you first,' he teases.

'Then we can talk about how I'm practically naked in the half an outfit you gave me.'

Aaron's laughter is rich and carefree. Some of the worry eases from my chest at the sound and I let him lead me deeper into the kitchen.

THE INITIAL BENEFIT of wearing skimpy clothing becomes apparent the moment we step outside. The white interior of Aaron's home obviously does a good job of deflecting the heat, because it's sweltering out here. I scratch at my scalp through the wig, already tempted to rip the damn thing off.

'Stop fidgeting with it,' he scolds.

I drop my hand and stick out my tongue. He chuckles like he finds me ridiculous then grabs my hand, lacing our fingers and guides me between rows of white houses. Sweat beads my nape, as other people begin to appear. They're dressed in similar clothing to us, easing some of my self-consciousness, except for the many muscles suddenly on display. My angles are softer and since I hit puberty, more rounded.

We move inland from the ocean and the houses thin out, until they give way to a paved square. A trio of stone statues stand tall in the centre. As we get close, I make out foreign words inscribed around the base. I don't recognise some of the letters, so don't have a chance of attempting to read what they say, but I can guess at the gods the statues represent. The one gripping a trident is probably Poseidon. The one with the lightning bolt held above his head, is definitely Zeus. That leaves Hades, his stone eyes seeming to track me as Aaron pulls me past.

We stop outside a shop filled with leather and metal and the man behind the counter gives us a toothy grin. He's got a patch over his right eye and his skin is weathered from too much sun.

'What do we have here?' he asks looking at me.

'Cytherea, Daughter of Aphrodite,' Aaron says.

My gaze snaps to him and I quirk an eyebrow in question. This is the first time he's let me know I'll be going by that name and it makes me feel off kilter. I understand the necessity for it, I just wish he'd have given me some warning. I look back to the man with the eyepatch when he comes over, studying me with his good eye. The visible parts of his body are pitted with scars and he smells ripe, like body odour and eucalyptus.

'Fit her for armour,' Aaron orders. 'Spare no expense.

The man grins. 'It would be my honour,' he declares then winks at Aaron. 'I'll do my best. Wouldn't want to displease your father.'

I glance at Aaron in time to witness him wipe a nervous expression from his face. Every time someone mentions his father, he skirts around the subject then swiftly changes it. I thought maybe they just don't get on, but now? What is so terrible about his dad that he obviously doesn't want me to know who he is?

The stinky man cups my elbow and I fight a cringe, as he leads me deeper into the shop. 'Let me get you measured,' he says, leering at me with his good eye. Ugh.

A muscle ticks in my jaw at the amused expression on Aaron's face, while he watches me get fitted for armour. Eyepatch has wandering hands, which I'd taken to slapping when he got a little too friendly, until Aaron threatened to gut him for it. The man's been nothing but respectful since, strapping specially moulded metal to the leather already hugging my flesh. The amount of armour is alarming though, making me wonder what exactly I'll be doing in the Games.

Aaron inspects the man's work when he's done, running his fingers over the shiny bits of metal and tugging at the straps holding it in place. He grunts his approval and drops a handful of gold coins in the man's hand. The man's eye light with glee.

'How does it feel?' Aaron asks gesturing me forward.

I take a nervous step, expecting to fall flat on my face. My eyes round with surprise when I don't. 'It doesn't feel like I'm wearing it.'

'That's why all the best warriors come to me,' Eyepatch says from where he's counting his money in the corner.

Aaron smirks then points to a wall of weapons behind me. 'Pick one.'

I turn to the wall, panic rising as I stare at the buffet of swords and daggers. 'I know why I can't use the bow...' I glance at Eyepatch, 'my *parent* gave me but why can't I just choose another. I don't know if I can stab someone.' If I have to defend myself, I prefer the idea of using a bow. It doesn't involve being inches from your opponent or physically feeling the damage you inflict on them.

Aaron steps up behind me and bends until his lips brush my ear. 'Apollo is associated with the bow,' he breathes. 'You shouldn't be seen as being proficient in anything that will link you to him.'

'I'm not *proficient* in anything else,' I say.

He reaches over and plucks a sword from the wall then hands it to me. 'You'll learn.'

I take it from him, wrapping my fingers around the jewelled hilt. It barely weighs a thing like the armour and is perfectly balanced. But it doesn't feel right. I place it back on the wall and look over the rest of the weapons. If I really have to do this, then I need to do it right.

Sunshine glints from a short sword at the very edge of the display, drawing me closer. I unhook it from its mount and study the engraved hilt. It's the only gold blade in the collection and a shimmer of light sparkles along the razor edge as I turn it in my hands.

'*A gift from Artemis,*' Apollo's familiar voice breathes into my mind.

My grip tightens on the hilt in response and I turn back to Aaron. 'This one, feels right.'

He nods then throws another gold coin at Eyepatch. The pitted man catches it without looking up, a toothy grin creasing his features.

13

I buckle a sheath onto my thigh and slot the blade into place, as I sit on the wall skirting the trio of statues in the square. Aaron disappeared into a shop ten minutes ago. When I realised how much attention he garners, I'd begged to stay outside. He seems oblivious to the staring, like he's used to it or just doesn't care. As soon as I left his side, I became invisible. I'm not the prettiest girl wandering around the square and it's...refreshing.

I sit in the shade of the statues and people-watch. Nearly everyone is plastered in armour and sporting muscular physiques. I chew on my thumbnail, wondering how Aaron expects me to compete against such opponents.

The relaxed laughter contrasts to their war-ready appearance and I try to see past it. The intimidation level drops when I imagine them in school uniforms and cliques start to form. I wonder if they have a clique for me. I never fit into one back at either of my schools but they seem more accepting of killers here. I snort at the direction of my thoughts. In Aaron's world, you have to be a certain kind of killer to belong, which rules me out here too.

Abrupt clattering draws my attention to a girl sprawled on her front a few metres away. Fruit rolls from an upturned bowl in front of her, bouncing across the cobblestones. She pushes onto her knees and reaches for the bowl. She isn't dressed in armour like the others but a simple, white dress tied at the waist with gold rope. Matching rope is woven through the long braid of red hair, hanging over her right shoulder. She's beautiful, with porcelain skin and soft brown eyes.

Several warriors in the square look over at her before turning away, despite her grazed elbows and how shaken she seems. She brushes a single tear from her cheek and hurries to gather the last of the fruit.

An apple bumps my sandalled foot and I pluck it from the ground. Aaron told me not to talk to anyone unless they spoke to me first but I can't just sit here and watch her struggle. The girl looks up in surprise when I place the apple in her bowl, chocolate eyes growing wider when I offer my hand to help her up.

'I am Delia, Oracle of Delphi,' she says eyeing my hand.

'Cytherea,' I answer. 'Um, Daughter of Aphrodite.'

She stares at my hand again, before finally accepting my offer of help. Her slender fingers wrap around mine, grip gentle as I help her stand.

'Thank you,' she says.

My smile falters when I try to pull my hand back and her grip tightens. A bolt of heat zings from her to me and everything around us grinds to a halt. I glance at the still-life painting of our surroundings then gasp when new scenery rises up in its place.

'W-what's happening?' I rasp.

Delia doesn't answer, just stares at me with glazed, unseeing eyes, as the rocks of Anthemusa surround us. I watch myself step from behind a dark boulder to our left. The breeze whips my other self's hair around her shoulders, strands like spun gold against the teal of her dress. She's sobbing as she stumbles to the water's edge, staring off at something in the distance. Before I can turn to see what has her attention, achingly beautiful women follow her onto the beach. They surround her, faces and hands smeared with something dark, like they're in a mess from eating barbecue. The brassy odour reaches me as I watch one woman suck the substance from her fingers, clearly savouring the taste.

'Oh my god,' I whisper. It isn't sauce at all, it's blood. They're covered in blood. Licking it from their fingers...

I stagger back but something snags my hand, refusing to let go. Delia seems to wake from her daze at my panicked attempt to get free and blinks at our surroundings.

'It's you,' she says looking from the sobbing me on the beach to the real me, trapped in her grasp.

I rip my hand from hers and back away. Anthemusa crumbles around us, leaving us back in the square, surrounded by a wall of curious warriors.

'What did you see, Oracle?' a tall male, asks.

'It's who?' another demands.

Delia glances around the wall of leather and muscle and smiles. My back prickles, pain slithering between my shoulder blades, at the thought of her outing me right here and now. She'll tell them what I am and not even Aaron will be able to save me.

Delia retrieves her bowl of fruit from the ground then stands and meets my gaze. A gap appears in the wall of warriors when she steps toward it, all of them seeming afraid to touch her. She gestures for me to follow and I hesitate just a moment, before I hurry out on her heels.

'Come on, Delia,' a tall female, whines. 'She's the winner of the Games, isn't she?'

Muted speculation fills the square at those words but nobody steps in Delia's way as she guides me from the group. I glance back at the shop Aaron disappeared into, wishing I'd just gone inside with him. An argument breaks out over who'll win the Games, none of the warriors being quiet, over the fact they think I can't win. Some of them eye me with annoyance though and I hurry to catch up with Delia.

She leads me from the square, down paved side streets and up to the steps of a circular building. Sunlight glints off the gold roof, making it gleam. She ascends the steps and disappears inside. I bite my lip, contemplating making a run for it, when she appears again in the doorway above. I sigh and traipse after her, stopping when I reach the top. Gold letters decorate the lintel of the entrance and I stare up at them.

'They say "House of Apollo",' Delia tells me from the other side of the archway. 'You're safe here, Inara.'

She offers her hand to pull me inside but I shake my head. 'No offence, but I'd rather not.'

She drops her hand and turns away. 'I understand.'

I follow her inside, careful not to get too close to the dishes of fire burning either side of the dark passageway. The flames lick up the walls, illuminating the way and perfuming the air with something floral. Delia leads me along several passages then into a large, inner chamber. A giant, marble carving of Apollo stands proud in the centre, bow drawn and stone gaze fixed on whatever he's hunting. I look up at the translucent gold roof, allowing sunlight to paint the room with a honeyed glow.

My gaze drops to the young girls in matching tunics, attending different tasks throughout the room. The closest of them places blossoms and floating candles into the pool surrounding the base of Apollo's effigy. They sing as they work, weaving the air with sweet harmony.

'They are Daughters of Okeanos,' Delia explains and I wonder why that sounds familiar.

She claps her hands once and the girls stop what they're doing to line up in front of us. A dark-skinned beauty steps from behind a pillar, blue eyes meeting mine, the reason it sounds familiar looking me in the face.

'You,' I say taking a step back.

'You recognise Diana?' Delia asks looking between us.

'She was hunting me,' I say. 'I hid in a tree to evade her.'

'I saw you in the burning tree,' Diana agrees. 'I left you there knowing the warrior and human girl approached.'

'Are you saying you *weren't* trying to kill me?'

'Diana has been tracking you for weeks,' Delia says. 'She wasn't supposed to let you see her.'

I glance between them. 'Why *was* she tracking me?'

'Aaron wasn't the first assassin to locate you,' Delia says. 'Apollo wanted to ensure your safety, so he sent several warriors to protect you.'

'I took care of the first three hunters,' Diana says.

I stare at the fragile-looking girl as my mind tries to process what she's saying. Death was following me around way before my transition kicked in, meaning Olympus wanted me dead a long time before they knew if my Siren abilities would realise.

'I owe you my life,' I say, brain still whirring over what the hell this all means. I feel sick at the thought that I might've been dead before Aaron ever found me. Not that what he did the night of the accident wasn't terrifying but, what's growing between us now...

'You owe me nothing,' Diana says. 'I serve the wish of my goddess.' She bows then moves away and the other girls follow suit, dispersing to return to their tasks.

'Her goddess?' I ask Delia.

'Artemis,' she says, 'Apollo's twin sister. She gave the order to the Daughters of Okeanos to protect you.'

The revelation that I have a divine aunt, makes me think of Aunt Gertrude and guilt rains through me. She's probably worried sick but at least she's safe now I'm gone. How many assassins visited her home while I was there? I shudder at the thought.

'You plan to compete in the Games,' Delia says as we walk a slow circle around the base of Apollo's statue.

'How do you know?'

She smiles. 'I'm an oracle, remember?' She points to the sword strapped to my thigh. 'Artemis gifted you that.' We leave the main chamber, back into the passageways and I follow Delia in silence as my fingers brush the hilt of the blade. She turns to me when we reach the exit. 'You think you have no allies but you're wrong, Daughter of Apollo,' she says then steps outside. 'Come, we must return to the square before Aaron realises, you're missing.'

She glances my way as we walk back. 'You want to know if the vision we shared is going to come true.'

'It's weird how you speak in statements like you're, answering questions I haven't asked.'

'Why ask when I already know the answers? I see only possibilities, though; the many pathways a being can follow. Everyone carves their own path, Inara.' Her warm gaze meets mine. 'Do you really think I'd be helping you if I truly believed that vision would come true? You have goodness in you, remember that.'

'But it's a possibility? I could get trapped on Anthemusa with those...for want of a better word, women.'

'Anything is possible. Your existence is proof of that.'

'What do you mean?'

'Aaron should've killed you,' she says. 'The hatred he has for your kind, should've sealed your fate the moment he found you, yet here you are.'

'Why *does* he hate Sirens so much?' I ask sensing there's something more than just the fact they're monsters.

'This is something he must tell you,' Delia answers, stopping at the edge of the square and pointing. 'He is searching for you.'

I look over to where she's pointing to see Aaron blinking in the sunlight from the doorway he's stepped from. When I glance back at Delia, she's gone. I blow out a breath, wondering how everyone keeps doing that. It's like being around members of the Magic Circle.

I turn back to Aaron and smirk at his confusion at finding me gone. I step in his direction but falter when a girl hurries from the doorway behind him, calling his name. Surprise fills his face when he sees her. She runs at him and he catches her, when she leaps into his arms. He spins her, both of them laughing. It's a joyful sound, echoing across the square to where I'm standing.

The girl smiles up at Aaron as they stop spinning and he places her on her feet. Her hazel eyes are warm and filled with affection as she tells him something I'm too far away to hear. She's beautiful; dark hair falling in spirals to her waist. The dark leather hugging her form, highlights her feminine superiority, making me feel inadequate in comparison. Unlike me, she's toned and athletic and more suited to Aaron. Flowery tattoos mark her skin from wrist fingertip, like she's wearing lace gloves. There's something very...womanly about her, despite her looking close to my age.

Aaron laughs at whatever she's saying and rests a hand on her shoulder. Their bodies remain close as they talk and an uncomfortable sensation uncurls in my stomach. Ice roars to life in my chest, licking my ribs like acid. I gasp against it, as wintry rage smokes through my flesh. The bracelets on my wrists activate, lighting up ready and an insidious voice breathes into my mind. It tells me to end the girl that's touching what's mine.

Aaron's laughter carries over the bustle of the crowded square again, piercing the cold hatred for a girl I don't even know. The world snaps back into focus and I take a step back. I blink down at my burning wrists, wondering what the hell I'm doing. The overwhelming need to kill Aaron's friend, grips my flesh. I press shaking fingers to my throat and try to swallow the aching burn back. My Siren voice didn't hurt the day I'd hummed in the shop to steal food but, I hadn't wanted to kill anyone then.

I turn from the square before Aaron can spot me, shaking with a sickening mix of rage and fear. I really am the monster everyone claims me to be. I killed to save Aaron but this...this is the overwhelming need to murder, he claims all Sirens have. I wanted to kill her, even delighted in the thought. If it hadn't been for the sound of his laughter... How long will it be before I truly hurt someone?

I run from Aaron and his friend, as fast as my legs will take me. I won't let myself become like the women on that island. I don't stop until I'm outside Aaron's home, sweating and panting because it took too long to find my way back. I stare up at the house wondering if he's beaten me here. Even if he hasn't, Logan is likely inside.

I turn from the door and head towards the cliff edge instead. I just need time to process, then I can make an informed decision about what to do. Do I tell Aaron about the wintry rage, or will it make him cold and wary of me again? The thought of him looking at me with distain again hurts.

I wander along the edge of the cliff until my breathing levels out. My shoulders cramp each time I look down at the black sand far below. Dizziness sweeps through me, so I lower onto the grass and yank off my sandals. Waves crash against the beach below, foaming and pretty, as the sun paints sparkles across the water. It's peaceful here, no planes or traffic in the distance. I flop onto my back and let my feet dangle from the edge. The breeze tickles my bare soles and I sigh out a long breathe.

This is what I need, a few minutes alone to decompress. I close my eyes and listen to the sound of waves lapping sand. It's calming and soothing and I let myself doze.

WHEN THE SUN grows hotter and the air is stifling, I sit up to look around. I don't know how long I've dozed but it's dark, silver moon-light bathing the rocks around me. My spine stiffens when I realise where I am. I shove to my feet and look around, wondering how the hell I made it to Anthemusa.

'Delia?' I whisper, wondering if this is real.

It *feels* real but so did the vision and I was just on the Guardian Isle atop the cliff. I walk from the shelter of the rocks, down to the ocean and hesitate at the sight of Callista, standing in the surf.

'Uh, hello?'

She whirls in my direction, dark eyes wide. The first thing that strikes me, is how beautiful she is. She looks no older than twenty-five, with dark hair cascading to her waist. Thick lashes, angular features. She has the body of a fifty's pinup, her movements sultry as she closes the distance between us. She cups my face but I cringe away at her icy touch. She snaps her fingers back in the same instance, like I've burned her.

'You're warm, like your father,' she breathes then joy fills her midnight gaze. 'How I have dreamed of this moment.'

'I'm really here?' I ask, panicked.

'No,' she sighs. 'Apollo would visit me the same way. I could touch him and he me, but he was never really here.' My panic ebbs at her explanation. 'Do you know who I am?'

I nod but can't bring myself to say it. The sultry creature before me doesn't fit my idea of what a mother should be. She hasn't aged since the dream I had of her when she was pregnant with me. I know it must be because she isn't human and I shouldn't hold it against her but... I don't think she'll ever measure up, not really. She'll never be the woman who raised me. She'll never be Grace Thompson. It isn't fair for me to compare them but I had it so good for seventeen years and I just want back what I've lost.

A spicy scent teases my nostrils and I look around. Instead of a bright, cerulean gaze, I see is empty night. His voice carries on the breeze, as if woven into the air.

'Did you hear that?' I ask.

'Not yet,' Callista pleads, frigid fingers gripping my arm.

I meet her panicked gaze. 'What do you mean?' I look down when her hand slips through my arm and see I'm fading. 'Oh.'

'Please come back,' she says. My heart aches for her loss. Grief is something I'm familiar with, something I understand.

'I'll try.'

I turn away as I continue to fade and follow the sound of Aaron's voice to the edge of the ocean. It grows bolder and instinct floods me, like my spirit is connecting back with my body. It's a heady sensation and I feel grass instead of sand beneath my feet.

I close my eyes and fall forward towards his voice. A strange sensation shudders the length of my spine, a sense of freedom I've never experienced blasting through me. I open my arms to it, welcoming the rush of air around my body, before something bands my waist and yanks me back.

14

I blink in the stark sunlight, trying to breathe against the steel bar constricting my chest. I look down at the muscular arms, then beyond to the black sand and waves below.

'Hell fire,' I croak.

'Are you crazy?' Logan snarls against the shell of my ear as he backs us onto the grass, away from the sheer drop. He spins me to face him, grip painful on my upper arms. He looks furious, dark gaze penetrating like Aaron's but colder. He smells spicy like Aaron, too: spicy but with a hint more musk.

'Y-you can let go now,' I say.

He glares at me. 'If I let go, will you try throwing yourself off the edge again?'

I glance over my shoulder to the beach below, stomach flipping when I realise what he means. My leap from the shore of Anthemusa almost became reality, right from the edge of the cliff.

'I was sleepwalking! I wasn't trying to jump.'

The severe edge to his glare melts, dark eyes heating with warmth that wasn't there before. *Now*, he looks like his brother. Heat creeps through my body as he continues to stare at me with that perceptive gaze.

'You can, um—you can let go now,' I say.

His gaze sharpens and he drops me like a hot potato. I stumble at the loss of support then watch him stalk away without a backwards glance. My throat ignites at the feeling of rejection, like it did at the square. I press shaking fingers to it then turn away in case Logan decides to come back. The feeling gets worse the more I try to swallow it away and I hiss in frustration. I don't know why I feel rejected by Logan and don't even know why I care. I don't even like him. I glance in the direction of Aaron's house then start running. I can't let him find me like this. He'll go back to hating me and the thought fills me with terror.

Something glitters on the ground as I reach the pathway that winds down the front of the cliff, down to the beach. I pluck the feather from the grass and smooth it between my thumb and forefinger, wondering what kind of bird would have feathers as long as my forearm. I cringe at the thought, hoping to never meet one and release the feather into the breeze. It floats away, glinting in the morning sun.

The sun has reached its zenith by the time I reach the black sand. The sugary grains coat and mould my feet, as I pad down to the waves. The cliff towers above me, the curve of the beach wrapping me in the illusion of privacy.

Water fizzes around my toes when I step into the surf. It's cool and refreshing and I unbuckle my shin-guards, throwing them back onto the beach to wade out a little deeper. I pull off the itchy wig and move deeper, until the waves kiss my thighs. Calm bleeds through me and the fire, finally, ebbs from my throat.

An eagle screeches above and I tip my face to it, lifting my arm to block the glare of the sun. I catch a reflection of movement in the bracelet on my wrist and freeze. I angle my arm, until the metal plate on my vambrace details the dark figure moving silently though the water behind me.

I drop the wig from my right hand and casually slide my fingers to the hilt of the blade on my thigh. I drop my left arm, find my balance then, spin to face my attacker. My sword clashes with his, before my eyes widen and I drop my weapon.

Aaron catches it before it hits the water and offers it back to me. 'That was good but you're not supposed to drop your blade,' he says then frowns. 'I heard you shared a vision with the Oracle of Delphi.'

'I didn't realise I wasn't supposed to touch her,' I defend at his chastising tone.

'What did you see?'

'Myself, on Anthemusa,' I say wading past him, back to the beach. 'Delia has been expecting me apparently.'

'Not everything Delia sees comes to pass,' he says tightly.

'But it's likely, otherwise what's the point in having an Oracle?'

He catches my hand as we reach the sand. 'I won't let that happen, Inara.'

I pull away. 'Why are you doing this, Aaron? You don't even know me, yet you're risking your life for me. How long have we been together, a week—?'

'Three.' When my mouth falls open, he says, 'I think whatever you did to bring Helen back then heal my arm, sapped your energy. That and being shot, and then the transition. You were unconscious for a while after we arrived.'

I shake my head. 'It doesn't even matter. The point is, how can you do such an emotional three-sixty in such a short amount of time? You wanted to kill me, Aaron. *Kill me.* You came to murder me because you hate what I am and now that suddenly doesn't matter?'

It isn't until the words are out that I realise, the real reason I'm so upset. I thought it was how my jealousy of seeing Aaron with that girl at the square made my throat burn but really, it's fear. Seeing them together reminded me that it's not just about me. Aaron had a life and friends before he came to hunt me down. He's choosing to risk it all, when he doesn't really know me. I'm afraid to entrust my fragile heart to a being who had wanted that very heart to stop beating. What will happen when he witnesses the growing darkness in me and decides he doesn't like what he sees?

'Is that what this is about?' he sighs.

'I don't know,' I say and turn away. 'I don't... You're asking me to trust you but the life I knew is gone. I'm not who or *what* I thought I was. I'm...not anybody anymore and, if I don't know who I am, how am I supposed to trust in anyone else?' I've got a track history of being a poor judge of character.

He steps in front of me and bends to collect my shin-guards from the sand. 'You'll need to put these on,' he says kneeling at my feet to buckle them into place for me. He stands and pulls the lyre from his tunic.

'Where are we going?'

'To answer some of your questions,' he says.

He strums the strings and the air trembles, rippling outward, like splash-rings on the surface of a pond. A doorway opens in front of us and Aaron takes my hand to guide me through. The beach gives way to a tree-filled park and I shiver in the frigid air. My gaze lands on the rows of obelisks, sticking from the ground like stone teeth.

'A graveyard?'

Aaron nods and leads me across a concrete path, into an older section of the cemetery. The scent of decaying flowers hangs heavy in the damp air, reminding me of things I don't want to remember. New gravestones give way to great monuments, rising from the earth like saintly monoliths. Mist clings to stone figures and rusted railings and sadness fills me at the forgotten graves.

Aaron stops at an immaculately clean, white-marble gravestone. An angel crouches atop the stone tablet, wings curled around her as she bows in prayer. A bouquet of wilting flowers, rests beneath her, suggesting someone visited the grave recently.

'Inara, I'd like you to meet my mother,' Aaron says, kneeling to clear stray leaves from the grave.

'Your...' I swallow a lump of emotion from my throat. 'I'm sorry, Aaron. I didn't know.'

He stands and turns to face me. 'You asked why I hated you,' he says and points to his mother's grave. 'This is why.'

'You hated me because your mother died?'

'Because you're a Siren, like the one who killed her.'

I glance between him and the grave, wondering how that can be true. If the rest of the Sirens are confined to Anthemusa, how is his mother's body buried here?

'But if she died on Anthemusa—'

'I was there,' he says.

That doesn't make sense either. 'If you've been to Anthemusa then how—?'

'Am I still alive?' he asks. 'I never made it to the island. I just retrieved my mother's body from the water before it could wash ashore.'

'Oh my god,' I whisper.

'I was too far away to hear the singing but close enough to watch her drown,' he continues, gaze distant. 'The Sirens didn't know I was there, or perhaps I'd be dead too. I waited for darkness to fall, before swimming out to bring her back. I was nine.'

'Aaron,' I whisper, a tear streaking my face.

'My father was furious,' he says, his own expression turning angry. 'He ordered Apollo to end the Siren that murdered my mother but Apollo fell in love with her, instead.'

I feel like I've been slapped. 'Callista is the Siren that killed your mother?'

His icy glare lasers on me. 'When I learned of your existence, I had my chance for revenge. You were a killer, like your mother and I was desperate to end you. My only fear was someone beating me to it.'

'I'm not...I'm not like her.'

The ice melts from his gaze and he cups my jaw. 'I was so ready to kill you.'

'Please stop.'

'Then I met you and realised, you're nothing like her. You have the beauty and the voice but you lack a Siren's power of deception; their killer instinct.' He huffs a laugh, gaze warming. 'You can't even stomach killing an animal, Inara. You're sweet and kind and courageous. And it's driving me crazy.'

I sniff. 'Crazy good or crazy bad?'

He kisses me, that amorous electricity of his, striking through me like lightning. I curl my fingers into his hair, desperate for more of the tight heat cinching my centre. His hands slide down my back, fingers tracing my spine before he grips my hips and pulls me flush against him.

'The good kind of crazy,' he breathes.

Warm delight smokes through me at his confession but I turn my face away when he tries to kiss me again. 'Your mum is right there, Aaron.'

He laughs and I turn in his hold to face the grave again. I try to read the letters carved into the white marble but it's in a language I can't decipher, except for her name.

'Mariah Lux. It's pretty.'

'She'd have liked you,' he says. His arms tighten around me when I shiver in the cold and he tugs at the end of my braid. 'You need new fake hair before we go back.'

'What about clothes? Can I at least wear jeans?'

'Jeans will draw too much attention on the Guardian Isle and it's too hot for denim.'

'Too hot for denim but not leather,' I scoff.

He smirks and starts pulling me back towards the path. 'Leather is hardy and protective against knife wounds.'

Ugh. 'I get it, half naked it is.'

Aaron's deep laughter breaks through the dank air, like sunlight burning mist from a meadow. I stare up at his profile, smiling despite the cold seeping to my bones. He's other-worldly beautiful when he laughs like that and it makes my insides quiver.

THE CEMETERY GATES open onto a residential road. Crispy leaves crunch beneath my sandals as Aaron leads me along the pavement. The sound of excited children permeates the air as we turn the corner. A playground comes into view, children running and skipping, stuffed tight into thick coats and woollen hats. It reminds me of how cold it is, while I'm walking around in a skimpy leather ensemble.

I cringe as we walk along the main road and people stare at us with wide eyes. Aaron doesn't seem to care, striding along in complete confidence until we reach a supermarket.

'I'm not going in there, dressed like this,' I say outside the entrance, people openly staring at us.

Aaron watches me cringe then pulls me into an alcove reserved for bicycles. 'If it bothers you so much, you can wait here. But I mean wait here, Inara. No disappearing while I'm inside again, to go share visions with the Oracle of Delphi.'

I huddle out of sight against the wall. 'We don't have Oracles in this realm, Aaron and I'll only move if I'm attacked.'

'Nothing will attack you in a place this public,' he says then leans in to press a kiss to my lips, like he can't help himself. 'Wait here,' he reiterates then strolls into the store.

I stare after him, wishing I had even a fraction of his confidence. A woman stares so intently at Aaron as he passes that she walks into the window beside the automatic doors. Aaron glances back at my startled laughter, a grin lighting his face before he's gone from view. My heart does a weird little hiccup at that smile and I turn away, huddling back into the alcove.

I shiver at the cold brick against my bare back and move away to bob up and down on the balls of my feet. I glance at the entrance as time ticks by, wondering why it's taking Aaron so long.

'Inara?' I spin to the familiar figure locking his bike into an available slot. He grins when he sees my face, raking fingers through his brown hair after he takes off his helmet. 'It *is* you!' he says then frowns. 'Uh, does Daniel know you're out dressed like that?'

'Joshua Forester.'

He was invited to the funerals, wasn't he? Aunt Gertrude posted the obituaries and let the relevant people know. Even though Joshua moved away a few years ago, he and Daniel stayed best friends.

'How is Danny Boy?' he asks. 'Is he back at uni after the break?'

'How haven't you heard?'

The smile bleeds from his lips. 'Heard what?'

'It was in the papers and on the news.'

He moves closer. 'Heard what, Inara?'

'There was an accident,' I rasp. 'They're gone, Josh. All of them.'

'What do you mean? What kind of accident. Who is gone?'

My mouth goes dry, voice paper-thin, as I describe the night of the accident, minus Aaron's presence. It sounds so surreal, like it's somebody else's life I'm describing. Joshua's eyes grow wet with tears as I speak, face creasing with pain. He pulls me into a fierce hug when I've finished, clinging to me as if I'm the one that died.

'You're freezing,' he says, drawing away to pull off his jacket. He wraps it around my shoulders, tears streaking his face. 'I didn't know,' he says. 'God, Nara I feel like...' He sniffs, 'I don't know what to say.'

'There isn't anything you can say,' I answer, snuggling into his still-warm jacket that smells like fresh bread. It must've been hanging in one of his family's bakeries.

'I should've been there for you...after,' he says. 'Where are you staying, with your grandparents?'

'Social Services claim they're too old,' I say. 'I'm stopping with my aunt.'

'Gertrude?' I nod and he frowns. 'Doesn't she travel a lot for work?'

I shrug. 'She tries not to now she has me but I'm not a child anymore, Josh.'

'You're not an adult either. Mum is going to flip when she finds out what's happened. She'll want you to come live with us.'

'Josh—'

'You were always like the daughter she never had and like my surrogate little sister,' he says. 'It makes sense.'

'Josh, I can't—'

'You can,' he insists then, 'God, I can't believe you've been going through this alone.'

The guilt in his tone brings fresh tears to my eyes. He loved my family like they were his own and cares that they're gone. My grandparents care but they're miles away. My aunt cares but she's been struggling to push through her own grief, while navigating work and me.

'Don't cry,' he rasps pulling me into another hug. 'I'm so sorry, Nara. So very, very sorry.'

I hug him back, burying my nose against the warm, comforting smell of bread. He smells familiar, like home and the fresh cinnamon buns he'd bring after Saturday morning football with Daniel. Joshua always gave me first pick, before he and Daniel inhaled the rest.

He wipes tears from my face when I finally pull myself together and meet his gaze. 'Sorry.'

'Don't apologise, Inara.'

'I've missed you, Josh.'

His smile is sad. 'Me too. What are you doing here?' He steps back and eyes my skimpy outfit, concern pinching his eyebrows together. 'Dressed like that?'

I try to sound nonchalant, 'I'm on my way to...a party. My, um, friend had to...um, pick something up from the shop.' Man alive, I'm crap at lying.

'A party,' he drawls, 'in the middle of the day on a Thursday? You do realise you're the worst liar in the history of liars, right?'

'Yes,' I sigh. 'I'm sorry, I—'

His phone pings and he fishes it from his pocket to grimace at whatever message shows on the screen. 'Hold that thought,' he tells me. 'I need to pick up something urgent for the bakery. When we get out—'

'I'm not going in there, dressed like this,' I cut in. If I won't do it for Aaron then there's not a cat in hell's chance, I'll do it for Joshua.

He frowns but concedes, 'When *I* get out, you're coming home with me and explaining what's going on.'

'But my friend—'

'Can come too,' he says. He squeezes my shoulder and gives me a stern look. 'Wait right here. I'll be out in a few minutes.'

He hurries inside and I blow out a frustrated breath. What were the chances of bumping into someone I know? I glance back at the entrance, willing Aaron to hurry up because I can't wait around for

Joshua. There's no way Aaron will agree to go with him and, even if he would, I wouldn't put Josh or his family in that kind of danger.

'All they had was this one,' Aaron says from right behind me, scaring me half to death. I whirl around to see him frowning at the wig in his hands. 'It's curlier than the last one but the same shade.'

'I should put a bell on you,' I hiss, pressing a hand to my pounding heart.

Aaron smirks but it fades when he steps close, his nostrils flaring. His gaze lands on Joshua's jacket around my shoulders and he frowns.

I shrug it off and hang it on the seat of Joshua's bike. 'I bumped into an old friend,' I say and step from the alcove. 'We should leave before they come back out.'

'What did you tell him?' Aaron asks as we make our way from the entrance.

'That I'm on my way to a fancy dress party and—Wait, how'd you know it's a *him*?'

We pause at the corner so I can pull on the wig and Aaron helps me tuck my hair beneath. Chestnut curls fall around my shoulders and I'm amazed he managed to find such a good colour match to the old one.

'I can smell it,' he says.

I blink at his admission then shake off the surprise and pluck at one of the curls. 'I don't suppose they have curling tongs on the Guardian Isle?'

He snorts and takes my hand, guiding me forward. I glance back at the supermarket, wondering how upset Joshua will be when he finds me gone. Will he look for me? Will he phone my aunt? I don't want any of them to worry but I'm also terrified of being forgotten.

'Inara!' Joshua yells as we reach the next corner.

I falter, turning back to see the daily paper clutched in his hand. He spots me almost instantly and starts running in my direction. Other people start to take notice, glancing at Aaron and I in concern.

'He knows I'm missing,' I say.

Aaron tightens his grip on my hand and pulls me around the corner. 'Come on!'

'Wait!' Joshua calls somewhere from view, desperation drenching his tone.

I hesitate, steps faltering as I look back but Aaron doesn't stop. He drags me forward, past the school yard then back towards the cemetery.

'Wait,' I pant.

'No,' he growls.

'Inara, please!' Joshua yells.

I grip the metal bar of the cemetery gate in response to the pain in his voice, my fingers slipping from Aaron's as we jerk apart.

'I just need to talk to him,' I say, stepping in Joshua's direction. His pace slows when he sees I'm going back, relief painting his face.

Aaron grabs my hand. 'He can't come with us and can't see us leave, Inara.'

'I just need to calm him down, so he won't worry when I'm gone,' I say tugging my hand free. 'Wait here. I'll be back in a minute.'

'The Hades you will,' he growls and the ground disappears from beneath my feet.

Gravestones come into view, the ground rushing past below as I realise, I'm slung over Aaron's shoulder. Again! I look up in time to see Joshua reach the cemetery gates, the air rippling between us. He reaches for me and I reach back as the graveyard disappears behind blue skies and black sand.

'Joshua!' I scream despite knowing it's too late. Aaron pulls me off his shoulder, sliding me down his front until my feet hit sand. I shove away and put distance between us. 'How could you?'

'You need to see reason!'

'That's rich, coming from you! I told you, I wanted to calm him down so he wouldn't worry.'

'It could've been a ruse! He could've been something else. You were at risk.'

'He had his chance to kill me while you were in the supermarket,' I scoff. 'There are very few people left that I can claim as family, Aaron. I didn't get the chance to say goodbye to Helen and now, because of you, it includes Joshua. Just like with my family the night...the night they died.'

Regret fills his gaze. 'Inara, I—'

'Just leave me alone,' I snarl then snatch the lyre from his hand. 'This was given to *me* by Apollo.' My throat ignites with phantom fire and I glare at Aaron, breath sawing in and out. I want to say more but can't now, so I whirl away and sprint up the beach.

THE SUN IS SETTING beneath the sea when Aaron finally finds me. His approach is silent and I jerk in surprise when he drops onto the sand at my side. I glare out at the ocean and clutch the lyre tight to my chest.

'You're still angry,' he says.

I stare at the still water, trying to find the burning rage from earlier but it's gone. I'm still hurting from the look on Joshua's face right before he disappeared but I understand why Aaron did it. I'm just sick of having my choices taken from me.

'I know *why* you did it, I just don't like the way you ignored my wishes. You didn't trust my judgement of the situation, Aaron.'

'You're right. Do you want me to take you back to him?'

'We both know it isn't safe, otherwise I would've used the lyre to do it already,' I huff.

He's quiet for a while then asks, 'What do you want to do, Inara?'

I meet his gaze because it's the first time he's asked me that. 'I want you to teach me how to fight, so I can defend myself. I hate how you keep slinging me over your shoulder whenever the fancy takes you; I hate feeling so weak.'

'You're not weak.'

'Oh yeah? Then why do I feel it?'

His hand covers mine, a current of electricity skating up my arm and making me shiver. 'Because you keep thinking of yourself as human, despite being half Siren, half god,' he says. 'You need to harness the abilities you were, born with.'

I think of the acid burn it took nearly an hour to ease from my throat. 'Don't expect me to sing.'

'I didn't mean your voice.'

We stare out at the ocean in silence, the last rays of sunlight streaking the sky behind the ocean. One by one, the stars appear, seeming bigger now I know about the gods. Are they up there now, looking down?

Aaron pushes to his feet then offers his hand. 'I have a surprise for you.'

'Is it another weapon because they don't excite me like they do you.'

He snorts a laugh. 'You'll see.'

The house is dark and silent when he pulls me inside. The lack of lamp-posts outside means there wasn't any light to guide our way here but Aaron managed. For some reason, the dark and quiet remind me of Logan. They suit him, like he belongs to the silence and shadows. I think of the coldness in his eyes earlier, darker than sin and twice as deadly, like the void between stars.

Aaron lights an oil lamp on the wall in his room and I blink in the sudden brightness. 'Those are for you,' he says gesturing to a neat pile of fabrics on the end of the bed I woke in.

I pick up the folded red square and shake it out. The fabric falls into the shape of a tunic dress and I can't help my stupid grin. I press it to my body, noting the length is longer than the belt I'm currently trying to pass off as a skirt.

'They're all the same as the red one,' Aaron says gesturing to the other coloured fabrics. 'I thought you'd like them better. They're less revealing and sit under your armour.'

'They're perfect,' I say and fumble with the buckles holding my armour in place.

Aaron takes over when it's obvious I'm getting nowhere fast, his fingers deftly stripping away layers of leather and metal. He kneels to pull off my shin-guards next. My mouth goes dry at the electric sting of his fingers against the skin behind my knees. Warmth weaves through me as I stare down at the crown of his head, wondering if he's going to peel everything away. I've never felt this way about anyone; never wanted the things I desire from him.

He pushes to his feet and strokes a chestnut curl from my face. His eyes are luminous as he stares down at me, seemingly glowing in the dim light of the room.

'I'll wait for you outside,' he says, voice deeper than usual.

I lick my lips and his gaze lingers on them for a prolonged moment, before he leaves the room. I stare at the door after he's gone, insides quivering with jelly heat. My fingers shake as I strip the skimpy leather from my body. I pull the red tunic on and smile down at the hem midway down my thigh.

Aaron smiles when I open the door. He gets up from where he's sitting against the wall opposite the doorway. 'Like them?'

'I love them.'

Blue fire flares in his gaze at my answer. 'Your armour fits over them,' he says again.

I grin. 'No more short leather.'

He huffs a laugh. 'No more short leather.'

He takes my hand and I frown when he leads me away from his bedroom. 'Where are we going?'

'You need food before you sleep because tomorrow, we start your training.'

15

The red tunic clings to my sticky skin as I crawl on my belly through the long grass. Dirt, sweat and blood crust my fingernails from today's training. It's been a long week of Aaron handing me my inadequacies on a platter and calling it training. This time, though, this time I'll make it to that damned water.

I stare at the bottle sitting on a flat rock like gleaming treasure, glass sweating in the sunlight. Dewy beads slide down the uneven surface, tormenting me. I peel my tongue from the roof of my mouth and try to muster some saliva to swallow. It's impossible, tongue gluing back in place at the attempt.

I glare at the bottle, knowing Aaron is out there somewhere, watching my prize. Today's challenge is to get the water. It sounded simple enough at dawn when he outlined the rules but he left out the part about having to get past him in the process. It's late afternoon, the sun a burning ball of fire in the sky and I'm desperate for a drink. Aaron downed the last bottle with a smug smile, as I'd glared at him over my shoulder during my retreat. I trace the cut he gifted me during that scuffle. It's one of many I've acquired during today's training, superficial but stinging with dirt and dried sweat.

I shift onto my elbows and squint through the thick grass. A tingle of awareness traces my spine, telling me he's definitely out there. It's an ability I've discovered this past week, an extra-sensory awareness warning me of approaching danger. I press my cheek to the baked earth as I try to gather strength for what's to come. A pearl of sweat slips from my forehead and melts into the dirt, and I wonder how the hell I have any fluids left in me.

Anger flares through me, bright and searing. I push from the ground and run for the bottle, my building wrath the only thing pushing me forward. The tingle down my spine turns into an insistent wriggle and the hairs on my nape stand tall.

I skid to a stop and inhale a deep breath through my nose. Warm spice infuses my senses and I draw my sword. The Artemis blade clashes with Aaron's when I spin to deflect his blow. I lean back on my heels, forcing him into my domain and surprise flashes in his eyes. He stumbles forward and I jerk my knee into his chest, while slamming my arm down against his shoulders. He grunts as he flips then thuds onto his back in the dirt, a cloud of dust bursting into the air on impact. His hand locks around my ankle then yanks me off, my feet.

I kick out with my free foot, hitting somewhere fleshy and punching an expletive from Aaron in response. He releases my ankle and I scramble away, pushing back onto my feet. I think of retreat for a single moment, before turning and jumping blindly back into the rising dust.

Aaron goes rigid when I land on top of him, like he didn't expect me to attack. I've spent the last week playing defence, so can't blame him. Today has been no different. I locate the water, try to reach it only to be stopped by Aaron, before retreating. Offence, is my only option if I want a drink.

I lock onto his wrists with both hands and bury my knee into the curve of his spine. He grunts when I yank his arms back, digging my knee in deeper and forcing his face against the hard earth. A smile tugs at my lips as an icy shiver dances down my spine.

Aaron twists from my grip in a move so smooth, I don't realise it's happened until I'm flat on my back. He reaches for his dagger but I shove from the ground and land on him again. I grip his throat in my left hand, pinning him to the ground and press the tip of my blade to the underside of his jaw.

We stare at each other, panting and covered in dirt. Adrenaline and rage surge through me, smoking a strange yet familiar sensation through my flesh. The ice in my veins is exciting and seductive, bleeding through the perpetual heat in my middle. Both sensations have grown this past week and I'm starting to feel torn by their opposing natures. Like the granular parts of me are in direct conflict. The fire is a deep, warm constant, while the ice comes and goes, calling to me and begging to accept what it's offering. I want it but shy away from its exotic rage. It's dark, frigid and all-consuming and, as I look down at Aaron now, a strange kind of thirst grips me.

His deep laughter rouses me from the wintry fog clouding my mind and I blink as if waking from a dream. Aaron was right about my inherited godly abilities being a part of me but I've inherited other stuff too—things not from my father's side of the family. The rage dissipates against the sight of his smiling face but the sandpaper burn remains in my throat.

'There you are, Goddess,' he breathes.

I sheath the Artemis blade and climb off him, too afraid to answer while my throat is burning. I leave him in the dirt and go fetch my prize. My soft tissues sigh in relief as I gulp the water. It's gone before I'm ready but Aaron pushes another into my palm.

'Slowly or you'll vomit,' he says. He goes to a cluster of bushes a few metres away and retrieves a canvas bag. I eye it warily when he offers it to me and he smirks. 'It's just food.'

I take it from him and peer inside, half expecting something vicious to pop out. It's crammed with little ceramic pots, filled with different kinds of food. I sink onto the stone where the water had been sitting and pull out one of the pots, before offering Aaron the rest. He's watching me closely, probably wondering why I'm suddenly mute.

Sweet bliss bursts over my tongue at the first bite of whatever cake is in my pot. I bite back a groan and devour the little piece of heaven that is still left. It's sweet and sticky and drenched in honey, and I want more. I look over to the bag to see Aaron grinning.

'Here,' he says offering another ceramic pot.

I hide my disappointment when it isn't more cake but dig in. It's some kind of spicy potato, with a yogurt dressing and I hum my pleasure at the delicious taste. I freeze when I realise, I've made a sound but Aaron isn't affected.

I risk speaking, the burn from my throat almost gone. 'Thank you.'

He collects the empty pots. 'You did well today.'

His praise sends warmth through me and I push to my feet when he does, elated that it's time to go. I'm desperate for a shower then bed, body aching more than I thought possible.

It isn't until we turn down the street leading to Apollo's temple and I see Delia waiting at the bottom of the steps, that I realise we're not going back to Aaron's home. The setting sun glows orange against Delia's white dress, clashing with the deep red of her hair. Her welcoming smile fades as we approach, her gaze raking over me.

'I'm lucky you've delivered her in one piece,' she scolds Aaron.

'If I go easy on her in training, she'll be killed when the fight gets real,' he says.

'There aren't intentional deaths in the Games,' Delia counters.

'He isn't training me for the Games,' I say getting between them and meeting Delia's annoyed gaze. 'I asked him to teach me how to defend myself and that's what he's doing.'

She purses her lips but accepts my explanation with a nod. I turn to Aaron, his gaze defrosting when it shifts from Delia to me.

'I'll return for you at dawn,' he says.

'You're leaving me here?'

'I can't enter the Temple of Apollo, Goddess.'

I frown at his new nickname for me. 'Why the hell not?'

'Artemis has deemed it a sanctuary for her Daughters of Okeanos,' he says. 'She's barred it from males but I'll be here at dawn when you come out.'

'Why are you leaving me?' I demand. I glance over my shoulder to where Delia is watching. 'No offence.'

'I have things I've been neglecting,' Aaron says.

I deflate at his admission, knowing I'm likely the reason he hasn't had time to do the things he needs to do. He's barely left my side in weeks.

'I'm sorry,' I say. 'Go do whatever you need and I'll see you later.'

'I'll be right here at dawn,' he promises.

I force a smile then follow Delia up the temple steps. The heat of Aaron's gaze warms my back until I step inside.

Delia leads me around the statue of Apollo, then through one of the archways at the back of the central chamber. The small, stone-walled room beyond houses a sunken pool. Ribbons of scented steam rise from the shimmering surface, beading my skin with moisture in seconds.

Delia claps her hands and four girls appear in response. They surround me and start pulling at my armour, stripping it away until I'm standing in my filthy tunic. I back up when a small hand tugs at the hem, meeting Diana's expectant gaze.

'You need to take it off,' she says.

I look around the many eyes on me and fold my arms over my chest. 'Why do you want my clothes?'

'Because your wounds need cleaning,' Delia says then smirks, 'but also because you smell.'

'I'll shower at Aaron's,' I say then back up when Daughters of Okeanos start to advance on me. 'Really, I'm fine,' I insist.

The floor suddenly disappears from beneath my feet and I squeal in surprise. I hit the water with a splash then gasp as I surface, perfumed oils stinging my numerous cuts and grazes. The cold length of a blade slides between my spine and the tunic, before slicing it from my body.

'Hey!' I hiss, hugging my naked chest.

The little brunette tosses the short sword onto the pool edge then turns to me with an exasperated sigh. Three other girls slip into the water to help her surround me, then they descend. The wig is plucked from my head, my braid unwoven and I'm scrubbed from head to toe by a flurry of small fingers.

I'm pulled from the pool when they're done. My skin and hair are instantly dry but nobody seems to care. A clean dress is pulled over my head and tugged into place over my body, before I'm gently pushed into a chair. My hair is brushed then braided into a fat rope down my back.

I squirm under their frowns when they're done. 'What?'

'You need food and rest to heal,' Diana says, concern in her sapphire gaze. She's the only Daughter of Okeanos I've heard speak and there's knowledge in her gaze, making her seem ancient despite her youthful face. 'The warrior has pushed you hard.'

I follow her gaze to the injuries marring my body. Purple bruises and red slashes, stain my pale skin. I reach for my face and wince as my fingertips brush tender flesh.

'Why didn't I notice this earlier?' I say.

'The medicinal oils in the water bring the injuries out to promote healing,' Delia says from the doorway. I turn to where she's standing then shield my gaze from a blinding flare of light.

Apollo appears in the wake of the light and smiles my way. 'Hello, Sunbeam.'

Delia and the Daughters of Okeanos drop to their knees and press their foreheads to the stone floor in supplication. I look from them to him then fold my arms across my chest in rebellion. If he's waiting for me to bow at his feet, he'll have a long wait.

'Isn't it dangerous for you to be here?' I drawl.

'Nobody is suspicious of my visiting one of my temples this close to the Guardian Isle Games,' he says. 'It's expected.'

I push from my seat and step around him. 'I'll be going then.'

He steps in my path. 'I'm here to see you.'

I glare up at him, wondering why he's acting like he cares. He had seventeen years to build a relationship with me. 'What do you want?'

Delia shifts on the floor and I frown at her terrified expression. My father is a god and I know I should be afraid like Delia...but I'm not. He's intimidating and ethereal, his skin gleaming like he's made from pure light, yet there's something very...*average* about his presence. It's like he's always been around me, like he claimed the last time we met.

He cups my face in a too-hot hand and fire threads through me. The searing heat lasts just a moment before he steps back and the fire retreats. I drop my gaze to my tingling skin to find the cuts and bruises gone, skin smooth and blemish free. Even the scar from the Fury attack has vanished. I brush my fingertips over the smooth skin of my thigh, where the puckered scar from Bedros's arrow was.

'I only came to see you,' Apollo says. 'If you wish me to leave, I will but I'd like you to stay.'

I sigh, 'You really want this?'

'I've spent so much time watching, wanting to know you. I'd like you to see me, to know me as your father.'

I chew my lip while I mull it over then sigh, 'Okay.'

The tension in the room dissipates at Apollo's resplendent smile and I squeak, when he pulls me into a hot hug.

THE SUN PEEKS over the buildings as I leave the temple, stretching my aching limbs. I'm dead on my feet, desperate for sleep but spending time with Apollo was worth it. I take a lasting look at the sun and smile, trying to wrap my brain around his ability to go from being in the temple, to the heavens in a blink. I actually like him and despite him looking more like a brother, he'd been...fatherly. We even had stuff in common.

My gaze drops to Aaron, sitting at the bottom of the stone steps. His back is to me, elbows on his knees as he rests his chin in his hands. I creep down to him, body tense with glee. I leap off the step above him and land on his back, wrapping my arms around his sculpted chest and laughing at his surprise. He jerks to his feet and shrugs me off and a warning prickle skates up my spine.

'Why are you angry?'

'I'd say I'm annoyed more than angry,' Logan says turning to face me, black eyes drinking me in. His lips curve with a dark smile and the shadows seem to reach for him, like they're seeking shelter from the rising sun.

'What are *you* doing here?'

'Aaron's been summoned by his father, so asked me to come for you in his stead. Did you enjoy your training session with the Daughters of Okeanos? I'm surprised you convinced them to do it.'

I look back at the temple and realise, it must be the excuse Aaron gave for my being somewhere related to Apollo. I find it hard to believe he'd warn me away from Logan then send him to collect me though.

'I'll find my own way back,' I say.

He catches my arm when I step around him. 'Aaron asked me to escort you, so here I am.'

I jerk from his hold. 'Why would he warn me away from you then send you for me?'

Logan smirks. 'Of course, he told you not to trust me; but aside from our mutual hatred of each other, we actually share something in common.'

'And what's that?'

He shrugs. 'We hate our fathers more. Call it a mutual hobby.'

I frown at his explanation, wondering once more what's so bad about Aaron's father that he still hasn't told me who he is. What could be so bad that he'd send his brother to collect me in his stead?

'Tick-tock, Princess,' Logan sneers.

I turn away. 'I'll just wait in the temple until Aaron gets back.'

'Have it your way but I have one more thing to say before you go.'

I pause on the bottom step and turn back. 'What?'

A white grin flashes against his dark features and he leans in close, blade-straight nose brushing mine. 'Sweet dreams.'

My frown deepens. 'What?'

Logan snatches me from the step and slaps a hand over my mouth and nose. Something soft crushes against my lips, a sweet fragrance permeating my senses. My body sags, feeling heavy and numb, and I go limp in his arms.

Logan scoops me up and leans in to bring his lips to my ear. 'Nighty-night, Princess,' he whispers.

My eyelids fall shut and darkness claims me.

16

I groan at the baking heat of Anthemusa and blink heavy eyelids open. I shove to my feet, frustrated that I'm here and look around the white-sanded beach. When I visit Anthemusa, I wake up tired like I haven't been sleeping at all and I'm exhausted from all the training. I pad to the water's edge, where Callista stands, lustrous hair billowing in the breeze like silk. It shines blue-black in the bright sun as she stares out at the water.

She smiles, 'You came back.' She reaches for my hand and I fight the need to recoil at her icy touch, wondering how she stays so cold when I'm sweating like a pig in the heat.

Her gaze tracks back to the setting sun. 'You're warm, like your father and I haven't felt his touch in a long time.'

'He doesn't come to see you anymore?'

'He does but he's no longer allowed to set foot on the island. I stand here and he there,' she says pointing to the ocean about two metres in front of us. 'He told me he was going to visit you?'

I nod. 'He came to his temple on the Guardian Isle.'

She turns her curious gaze to me. 'You don't mind staying with the Oracle of Delphi? Does it not frighten you that she sees what's to come?'

'I'm not staying at the temple.'

'Then where...?' Her expression hardens. 'Not with the warrior?'

'Aaron's training me,' I say, surprised by the sudden shift in her demeanour. Gone is the soft-spoken woman with a serene expression.

Her black eyes glitter. 'You're using him to train you?'

'I'm not using him, I love—'

Her free hand connects with my cheek in a cold, hard slap. 'You leave him and come to Anthemusa, right now,' she orders, voice an ethereal sneer. It's a beautiful, mesmerising sound but useless against me.

I rip my hand from hers. 'Why would you want me to get trapped here when I'm free and protected?'

'What about protection from *him*? You don't know him, Inara. He's dangerous to you—*Love* is dangerous to you.'

I already know love is dangerous. Letting people in enough to love them makes me vulnerable to the pain of losing them. I didn't think I was in danger of ever loving Aaron but I was wrong and now it's too late.

'I don't want to be trapped on this island,' I say.

'Then kill him and eliminate the threat he poses.'

'What? No! I can't kill—'

'You're Siren and my daughter. It's in your blood to kill, Inara.'

'I don't care, I won't hurt Aaron.'

She gets in my face. 'You *will* return to me then.'

'No.'

'I will drag you here myself,' she hisses.

'Good luck with that, when you're stuck here.'

A smug smile curves her lips. 'I'll give you until the Guardian Isle Games to kill him or say your goodbyes, before I send someone to retrieve you.'

I stare in shock because I didn't know that was a possibility. She smirks at my lack of response and Anthemusa crumbles around me.

A FLASH of lightning illuminates Aaron's empty bed across the room. It's empty because he's in bed with me, holding me as the storm rages outside. His fingers comb the curls of my fake hair, breaths brushing my forehead.

Callista's parting words bleed ice through my insides and panic forms a tight knot in my stomach. If she succeeds with her threat, I'll never see Aaron again. He'll be far away, out of reach. The need to be closer to him, overwhelms me and I seek his face in the darkness.

He goes rigid when my lips meet his, then grips my nape and weaves his tongue with mine. I moan, a wave of rough passion rushing between us. His kiss is fierce, like he'll never get another chance and I match his need with my own. Then I frown because the connection isn't there anymore, or that delicious, electric sting.

He holds me close when I try to pull away, deepening the kiss until I shove at his chest and break free. The next flash of lightning illuminates his face and I jerk back when I realise, it's Logan. I scramble to get away from him and fall from the bed, landing in a heap on the wooden floor.

'What the hell were you doing?' I snarl up at him.

He stands; towering over me, points at the oil lamp on the wall and it flares to life. '*You* kissed me.'

But I'd thought he was Aaron—again. 'You were holding me,' I accuse, 'stroking my hair!'

'You were crying and I had to do *something* to shut you up.'

'Why did you kiss me back, though?'

'Why are you so upset? Is it because you enjoyed it so much?'

'Keep your goddamned hands off of me, Logan.'

He smirks. 'Is that a threat, Princess?'

I shove to my feet, throat igniting with the burn of my Siren voice. I back away but he counters my steps, until I'm trapped against the wall. Enticing frost, crusts my insides, mouth watering with the promise of violence.

'What's wrong?' he sneers. 'Cat got your tongue?'

I tilt my head and lick my lips. His gaze drops to my mouth, dark and hungry. I smirk as I pull my fist back then punch him square in the face. His nose crunches under my knuckles, just like Aaron's did in the beach hut. My hand screams with pain but the look on Logan's face is worth it. The ice in my middle delights in his anguish but it isn't enough and thirsts for more.

Logan glares at me, blood dripping from his nose before the emotion drains from his expression. The lamp flicks off, leaving intermittent flashes, to light the room instead. He becomes a shadowy figure, looming over me in the darkness; a wall of lightless muscle in the suddenly frigid space. His hand clamps around my throat and my feet lift from the floor. He squeezes, cutting off my oxygen as I scramble against him.

Another dark figure slams into him, ripping his grip from my neck. I sink to the floor, clutching my bruised throat as I suck in gulps of air. I stare into the middle of the room where Aaron and Logan are tangled together, exchanging punches. It's difficult to keep track in the flashes of lightning. They're moving so fast and look so similar, that I can't decipher which one is which.

I get up and stare down at the snarl of arms and legs, trying to figure out how I'll pry them apart. The air is thick with the sound of fighting and they swear at each other, completely ignoring me. My panic melts into frustration. They're clearly, evenly matched and both too stubborn to submit. Logan snarls something in their language and Aaron bites out a retort. They've officially frozen me out of the argument, so I huff and head for the door.

The tide kisses my toes as I watch the distant lightning storm. The sun will rise soon, so I'm not too afraid to sit and watch the performance. The coming dawn marks another day closer to the Guardian Isle Games, which is one day closer to Callista's threat.

Aaron drops onto the sand beside me and wraps an arm around my shoulders. He pulls me against his side and I sigh as I rest my head on his shoulder. We sit like that for a while, watching the sun rise.

'I think Logan likes you,' he says, breaking the comfortable silence.

I rub my bruised throat. 'He's got a funny way of showing it.'

'You're the first female to make him react like that,' he says.

The curvaceous girl with tattooed hands, flashes into my mind and I work my bottom lip between my teeth. I wonder if Logan ever tried kissing her, after Aaron brought her to their home. I bite back the question and turn my gaze to Aaron. My eyes go wide at the sight of him, bruised and bleeding.

'Oh my god!' I gasp.

Blood spills from his split lip when he grins. 'Logan fared much worse,' he says then frowns and cups my jaw. 'I'll heal, Inara.'

I climb into his lap and cup his face in return, forcing myself to brave the memory of healing his arm. The perpetual heat in my middle flexes and hot tingles infuse my flesh. I fight a wince and stroke his cheeks. He smiles and wraps his arms around me, unaware of the building inferno in my chest. I brush his lips with mine and he moans. I slide my tongue against the seam of his lips and opens to my kiss, eyes falling shut as the first tear rolls down my face.

Heat blisters through me, flames spreading from the lava in my centre, out into my extremities. I stay lax in Aaron's arms so he won't figure out what I'm doing and kiss him back. The cuts and bruises fade from his skin as I watch and he's seemingly oblivious. Last time I healed him it hurt us both and I don't know why it's different this time.

His eyes open as I break the kiss, a whimper wrenching from me. He shoves me away the second he realises what I've been doing and I land on my back, too drained to move. His face appears above mine, mouth a tight line of anger. He reaches to touch me but hesitates.

'I'm done,' I pant. 'Just leave me here and I'll come find you when I can get up.'

He growls and scoops me from the sand, electricity stinging my skin as he sits with me cradled against him. We're quiet while he fumes and I watch the sun burn mist from the ocean.

'Did you ever bring that girl back to meet Logan?' I ask after a while.

His anger fades to confusion. 'What girl?'

'Wavy hair and hazel eyes,' I say still staring out at the ocean, too chicken to meet his gaze. 'She had flowery tattoos from her fingers to wrists and looked like she could be a glamour model.'

'You mean Amaryllis,' he says, a smile in his voice. 'You don't need to be jealous, Goddess. She's just a friend.'

My gaze snaps to his, throat itching like it's going to burn. 'I'm surprised you could breathe with how tightly you were wrapped around each other.'

'We tried to be more than friends once,' he admits.

A sick feeling grips my stomach. 'You did?'

'Kissing Amaryllis was like kissing a sister and she felt the same way.' He grips my chin when I try to look away, forcing me to hold his gaze. 'Nobody has ever made me feel like you make me feel, Inara.'

The sick feeling eases but that still doesn't explain the other issue. 'You left me with you brother.'

His muscles tighten. 'I had no other option. My father wanted to see me before the Games begin.'

'He couldn't wait?'

'My father waits for no one, not even his children. If I hadn't gone when he summoned me, he would've had me retrieved. I put him off for as long as I could but the Games begin tomorrow, so I was out of time.'

'Tomorrow?' Callista's warning cuts through me. I've got until tomorrow until she sends someone to fetch me. My time with Aaron is nearly over and it's suddenly difficult to breathe.

'You're ready,' he says mistaking my panic as fear of competing in the Games. 'Your instincts are flourishing and I'll be with you the whole way.'

'You're right,' I say forcing a smile. I climb from his lap, legs still shaking and turn to leave.

He shoves to his feet and catches my hand. 'What's wrong?'

'Nothing,' I lie, even as my throat threatens to close with fear. Callista is coming for me and there's nothing I can do.

The sound of clanking metal draws my focus back to Aaron and I turn to find him stripping. 'What the hell are you doing now?' I demand, as more of his tanned skin is revealed.

He doesn't stop until he's down to his leather skirt thingy, then he looks at me and says, 'Strip.'

'What?'

'To your tunic,' he says, starting to unbuckle my armour. 'It's hot and the water is cool.'

I glance from him to the ocean in understanding. 'Oh.'

The tunic suctions to my skin as waves not yet warmed by the sun, crash around my hips and make me shiver. Aaron grins when he feels it and I grin back. He was right, this is refreshing.

The grin bleeds from my lips when he pulls me deeper and the water kisses my shoulders. 'That's enough. It's too deep.'

'Teaching you to swim will be easier if you can't touch the bottom,' he says.

'I didn't come out here for a swimming lesson, Aaron.'

He tugs sharply on my hand, forcing me deeper until the sand disappears from beneath my feet. Aaron catches me before my head dips below the surface and holds me against him. I cling to his suspended form with a death grip.

'Take me back!'

'You punched Logan in the face, yet fear the water,' he mocks as we drift further from shore.

'The ocean hates me more than your brother,' I say. 'It's bigger than Logan and has tried to drown me on several occasions.'

'Not the ocean, nor my brother hate you, Inara.'

'I don't care! Please, just take me back to shore, Aaron.'

'Do you trust me?'

'No.'

He smirks. 'Be honest.'

I glare at him. 'Fine, I trust you. Now take me back.'

'Then trust that I won't let the ocean drown you, Inara.'

I stare into his bright gaze and sigh, slowly forcing my muscles to unlock. 'I don't like this one bit.'

'Really? I couldn't tell.'

~

THE SUN IS high when I splash towards the shore. There's nothing graceful or fast about my swimming but at least I'm doing it. *Me*: the professional at drowning. Aaron glides past like a pro, then gets to his feet and waits for me in the shallows.

'I did it!' I pant as he helps me stand.

Daniel would've been so damn proud and it's all thanks to Aaron. I throw myself at him when we reach our abandoned clothing on the sand, slinging my arms around his neck.

He wipes a tear from my already dry cheek. 'What's wrong?'

'I never thought I could feel this way again, Aaron. I was lost and alone but you found me and I feel so happy.'

He cups my jaw. 'You're nothing like I expected. Gentle and absurd, crying because you're happy. I never thought I'd ever... You're beautiful to look at but you're exquisite on the inside and I, I love you, Inara.'

My being lights with joy and I start to smile, before it fades in the wake of my mother's warning. Silence stretches between us and fresh tears drip from my chin. It's one thing for me to love Aaron but when I'm gone, he'll be in pain. I've known since he found me that my life will likely be short. I never should've let it get this far. The day he kissed me in the woods, I should've shied away, not led him to believe we had a future. He charmed me with his pretty promises but I'm destined for pain. He doesn't have to share my fate though.

'Happy tears?' he asks.

'You can't love me,' I rasp, backing away like I should've been doing all along.

Why did I let this happen? Back when he told me he wanted to keep me, I never envisioned I'd feel this strongly about him, never expected either of us would grow to love each other. I cared for him back then but now...

'Why not?' he demands.

'I kissed Logan,' I say wanting Aaron to hate me. If he hates me, he'll realise loving me was a mistake and it will be easier for him when I'm gone.

'I know. It's the first thing he told me during our fight.'

'Then why aren't you angry with me?'

'Because I trust you. I'm offended you'd mistake Logan for me but I'm not angry, Inara. Why are you so desperate for me, to be? Why do I feel like there's something you aren't telling me?'

I look away. 'There isn't.'

'You're not a very good liar.'

I close my eyes and blow out a breath before meeting his gaze. 'I saw Callista last night.'

He goes rigid. 'What?'

'Sometimes when I sleep... Sometimes I find myself on Anthemusa with her and we...talk.'

He goes so tense it's like he's turned to stone. 'You inherited Apollo's ability of divine visitation?'

'If you say so. It isn't like anyone really explained any of this to me.'

'The gods can leave their corporeal forms in one place and send their inner essence somewhere else,' he says. 'It's a rare ability for demigod offspring to inherit.'

Inner essence? 'You mean their souls?'

'They don't have souls but I suppose I can see why you'd liken the two. Why didn't you tell me about this sooner?'

'I don't plan to visit Anthemusa, Aaron. I just go to sleep and wake up there with *her*. I used to think I was dreaming and she was nice until last night.'

'What happened last night?'

'She threatened me.'

His irises flare electric blue as he growls, 'What did she say?'

I blink at the neon gleam of his eyes. They've glowed before but this is so vivid. So...inhuman.

'I have until the Games begin to go to her, or she'll send someone to retrieve me.'

A muscle ticks in his jaw. 'Did she mention who she'd send?'

'She didn't get chance. I got upset and it woke me up.'

'Upset?'

'She said things that made me angry; things I won't do no matter how much Siren blood runs through my veins. But this is the reason you can't love me, Aaron. When she traps me on that island with her, you won't exactly be able to visit. I know what it's like to lose the people you love and I won't put you through it.'

'You're not going anywhere.'

I flinch at the press of his anger against my skin. It's prickly and intense and makes me want to vomit.

'I might not get a choice, Aaron.'

'I won't let Callista steal anyone else from me,' he snarls. 'You can't just give in, Inara! Fight for me. I know it isn't in your nature but please, at least fight as if you love me back.'

'You think I don't love you?' I cry. 'Why the hell do you think Callista got so angry and said all that stuff to make me reciprocate? She's happy for me to stay free from Anthemusa if I...' I shake my head and look away. I can't even say it.

'If you, what?'

'It doesn't matter.'

He grips my shoulders until I meet his gaze again. 'No more secrets, Inara. What does Callista want you to do?'

'I won't say it! It's too disgusting and I'm not like her. I won't... I won't, Aaron!'

He pulls me into a hug. 'I'm sorry, you don't have to tell me.'

I press my face to his chest and let the sound of his heart, anchor me to the moment. He's here and alive and my fear is for something that hasn't even happened. I breathe deep until I'm calm enough to speak again.

'She didn't like it when I told her that I love you.'

I peek up to see him smiling, eyes warm. The sensation of belonging, overwhelms me and my heart begins to race. His lips press to mine, soft and salty from our swim. I slide my fingers through his wet hair, his electricity a delicious sting against my flesh. It knits the frayed fibres of my soul back together, his love seeping into the crater left from losing my family. Whatever happens after this moment, Aaron will always be a part of me.

17

Moonlight streams in through the window, painting silver patterns on the wooden floor. I'm curled up on my bed, fully dressed, watching Aaron sleep peacefully across the room. I don't know how he can he sleep at a time like this, dressed in leather and metal. He wants us to be ready in case Callista follows through with her threat but this seems ridiculous.

The only consolation is that I get to study him while he sleeps. His usually tanned skin gleams alabaster in the silver light, dark hair wild against his pillow. His lashes are thick crescents against high cheekbones, the kind most girls would kill for. He sighs, full lips curving with a smile, before he murmurs my name.

I get up to tiptoe closer, hoping he'll speak again but something clatters against the floor and I freeze. Aaron stirs but doesn't wake, turning his back to me as he settles once more. I blow out a breath and look down at the lyre, glittering on the floor at my feet. Suddenly, all I can think about is Helen and the possibility of never seeing her again.

I pick up the lyre and glance at Aaron before strumming the strings. It's stupid to leave but I can't miss the chance to tell Helen goodbye. There's a very high probability I'll die or end up on Anthemusa, even with Aaron's assurances that I won't. The room ripples and I blink against the sunlight on the other side of the portal I've opened. I step through into Helen's bedroom before the brightness wakes Aaron then watch the doorway fade behind me.

The sound of the television gets louder as I creep downstairs. I hesitate at the bottom worried Helen's parents will see me. Not only am I technically still missing, I'm dressed in full armour with a blade strapped to my thigh.

I sigh in relief when I find Helen sitting alone on the sofa in the front room, shouting abuse at the TV. The vibrant red of her hair is a surprise but not unexpected. The girl dyes her hair so much I'm shocked she has any left. The shade reminds me of Delia and I smile as I watch from the doorway. Helen glances my way then looks back at the TV, before snapping her attention to me.

'Oh my god!' she squeals and nearly trips over the coffee table on her way to tackling me. She hugs me before shoving me away. 'I've been freaking out since that prick carried you off! Then Joshua Forester turned up, spouting stories of you being kidnapped in a graveyard. What the hell is happening, Inara? We're supposed to be best friends, yet I know nothing.'

'How much does Josh know?'

'I didn't tell him anything if that's what you mean. Not that I *could* tell him anything, since you've told me *nothing*. You could've at least said goodbye, Inara. I didn't know if I'd ever see you again.'

'Do you really think I've had a choice, Helen? You saw I was unconscious when Aaron took me and it hasn't exactly been a tea party for me either.'

'You should have come back!'

'And risk getting you killed again? I shouldn't even be here right now. I only came so I could see you before...' I sigh and turn away. 'You know what, I shouldn't have come.'

She catches my hand. 'I'm sorry, okay! I just... I was worried about you.' Her voice cracks. 'I thought those monsters...' She shrugs and gives me a trembling smile. 'Please don't go, I'm glad you're here.'

I sigh. 'They don't have phones on the Guardian Isle, or I definitely would've called you.'

She pulls me to the sofa. 'No phones—How do they live? No, wait... Tell me about what you've been doing and how you saw Josh.'

'Aaron's home is like being in Ancient Greece,' I say. 'He's been training me to fight and barely leaves my side except for, you know, personal moments. Josh saw us during a quick trip to buy a new wig.'

'You came back for a wig,' she says eyeing my fake, brunette curls.

I nod. 'Aaron thought Josh might not be human so decided to rescue me. Josh saw me slung over Aaron's shoulder and assumed I was being kidnapped. Between the monsters and training—Oh my god, I haven't told you about meeting my birth mother!'

Helen's eyes go wide. 'You met your mum?'

I nod. 'She's as charming as a black widow spider.'

'I'm sorry for being a dick when you got here,' she says. 'I was mad that you hadn't tried to contact me and never considered you might not be able to. I want to know everything, Inara but most importantly, what happened to my wig?' She smirks. 'Actually, tell me why you're dressed like a cast member from that film *300*?'

I huff a laugh and the tension between us dissipates. No matter the situation, Helen always knows what to say to make me smile. She's brave and ballsy and taking everything that's happening in her stride. She died because of me and still wants to be my friend. If that isn't love, I don't know what is.

MY TIME with Helen passes too quickly. We make hot chocolate then go upstairs to her room to talk. Despite the horrors of last time, it's comforting to be here. It feels safe... Insulated, like I'm hidden away in a familiar haven from my childhood. I don't want to leave but staying means putting Helen at risk again. The longer I'm here, the greater danger she's in.

Helen rummages through her bag and pulls out a mobile phone. She presses it into my palm.

'I want you to take this and call me when you get there,' she says.

'Something tells me I won't get reception on the Guardian Isle, Helen.'

'Just try, okay?'

I tuck the phone into my tunic and pull out the lyre. Helen's bottom lip trembles at the sight.

'Goodbye, Helen.' I strum the stings and the room shivers, a doorway forming to my left.

'You owe me a new wig,' Helen says, trying to smile.

'Yeah,' I answer. 'I miss you too.'

I dash through the doorway before she can see my tears then bite back a curse when I see the sun is high in the sky. Aaron's going to be livid. I set off running across the sand to the grassy pathway that leads up the cliff. I falter when I reach the top and find Aaron prowling in front of his house. His expression when he sees me, makes me consider retreat.

He stalks up to me. 'Where have you been?'

'I couldn't sleep, so went for a walk.'

'A walk! Gods, Inara I thought Callista made good on her promise!' He holds his hand up, thumb and forefinger millimetres apart. 'I was *this* close to going to the Flowery Isle to rescue you.'

'That's suicidal,' I scoff knowing there'd be no point. Once I'm on that island, there's no escape for me. He'd be following me to his death.

He grips my shoulders and bends to bring our gazes, level. 'I'd follow you anywhere, Goddess—The Flowery Isle or the gates of Hades, it doesn't matter.'

I stare at him, horrified. 'Promise you won't follow if I get trapped on Anthemusa, Aaron.'

'No.'

He actually means it. 'I can't watch you die, Aaron.'

'Then do what you promised and fight.'

'I *am* fighting! You can't say stuff like that to blackmail me into getting what you want.'

'You think I don't see it, Inara? I know you'll sacrifice your freedom if you think it will save my life but I won't let you. If we fail in this, then we fail together. If you go down in battle, so will I.'

How did he see through me so easily? I glare and he glares back, both of us panting.

'Don't do this,' I beg.

'Don't force me to,' he answers.

Dread weaves icy fingers through my insides. Deep down, I know I'm going to lose him.

THE THUNDERING of the crowd shudders through the walls of the prep room below the arena. I tremble as Diana paints blue paste onto my skin, drawing a wide band of colour between my eyebrows and cheekbones. It dries in the heat, making my emerald eyes look bright. My tunic matches the aquamarine stripe, as does the ribbon woven through my braid.

Armour is pulled over my tunic, wavelets of petite fingers strapping leather and metal into place. The Artemis blade is buckled to the top of my right thigh then Delia tugs the chestnut wig over my hair. I pluck the phone Helen gave me from the curious fingers of a Daughter of Okeanos and slot it into my tunic with the lyre. I haven't had chance to see if I get any signal yet. Aaron didn't let me out of his sight until we reached the stadium and he handed me over to Delia.

'You're ready,' she says.

I meet her warm gaze then tremble against another earth-shaking roar from the crowd above. It feels like I'm about to be fed to the lions. Every contestant I've seen is athletic and muscular. They emulate the image of what a gladiator should be, while I look like I'm going to a fancy dress party.

I look into Delia's eyes as I try to find the courage to leave the prep room. She's so graceful and calm, red hair a cluster of loose curls, pinned around her porcelain face. Her brown eyes are lined with kohl and gold jewellery adorns her neck, arms and wrists. It makes soft, jingling sounds each time she moves and matches the gold rope cinching her white dress at the waist. I take a deep breath at her warm smile and step through the doorway.

Other competitors pay me no attention as Delia leads me along the stone corridor. If anything, they're more concerned about not touching Delia as she passes. They look menacing in their armour, various shades of war paint striping over their eyes. They make me feel tiny as they rush past. The air grows less stifling as we reach the exit and I lift my hand against the glare of the afternoon sun.

I turn at the sound of chuckling and find Aaron standing beside me. Blue eyes burn bright against the indigo paint on his skin. His armour is silver strapped to black leather, hair a wild mess against tanned skin. His smile is a white flash as he takes my hand.

'Are you ready, my goddess?' he breathes against my ear.

'No,' I rasp blushing furiously under Delia's amused gaze.

'The Daughters and I will follow,' she says taking my other hand. Her eyes glaze over, fingers tightening around mine.

I slip my hand from Aaron's and wave it in front of her face. 'Delia,' I whisper-hiss, not wanting to draw attention from anyone else.

The air shivers, stadium falling away to the vista of the ocean. Callista emerges from the water like a mermaid, rising from the surf. She climbs the beach; more Sirens appearing behind her. Long dresses cling to instantly dry skin, confirming it's a Siren quirk. Callista grins then leads the others inland, movements sultry as they pass where Delia and I are standing then disappear behind a cluster of rocks.

I slap Delia across the face. 'Wake up!'

She blinks from her daze and looks around. 'Why are we on the beach?'

'We aren't,' I hiss.

'A vision then,' she says and the beach fades to reveal the stadium.

Aaron yanks us apart and turns me to face him. 'What did you see?'

'Callista isn't sending someone to fetch me, she's coming here herself!'

'Sirens can't leave Anthemusa, Inara. The vision must have been there.'

'The sand is white there but was black in the vision, Aaron. I'm not wrong. Callista is coming *here* and she's bringing friends.'

'Only competitors allowed in the Hold,' a gruff voice barks at Delia. A male with pitted skin and a plethora of scars, storms in our direction.

'Where was the sun in the sky in your vision,' Aaron asks ignoring the man.

I remember the heat of it on my back. 'I was facing the ocean and the sun was behind us.'

'Then we have until tomorrow.'

'How do you know? What if she's already here?'

'Anthemusa is off the west coast of the Guardian Isle,' he says. 'If the sun was at your back in the vision, then it was still rising. That means it's morning when she gets here and, if she were here already, we'd know.'

'How?'

'The need to kill runs too strongly in them,' he says. 'They wouldn't be able to move among us, without satiating their bloodlust.'

'You heard me,' the man snarls at Delia. 'If you're not a competitor, get out.'

She raises a hand when he moves to grab her. 'By all means, touch me and view your fate.'

Recognition and curiosity, proceed the fear that finally settles on his face. 'I didn't recognise you, Oracle,' he says respectfully. 'Please, take your seat in the spectator section of the arena.'

Delia's cold expression warms as it pans to me and I flinch when she squeezes my fingers. 'Apollo be with you, Daughter of Aphrodite,' she says.

I stare after her while Aaron snarls something at the man. If Anthemusa is off the coast of the Guardian Isle, does that mean it's the island on the horizon? How can I have been this close to it all along, without Aaron telling me?

'We have to warn them,' I say glancing around the Competitors' Hold as the man leaves.

'If you tell this hold of warriors who you are, you won't leave this place alive,' Aaron warns. 'If we fail, we fail together, remember.'

'Then what do we do? We need to warn them, Aaron.'

He cups my jaw. 'We'll fight in the Games today, then leave tonight when it's dark.'

'And go where? I just...want them to leave me alone.'

He tucks a curl behind my ear. 'Then we'll go. Tomorrow we'll leave and never come back.'

He'd leave his home and friends, for me? 'But, how do you hide from gods?'

'We've succeeded so far, haven't we?' He seems so confident but it feels hopeless to me.

The roar of the crowd dies to nothing, leaving a deafening silence in its wake. A woman in white robes, steps into the Hold and looks around the competitors with a smile. Her high, clear voice penetrates the silence and Aaron stiffens at whatever she says. The others in the Hold start murmuring but I can't understand her foreign words.

Warriors start to scan those around them and I nudge Aaron. 'What's happening?'

He looks down at me with an unfamiliar expression. It takes a moment to realise, it's panic. The fact he's panicking streaks terror through me because I didn't think he was capable of the emotion.

'Each year a new rule is implemented to make the Games more interesting,' he says. 'This year they're teaming the competitors on basis of their parentage.'

The meaning of his words, register. 'We'll be separated?'

'They're trying to force alliances, so the strongest competitors don't form their own,' he explains. 'This way, gives the weaker fighters a better chance, prolonging the Games and making them more exciting.'

'More exciting,' I recite in a flat tone.

'Breathe,' he says. 'It will be okay. We'll find each other inside the Gaming Zone.'

'What the hell is the Gaming Zone?' He hasn't really explained anything about the Games to me in detail and I haven't asked. I trusted he'd be with me through it.

'The arena is the finish line,' he says stroking my face. 'Don't be afraid, Goddess. I'll find you.'

'You haven't taught me enough to survive on my own. I—I'll die without you.'

He brackets my face in his hands. 'Competitors don't die in the Games and you won't be alone. You'll have the protection of your sisters until I find you.'

'Sisters?'

'The other Daughters of Aphrodite.'

Oh yeah, that's what I'm pretending to be.

The clash of a metal gong stops our conversation, drawing everyone's focus to the white-robed woman.

'What's she saying?' I whisper.

'First to be called: two daughters and one son of Persephone,' Aaron translates.

One male and two females, step from the gathered warriors and go stand in a group behind the robed woman. They share the same skin tone and brown hair. Their armour has variations of the same emblem engraved in the metal and I look down at mine. An open-winged dove decorates my breastplate and I realise, it must be the symbol of Aphrodite. My gaze moves to the eagle engraved on Aaron's armour and I wonder which god it represents. He still hasn't told me who his father is but I guess I'm about to find out.

He pushes me forward and whispers, 'That's you.'

My heart races, as I follow three Daughters of Aphrodite to the robed woman and join their group. All three stare at me, each stunningly beautiful in their own right. In their armour, they look like models from a perfume advert, selling something probably called 'Warrior'. I fix my gaze on the ground, the weight of their stares pressing down on me. I wait for one of them to ask why I'm standing with them but none do. The robed woman announces another name and I look up at the commotion it causes from the other competitors.

'Why is the Son of Zeus even allowed to enter?' A Daughter of Aphrodite scoffs. 'He's sure to win.'

'That isn't set in stone,' another counters. 'There are four of us and only one of him.'

'Have you ever taken on a demigod from one of the top three?' the first to speak asks. 'They're nearly impossible to beat.'

A grin lights the second girl's face. 'I'd take the Son of Zeus on if he asked. Those fiery blue eyes, drilling into me...' She moans.

The three giggle, gazes tracking to where the Son of Zeus steps from the crowd. Aaron's gaze meets mine, those 'fiery blue eyes' penetrating my armour until my eyes sting. His expression is measured, like he expected the betrayal burning through me. He mouths something to me but I'm too upset to understand, mind too focused on wondering why he didn't tell me.

'Just great,' the girl beside me hisses, jerking my gaze from Aaron's. 'This year is going to end in a personal fight between those two again.'

'I thought they agreed never to enter the Games at the same time again,' Second Girl huffs.

'He's one demigod I'd gladly not fight,' the first states.

'He's as pretty as his brother but scares the crap out of me,' Second Girl agrees.

Brother? I peer around them to watch Logan stride up to the robed woman. Competitors, part under his menacing gaze. He spots me and smirks, deviating from his path.

'Seek me out in the Gaming Zone if you wish to form an alliance, Princess,' he says when he reaches where I'm standing. He grins at my responding glare and continues to the robed woman.

'How are you acquainted with the Son of Hades?' the first Daughter of Aphrodite to speak, asks.

All three stare at me while I glance at Logan. Finding out he's the Son of Hades, isn't as much of a shock as finding out about Aaron, though both make sense. Aaron's electric touch is sort of a given and Logan seems like he belongs in the shadows. I feel stupid for not figuring either out sooner.

The robed woman starts speaking again, saving me from answering. We're ushered from the Hold in our sibling groups; deafening roar of the crowd eclipsing the drumming of my heart. I stare up at the spectators lining the cascading stands of the circular arena. Delia's red hair draws my gaze, like a beacon amid the sea of cheering. Diana is beside her on the front row, watching as I step into a chariot with the Daughters of Aphrodite. Delia points to her eyes then to me, reminding me she'll be watching. I nod my understanding, as a whip snaps and the chariot jolts forward.

18

I sit on the ground, waiting for the three demigods to decide the best route to take. None have spoken to me in the hours since we left the stadium because my opinion isn't valued. Not that I'd know my way to the finish line if they did ask, so I'm happy to stay quiet while they argue.

The tall, buxom blonde with silver eyes and golden skin is Talia. Adonia is shorter and oriental looking, with thick black hair and pale blue eyes. Cali is voluptuous, with hazel eyes that remind me of Aaron's friend Amaryllis. She has perfect, mahogany curls that hang obediently to her hips, despite the windswept chariot ride we took to get here.

Talia's gaze meets mine, the others falling silent when she approaches. 'What's your name?'

Even when I stand, I still have to look up to meet her assessing gaze. I've never considered myself short but Talia has at least a foot on Aaron, with tight muscles in her arms and shoulders.

'Cytherea.'

She points to the Artemis blade strapped to my thigh. 'Can you use that or is it for decoration?'

'You don't look like you can even lift it,' Cali says.

'I can use it,' I defend.

'None of us knew you existed,' Talia says. 'It's obvious you were raised in the Realm of Man but when were you born—How old are you?'

'Seventeen.'

'She's just a baby!' Cali explodes.

'How did someone so young enter the Games?' Adonia asks.

They start bickering before I can respond, not caring about my answer. I fold my arms across my chest in frustration and wonder how they can be mad about my age when none of them look a day over twenty.

'I won't risk losing because I'm busy babysitting *her*,' Cali snarls.

She stabs a finger in my direction and anger flares through me, igniting the bracelets on my wrists. My throat burns and I spin away, worried I'll do something to reveal what I am.

'Wait!' Adonia calls after I've put some distance between us.

I turn as she catches up. 'Nobody is forcing any of you to stay with me,' I hiss.

She catches my hand when I keep walking. 'I don't know how you were able to register for the Games, little sister but it isn't safe for you to go on alone. The reason the entry age for the Games is no younger than fifty, is to prevent inexperienced demigods like you from getting killed.'

'Did you just say fifty?'

I stare at her youthful face then glance over to Talia and Cali. Callista didn't look a day over twenty-five either. Does this mean I won't age? I never really thought about my parents being immortal. If I don't get killed, will I live forever too? Dread, slides through me. Getting trapped on Anthemusa suddenly feels less of a life sentence and more of an eternal damnation.

'You didn't know?' Adonia asks.

'He never told me,' I rasp.

If the minimum entry age to the Games is fifty, how old is Aaron? He's half human, so what happens if I'm immortal and he isn't? How much time will we have left if we survive this? I love him, so will take whatever time we have left but it hurts. I don't want to live without him. I *won't*. A plan cements itself in my mind, like Aaron has cemented himself in my heart. If he dies, I'm not sticking around to live the same half-life I did after the crash.

Tingles, skate the length of my spine and the air around me grows thick. I turn a slow circle, muscles coiling with dread at the sensation I've honed through my training with Aaron. An internal alarm is warning me danger is approaching and I follow its guidance, squinting into the distance as the sun slips beneath the horizon. Instinct tells me to run into the woodland at my back and hide.

'We need to go,' I say.

'You don't decide where we go,' Cali says stalking in our direction.

'Something is coming,' I argue, closing my eyes. I reach out with my senses to the vibration in the air, picking through it the way I've practiced. 'Four...no, five heavy-set runners are coming this way.'

A blast of heat slices the air and I snap my eyes open to the faint flickering over Cali's shoulder. I body-slam her out of the way, as a flaming spear impales the baked earth where she'd been standing.

Talia, hauls us to our feet and starts dragging me at a dead run towards the tree line. Crippling pain shudders the length of my spine as we reach the woodland. When I falter, Talia plucks me off my feet and slings me over her shoulder. She doesn't break stride, as she launches into the nearest tree and pulls us into the canopy.

She drops me onto a thick branch and I dig my fingernails into the bark, as five rival competitors trot by below. The flames of their torches are bright in the lightless wood, illuminating broad-muscled physiques, laden weapons. The huge males crash through the foliage like an armoured vehicle, snapping branches and leaving a path of destruction in their wake.

'What warriors track prey into the woods and don't check the canopy,' Cali scoffs once the torches disappear from sight.

Talia smirks. 'Sons of Ares, all muscle and no brains.'

The three snicker then climb down from our hiding place. I prise my fingernails from the bark, swallow back an impending panic attack, then climb down to join them.

'You knew they were coming,' Talia says the moment my feet touch the ground.

I nod, unable to speak. A white-hot pebble is wedged in my throat, voice a burning ball of acid I can't swallow. I grit my teeth, refusing the icy need to let it out.

'Was your father an Oracle?' Cali asks.

I shake my head and walk away, not stopping until the painful throbbing in my throat eases. I turn to meet their expectant gazes when I finally stop, surprised they followed me without pressing for an answer. But I need to tell them something.

'I can feel it,' I say. My ability to sense danger is a Siren instinct, so I need to tread carefully on how much I tell them.

'Feel what?' Talia asks.

'When danger approaches.'

'That's a useful talent,' Adonia says.

'You're more skilled than we gave you credit for,' Talia agrees giving Cali a pointed look.

She holds her hands up in defence. 'Fine, I was wrong. A skill like that could be useful.'

'We can get close to the arena without the need to fight,' Adonia says, 'reserve our energy and resources for the more difficult battles near the finish line.'

'That's where our alliance ends, though,' Talia says. 'We're all here to win, so a mile from the finish line, we're on our own.'

'Agreed,' Cali says.

Adonia, puts her hand atop Talia and Cali's. 'Agreed.'

I sigh when they look at me expectantly and put my hand atop theirs. 'Agreed.'

THE NIGHT IS a blur of sweat and tree sap. We weave between trees, following the path of destruction left by the Sons of Ares. We stop when my spine prickles in warning and dodge several hunting parties. My adrenaline spikes with each near miss and I'm jittery by the time we breach the woodland. Dawn is breaking on the other side, making the previous hours of darkness seem like a nightmare.

I watch the ocean as we follow the coastline, dreaming of the moment I'll be allowed to wash the grime from my skin. We round a curve in the coast and stop at a string of indigo smoke, rising into the sky. I join the others to crouch behind a large cluster of rocks at the base of the cliff to scrutinise the area.

'It's a trap,' Cali whispers. 'Nobody would be stupid enough to light a fire out in the open in the middle of the day.'

'A trap Athena's offspring are walking into,' Adonia whispers back.

We follow her pointed finger to the two males and two females, creeping into view ahead. They have owl emblems carved into their armour and keen stares. We use the rocks as cover, as we edge closer to their vantage. When we're close enough to hear, we realise they're hoping to outnumber whomever set the trap.

Talia nudges my elbow and I look over to see Adonia and Cali flanking her with weapons drawn. They look excited and I fight a sigh. They appreciate my ability to dodge unnecessary conflict because it will give them a better chance at winning, but they love to fight, like Aaron.

Talia pulls the Artemis blade from its sheath and hands it to me with an encouraging smile. She's been my protector during the night, taking on the role of big sister with ease. The others look up to her and it's easy to understand why. She's strong, beautiful and wise in a way the rest of us aren't. I wrap my fingers around the hilt and try to steady my shaking hand. Talia grins with approval then signals for us to be quiet.

We stalk Athena's offspring who are too focused on the smoke to notice our approach. Adonia clamps a hand over the mouth of the male at the back of the group. She presses a blade to his throat as his amber eyes go wide. She brings her lips to his ear and whispers something. His face contorts with anger then he nods and disappears in a flare of light.

Talia grabs one of the girls by her hair as she covers her mouth. She drags her to the ground and kneels on her chest. A dagger is pressed between the girl's armour, stilling her struggles. She glares up at Talia and nods, before disappearing in a flash of light like the boy. I look around, wondering where the light takes those that surrender.

The remaining Son of Athena turns our way and calls a warning to his sister, as Cali is about to attack. The girl drops to her knees, avoiding Cali and knocking an arrow into her bow in one, fluid movement. Her first arrow bounces off Cali's armour but the second finds flesh. Cali falters and stares down at the shaft protruding from her abdomen. The axe slips from her fingers and she grabs the arrow, trying to tug it free.

Talia crashes into the girl and the boy darts for Cali. I throw myself in front of her, his axe clashing with my blade. A flash in my peripheral vision signals the last girl's surrender but the boy isn't ready to relent. He's strong, the muscles in his shoulders bunching as he bears down on his axe. The Artemis blade begins to slip in my sweaty grip and he grins.

'Yield,' he demands as my knees wobble.

My anger boils over at the victory already painting his face, wintry rage smoking though me. I let it bleed through my flesh and bite back a moan at the surge of delicious ice. I straighten my legs with sudden ease: seductive frost, coating my insides and hazing my vision. An ache quivers across my shoulders as I stand tall and grin at the boy.

His smile slips, surprise registering in his gaze as his muscles strain against my new-found strength. Sweat drips from his chin as I push forward, forcing him backwards. I breathe deep, tasting his intoxicating fear.

My voice gets dangerously close to ringing: 'Yield.'

A thin barrier is the only thing separating what I should and *want* to do. The delicious ice flooding my flesh, wants me to finish him; to taste the fear and hate pouring off him like yummy smoke. Siren song licks my throat at his defiance, the thought of him wanting to play a little longer, enticing it out. I grit my teeth against the agony of holding it in, praying he yields before I lose the battle with myself.

One of his legs, buckle; the axe slipping from his grip. I slam him onto his back and press the tip of my blade to the hollow of his throat.

He growls low and long then snarls, 'I yield!'

Light, flares between us and I hit the dirt as he disappears. I stay on my hands and knees, panting as I try to swallow the burn of my voice from my throat. When it fades enough to speak, I push to my feet and turn to help Cali. Talia and Adonia are standing in the spot where she'd been and Cali is gone.

'Cali's injuries were too great,' Adonia says then smirks. 'She won't be happy.'

'She'll sulk for weeks,' Talia agrees and they both start laughing.

We move closer to the plume of smoke and take refuge behind another cluster of rocks to scope the area. A small fire crackles in front of an opening in the rock face, the scent of smoke and burning fish thick in the air.

'The noise of the fight must have alerted them,' Talia whispers.

Adonia huffs an annoyed sigh, before her gaze sharpens and eagerness fills her face. She shifts into a hunting crouch and lasers in on a particular spot across the clearing.

'What do you see?' Talia asks.

'Over there,' Adonia says.

She springs over the rocks and darts into a cluster opposite, reappearing a moment later, dragging a struggling girl with her. I frown at her lack of armour and the jeans she's wearing. Familiarity, washes through me and I shove to my feet. Delia's red hair has me scrambling over the rocks to them. She screams as Adonia grips her hair and drags a blade down her cheek, growling at her to yield.

'No!' I shout, dodging Talia's efforts to restrain me.

I slam into Adonia but she twists on her way to the sand, punching me so hard in the face it spins me away from her. I grip my jaw and stagger onto my feet, weaving a few steps as I blink spots from my vision.

'What are you doing?' she snarls.

I spit the blood from my mouth and rasp, 'She isn't a competitor.'

Talia puts a steadying hand on my shoulder and reasons, 'She's in the Gaming Zone, little sister.'

'She isn't wearing armour or carrying a weapon,' I point out.

They look at Delia as she groans on the sand and Adonia murmurs, 'You're right.'

I shrug from Talia's grip and drop to my knees beside Delia, wondering what the hell she's doing in the Gaming Zone. She's face-down on the sand, red hair flared around her shoulders, as she comes around. I hesitate, wanting to help but not wanting to touch her in case I get sucked into another vision.

'Delia,' I say but she doesn't respond. I blow out a breath and gently ease her onto her back, brushing hair from her face and feel the colour drain from mine. 'Helen?'

When Aaron said humans couldn't come to the Guardian Isle, I assumed he meant it was a physical impossibility. Helen's eyes flutter open and I want to cry at the fragility of her grey gaze.

'How are you here?' I ask.

She sits up blinking, blood snaking a crimson ribbon down her cheek where Adonia cut her. She trembles as she tries to stand, so I grab her arm and help her up.

'I followed you through the doorway,' she says.

I stare at her in disbelief because I'd assumed someone or *something* had brought her here against her will. But she's telling me she came here on purpose. I frown, wondering how I didn't notice her, then remember how panicked I was when I got back and realised it was daytime.

'You came here of your own free will?'

'Of course, I did.'

I lose it. 'For God's sake, Helen I know you're stubborn but you've never been stupid! This isn't the Olympics. There are reasons humans aren't allowed here!'

'You think I don't know that? I wouldn't die for you if I had to?'

'You already died for me, remember?'

She opens her mouth to respond but flinches, when Talia steps close and grabs a length of Helen's red hair. She bends to sniff it, silver eyes going wide with surprise.

Helen snatches her hair back. 'There's this thing called personal space, you know.'

'It's true,' Talia says, 'she's human.'

'*She* has a name,' Helen huffs.

Adonia sniffs Helen and says, 'We need to get her out of the Gaming Zone before she's accidentally killed.' She bends to examine the cut on Helen's cheek, ignoring her protests to poke at the wound. 'Human's don't heel fast. This could get infected without treatment.'

I pull Helen to me and take the lyre from my tunic. Adonia draws her sword at the sight, the fear on her face insulting, considering what we've been through in the last day together.

'Put it away, Nia,' Talia says.

'She has Apollo's key. You know what that means—what she is,' Adonia argues.

'We'd already be dead if that's what she wanted,' Talia says.

Adonia stares at me, indecision clear on her face. 'Unless, she's toying with us.'

Helen huffs and steps in front of Adonia's blade. 'We were in the middle of a conversation,' she says then glares at the lyre in my hand. 'You wouldn't dare.'

'Put yourself in my shoes, Helen and tell me you wouldn't do the same,' I say.

She bristles but I slap a hand over her mouth. I glance around as the air thickens, my spine prickling with the threat of danger. Something is coming and it's big and close. There isn't time to open a doorway without being seen, so I have to get Helen to safety.

'How many?' Talia asks reading my reaction.

'More than I can count.'

'They'll kill Helen before they realise, she's human,' Adonia says.

I tuck the lyre into my tunic and tell Helen, 'Don't stop running until I say. If we get caught, for God's sake let us do the fighting, okay?'

She nods, face pale as I pull her into a dead run.

HELEN HAS ALWAYS BEEN ATHLETIC, loving contact sports and enjoying anything physical. Demigods are stronger and faster than humans, though. We keep slowing our pace so Helen can keep up; the gap between us and those tracking us narrowing. The fear of losing Helen threatens to suffocate me. If it comes to it, I'll reveal to everyone that I'm Siren so they focus on me and give her chance to escape.

The beach widens, ebony cliffs rising on our left as the ocean spreads in a streak of blue to the right. We pause on the black sand, looking for the best place to hide. Pain grips my shoulders and shudders down my spine, cracking loudly as I arch against it. Helen stares at me wide-eyed but I shake my head and drag her across the sparkling sand. Maybe we can hide her in the rocks then lead the others away.

'There,' Talia shouts pointing at the face of the cliff. 'We can lose them up there.'

I squint at where she's pointing, until a nearly-invisible staircase snaps into focus. It's carved into the black rock, steps steep and precarious. I look at Helen, doubled over and panting as we reach the bottom. Blood and sweat stain her top and her limbs are shaking with exertion.

'Leave...me,' she pants.

'The hell...I will,' I pant back.

Talia tosses Helen on her shoulder and says, 'Adonia will lead and Inara will bring up the rear.'

Adonia, starts climbing, followed by Talia and her cargo and I slip into position at the back. Helen's lack of argument at being carried is testament to how weak she is. Pain cramps my shoulders as we climb steps that look like they were carved thousands of years ago. I grit my teeth at the spikes of agony, tears streaking my face as I force myself to climb. The pain always seems to come at the worst moments, always when I need to escape.

I dig fingernails into the dirt at the top of the cliff and claw my way onto solid ground. I pant into the coarse grass as my spine releases several crunching pops. Bone grates against bone and Talia has to drag me in from the edge. A scream rakes out of me as my spine tries to bend at an impossible angle, flipping me onto my back.

Helen's fingers curl around mine. 'I'm here, Nara.'

The pain fades at the sound of her voice and I slump onto the grass. 'I'm still...pissed at...you,' I pant.

'Makes a change from me being pissed at you,' she says then, 'What was that, Nara? What's wrong with you?'

I close my eyes at her worried expression and mumble, 'Don't know.' I squeeze her cold fingers in mine. 'Got to get you home.'

She snorts. 'Rest a moment. I'll be here when you're done.'

19

We watch the competitors race across the sand. There's no formation to the large group, as if they're running scared.

'The group is too big to be a planned alliance,' Adonia says.

''It's as if they share a common fear,' Talia agrees, 'one that has compelled them to join forces.'

My gaze tracks to a slow, almost lethargic figure as it emerges from around the headland. Recognition flares through me, fire engulfing my lungs as if I'm meeting kin. I gasp at the acid licking my throat and shove to my feet.

I wave my arms above my head. 'Up here!'

Talia drags me back onto my stomach and hisses, 'What are you doing?'

'They aren't tracking us they're running from her!'

Talia follows the direction of my pointed finger, to the curvaceous figure following the pack of terrified demigods.

'It can't be.'

'It is,' I say shaking off her hold and pushing back onto my feet. 'Hurry, we have to help them!'

Talia, Adonia and Helen join me in waving and shouting to the others. The boy at the head of the pack turns in our direction. He slams against the rock face and starts climbing, the others following his lead. We drop to our knees at the top of the cliff and shout for them to climb faster.

The Siren, slinks after them, sauntering towards the cliff as if the effort of the chase bores her. She's ethereally beautiful, with ice-blonde hair and deep-purple robes.

Talia drags the first demigod over the lip of the cliff before helping Adonia with the next. Helen starts tending to the first male, giving him water from a canteen. Another two demigods are dragged onto the cliff and dropped onto to the grass, each taking only a moment before helping to pull the others to safety. Everyone is helping, except me.

I stand, frozen on the edge, unable to tear my gaze from the velvety stride of the approaching Siren. She moves like silk over marble, hair shining like cascading ice to her hips. The purple, ankle-length dress kisses her perfect curves, hugging her frame like water. She's achingly beautiful and yet, there's darkness in her. I feel the artic brush of it, like icy breath on the back of my neck.

She reaches the base of the cliff and pops her hands on her hips, as she looks up with lazy intent. Her gaze finds mine, surprise registering through her breath-taking features. Recognition flares between us and a smile tugs at her perfect lips. It's like being smiled at by an angel and I feel trapped in her midnight gaze.

A responding smile pulls at the corners of my mouth, iciness pulsing through me. The Siren's smile widens, like she feels what I'm feeling and I realise, she's expecting my help. My smile dies and I shake my head as I glare down at her. We're not the same. Her beautiful face, twists with a sneer. I *sense* her intent, the chill of her presence swelling around me. My gaze snaps to the demigods still climbing and I scream at the them to hurry.

I'm too high up for the Siren's song to reach me but I feel the press of it against my skin. Cold delight skates down my spine, before I crush it deep and lock it tight behind the incendiary heat at my centre. Nobody else reacts to the sensation and I realise that, like when I sense danger, this ability is a Siren thing. We're like spiders, sitting in our webs, sensing vibrations along the gossamer threads.

The song, sinks into my skin and oscillates through the marrow of my bones. It's seductive and delectable and forces the acid of my own song to spill into my mouth. Enticing fire coats my tongue, coaxing my lips apart...

Screaming, jolts me from the Siren's spell and I glance around in a daze. It takes a moment to understand that I almost joined her in her song, despite my refusal moments earlier. I stare at Amaryllis and the blond boy from the head of the pack, restraining a huge male with dark curly hair. His unnatural, amber gaze glints in the sun, as Amaryllis and the blond fight to stop him from climbing back down the cliff. I follow his terrified gaze to a female demigod still clinging to the cliff face. She's frozen there, like a living statue carved against the black rock.

The curly-haired boy drops to his knees, desperation on his face as he stares at her dream-like expression. Sunlight shines from the hammer engraved on his breastplate but I don't know which god it represents.

'I have to help my sister,' he snarls.

'If you go down there, you're as good as dead,' the blond says.

'Why isn't she doing anything?' Amaryllis breathes. 'That thing is just keeping her there, like this is a game.'

I look at the Siren and find her dark gaze fixed on me. She says something I can't hear and the girl shoves away from the cliff. The curly-haired boy screams as she plummets to the ground, a cloud of black sand exploding around her on impact. The world stills, until the cloud settles and the boy roars in despair.

The Siren looks up at the sound and grins, unearthly face smeared with crimson and the girl's mauled body in her arms. Those midnight eyes shift back to me and her smile widens. She lifts a delicate hand and licks blood from her fingers.

The curly-haired boy rips from those holding him and shoves to his feet. He holds out his hand and a blinding flash delivers an enormous hammer into his palm, matching the image engraved on his armour. It glows like the bow Apollo gifted me, the one fashioned by Hephaestus and suddenly I know who this boy's father is.

He hefts the glowing hammer over his head, muscles bunching under its weight. Talia grips my arm and starts pulling me away from the edge. I look around to see others doing the same and search for Helen. Adonia is already leading her to safety, so I stop resisting Talia's grip and turn to run with the others from the impending destruction.

I glance back to see the boy still standing there, tears streaking his face. He's staring down at his sister in the grip of that monster and all I can think about is my brother's funeral. The flowers. The wake. The hundreds of people who came to see him off. I tug from Talia's grip and turn back. She shouts my name but I ignore her, as I slip my hand into my tunic and find the small pouch Aaron gave me before the Games.

The boy glances my way when I join him on the edge. His eyes shine amber behind the curly curtain of his brown hair. The muscles in his arms are pronounced, moments away from sending us to our deaths.

'Run,' he grunts.

The coin is warm from being pressed against my body, as I shake it from the pouch. The boy stares at it, gratitude shining in his eyes when he realises my intent. It thuds onto the sand beside his sister and the Siren's head jerks up from feeding. An unnatural shadow floods the beach, slowly condensing into a dark mass beneath the sand. It moves under the grainy surface toward the Siren, an ancient leviathan seeking its prey.

Charon's bony fingers reach from the sand to collect the coin, before coming back to retrieve the girl. The Siren hisses when his fleshless arms encircle the girl's torso, seeming to embracing her in a final hug. The Siren fights for her kill but is no match for the Ferryman. He pulls the girl from her grasp with ease then retreats, bathing the beach back in sunlight.

The Siren's gaze snaps up to me, black eyes pools of fury. I smirk and give her a one-fingered salute. She snarls something I can't hear then grips the stone steps and starts to climb.

'Go,' the boy grunts, 'now!'

I turn to run but it's too late. The blow from his hammer sends a shockwave through the ground, before it crumbles under my feet. I lurch forward, reaching for the newly-made edge. My fingertips graze rock, just out of reach then someone catches my hands.

I swing forward and smack against the cliff face. Hot wetness gushes over my face and into my eyes and mouth. I look up to see who caught me but there's too much blood in my eyes. One of my blood-slicked hands slips free and Talia swears from above. Another pair of hands join hers around my wrist and start to pull.

I wipe at the blood with my free hand and see the boy, hanging from his hammer beside me. His tanned skin is grey with fatigue, amber eyes agonised as I reach for him. He stares at my offered hand, as if contemplating whether to take it.

'I know loss,' I tell him. 'Your sister would want you to live, like I know my brother would want it for me.'

The sadness in his eyes, resonates down to my soul and I see myself reflected in his pain. We stare at each other for a prolonged moment, before he accepts my help. His hand is so big it engulfs mine, fingers reaching past my wrist. I grit my teeth in realisation of what's about to happen but it doesn't prepare me for the pain.

His hammer disappears in a bright flash and my shoulder dislocates with a loud pop under his weight. Someone curses from above as I scream and black spots invade my vision. We're dragged to safety and the weight of the boy is lifted. Someone shoves down hard on my shoulder, popping it back into the socket.

Helen is sobbing beside me as I contemplate my life choices. I drift in and out of consciousness, until familiar spiciness teases my senses.

'Aaron?'

'I'm here,' he says.

He's holding me, though I don't remember him picking me up. He presses something cool and damp to my face and gently wipes blood from my eyes. I force them open then burst into tears at the sight of him.

'Easy,' he soothes.

'You're late.'

He brushes a curl from my face then wipes away more blood with a piece of cloth I can see has been torn from his tunic. 'Sorry it took me so long.'

I blink heavy eyelids. 'All that matters is you're here.'

He presses a kiss to my forehead. 'You'll heal faster if you sleep.'

'Helen is here,' I say fighting unconsciousness. 'I'm sorry, Aaron. I used the key to tell her goodbye but she followed me back.'

'I'll make sure she gets home safe but you need to rest, okay? Stop fighting it.'

'The Sirens are here, Aaron. What if one finds you while I'm sleeping?'

'Here, this will help.'

He takes a small pouch from his tunic and pulls out a purple petal. He presses it to my nose and I frown at the familiar fragrance. My eyes widen when I recognise the scent from the day Logan abducted me from outside Apollo's temple.

'Why?' I ask, as my body goes numb.

He presses his forehead to mine. 'Because you'll heal faster. It's okay, I promise I won't leave while you sleep, Goddess.'

The anger and fear build inside with nowhere to go. I'm on the verge of a panic attack and can't do anything about it. Once again, he's disregarding my choices. I work my mouth, trying to speak and Aaron brings his ear to my lips. My voice is reed-thin and lacking the conviction of the boiling anger I'm feeling. I've picked up enough of his language to know the words I murmur are a crude insult. He jerks away, surprise painting his face and a wisp of satisfaction smokes through me, before I pass out.

20

The narcotic qualities of the purple petal, leave a dull ache in my skull, made worse by the steady thudding in my left ear. I blink in the dim light and try to focus through my fuzzy thoughts. It takes a while to realise the sensation of my head bobbing up and down is because it's resting on a warm chest. It explains the thudding sound. My senses sharpen and I start to wonder *whose* chest I'm resting on.

I slide a hand to my thigh and grip the hilt of the Artemis blade. A hand clamps over mine when I start to inch it free. An arm girdles my waist when I fight back, trapping me against a hard body. I abandon the blade and dig my nails into flesh, faltering when Aaron swears in response.

'Aaron?'

He loosens his grip when I retract my nails then I blink up at his face. I climb his body until our faces are level and study his shining eyes in the light of the campfire; two sapphires set amid dirt-encrusted skin. Love for him wells up inside and my tears splash his face. Rough hands bracket my face and pull me in for a kiss but I shove away. The anger comes roaring back and I roll off him, landing with a bump on the parched earth.

I get up and stalk away, picking around sleeping bodies circling the fire. I can't hear Aaron but know he's following, so keep walking until we're far enough for our words to be private. I turn to glare at him, hugging my elbows, then notice my armour has been removed. The only things left are my weapons. My filthy tunic is stiff with blood and sweat and the idea that Aaron undressed me feels like another violation.

'Inara—'

I slap him hard across the face. 'You drugged me!'

He rubs his cheek. 'You needed to heal but refused to sleep. I had no choice.'

'*I* was the one without a choice because *you* took it from me!' I snarl. 'You forced me to lose what little control I had left, Aaron and I didn't know if... I didn't know...' Traitorous tears clog my throat and I start sobbing.

I don't know how to make him understand. If he dies, I won't survive it and I've spent the last couple of days thinking I might never see him again. All I needed was to know he was solid and real against me. Hear him speak and hold him close for a while.

He pulls me into a hug. 'I'm right here,' he says seeming to know my thoughts. 'I vow that I'm going nowhere, Inara.'

I cry against his chest until my eyes are sore. I'm not strong like Aaron. If I survive, I'll need therapy for years just to sleep at night.

'I hate this.'

'I'm sorry,' he says actually sounding it this time. 'You were in pain and I couldn't bear it. I knew the Morpheus Flower would take the pain away, so I did what I thought was best.'

I draw back to meet his gaze. What he did, came from a good place but, 'You can't take my choices like that. It might be acceptable in this place but... It's wrong, Aaron.'

'I'm sorry.'

He wipes my tears and warmth threads through me at the tender look in his eyes. He's my life and soul, the single reason I'm still breathing and it scares me how much I've come to care for him.

'I love you,' I tell him.

He smiles. 'I love you.'

He presses his lips to mine, warm electricity stinging my skin. I moan and he growls, tugging me closer. He yanks the wig from my head and drops it at our feet, wrapping my braid around his fist. He holds me tight and devours my mouth and I melt against him.

We're panting when we finally break apart, breaths mingling in the small space between us. I lick his bottom lip, addicted to his taste, then frown when he winces. My eyes narrow and I take his hand to turn him back towards the light of the fire. My eyes go wide at the cuts and scrapes covering his skin, fingers trembling as I trace the old scar stretching diagonally down his torso. It leads to a fresh injury on his left hip, zipper-shaped stitches snaking over his hipbone.

'What the hell happened to you?'

'Homemade stitches,' he says then shrugs. 'Logan and I crossed paths and I couldn't yield until I found you. I didn't have the luxury of letting it heal, so I improvised.'

'You *improvised*? I could've done a better job with a staple gun, Aaron.'

'Sewing isn't one of my strengths and Logan came off worse.' He smirks. 'He won't be happy at my forcing him to yield.'

I roll my eyes at his stupid answer and reach to press my palm to his stitches. Aaron snatches my hand away and I glare at him.

'Let me heal you,' I say trying to pull free.

'It causes you pain and drains you and I'm healing already,' he argues.

'It doesn't look like it.'

'It's taking longer because I haven't had chance to rest,' he says. 'I won't put you through pain for the same end result, Inara.'

'It doesn't cause me pain.'

'And Logan and I are the best of friends,' he scoffs. 'We're not doing it.'

'So, you get to decide what we talk about now too?'

'I just don't want you hurt!'

'Fine, then let's talk about how you're the Son of Zeus,' I say. 'Or, how Logan is the Son of Hades.'

He looks startled by the abrupt change in subject then sighs, 'How could I tell you and expect you not to hate me?'

'Why the heck would I hate you for it?'

He rakes his fingers through his hair. 'My father is the king of the gods, Inara. He's the one who ordered your death.'

'Yeah, I figured. And?'

'How can you still look at me with love when you know I was sent to kill you, and my father was the one who ordered it?' he asks. 'Without his wrath you'd still be living a comfortable life in the Human Realm.'

'My life was never comfortable, even before I transitioned, Aaron.' I look away feeling vulnerable in my admission but I need him to understand. 'I miss my family and Helen but... I never truly fit in there and we both know the reasons why.' I meet his gaze. 'Do you love me?'

'You know I do.'

I tilt my head and ask, 'Despite knowing I'm part monster?'

'You aren't—'

'I'm the monster you set out to kill, Aaron so answer the question. Do you love me, despite knowing I'm Siren?'

His jaw tightens. 'Yes, I love you.'

'And I don't care who your father is. I love you, despite knowing you once wanted me dead. I probably need my sanity checking because you're my safe place now. Not the Human Realm. *You.*'

He huffs and pulls me close, lips fusing with mine. Our chests press together and I feel his heart racing. His flavour tickles my senses until I'm dizzy with his electricity. I hug him as I catch my breath and the warmth of his love blooms through me. It saturates my flesh in the same way his anger does and I realise, feeling the emotions of others is another Siren sense. And feeling Aaron's love in this moment is everything. It's something to be told by another that they love you but to feel it... It's a honey-warmth that sinks bone-deep. He kisses the top of my head and whispers something in his language. A fresh wave of warmth thrums through me, the words foreign yet, somehow, I comprehend their meaning.

'I love you too,' I answer.

His arms tighten around me and we stand for a long time, just holding each other. It feels like he's holding me together.

'Sorry,' he says a while later, as he helps pull the wig back into place.

'It's okay,' I sigh as we head back to camp. I look around the sleeping bodies as we pass, until we reach his sleeping mat. 'Why have we stayed in such a large group?' I whisper as we lay on our sides facing each other.

He brushes a crusty curl from my face and says, 'Safety in numbers.'

'None of these muscle-bound warriors are brave enough to face a Siren yet gave me a hard time for not looking like an Amazonian,' I scoff.

Aaron loops an arm around my waist and pulls me closer. 'I like the way you look.' He traces a finger down my spine, making me shiver. 'And they're afraid because they should be, Inara. You didn't grow up here, didn't spend your childhood listening to stories of flesh-eating beauties waiting to lure you with their song. Didn't have nightmares about why the beaches of Anthemusa are white.'

'Why *are* they white?'

'It doesn't matter.'

I jab his side. 'Tell me.'

He sighs, 'They used to be black, like on the Guardian Isle. It's why the rocks are black on Anthemusa, because it's the true colouring of the landscape there.'

'Go on,' I press when he hesitates.

'You can't see the black sand anymore because it's hidden beneath a blanket of the Sirens' victims.'

'I never saw any bodies when I visited—'

'Not bodies, Inara. The sand is the ground-up remains of thousands of years of their bones.'

I stare at him in horror, as memory of the sugary sand between my toes brings bile to my throat. It's made from the bones of people? I walked on the remains of people! I spin away and retch against the dirt but haven't eaten in what feels like forever. Tears sting my eyes as I force my brain around it. So many people. The Sirens have taken so many lives.

Aaron rubs my back. 'Tomorrow, we'll reach the finish line and be gone.'

I wipe my mouth. 'And then what?'

'We can be out of sight long enough to open a doorway with the lyre and get you and Helen out of here.'

'But the Sirens on the Guardian Isle—'

'Once we reach the finish line, the gods will know what's happening in the Gaming Zone.'

I turn back. 'Don't they already?'

'They aren't allowed to watch what happens out here in realtime, so they aren't tempted to aid their offspring. They know if one of their offspring yields and is taken to the infirmary but that's it.'

'Then why doesn't anyone yield, so we can tell them faster?'

'Think about it,' he says. 'Only a god can release a Siren from the Flowery Isle, meaning one of them is in on this. All the gods watch the finish line, so they'll all be aware at the same time, when someone crosses it.'

'Which one do you think did it?'

He shrugs. 'I can't think of a god that would unleash Sirens onto an island of their offspring.'

'Maybe it's a god that doesn't have any offspring here.'

'It's forbidden to release any Siren from their curse,' he says. 'If the god that did it is discovered, the consequences will be dire. They'll probably even assist my father in returning the escaped Sirens to Anthemusa. Unless he simply destroys them instead.'

I flinch. 'Destroy?'

'That doesn't include you, Goddess.'

'If Zeus figures out—'

'That *won't* happen, Inara.' He cradles my jaw. 'I didn't mean to frighten you.'

I sigh and lay down again, fatigue weaving through me. I'm physically and mentally drained.

'This is so screwed up, Aaron.'

'You should try to sleep,' he says.

'I'm sick of being unconscious. I wouldn't mind it so much if I actually felt rested after and I'm afraid of visiting Anthemusa again.'

'If that happens, just remember I'm holding you here,' he says.

I trace a scar on his chest as I mull it over. If I don't sleep then neither will Aaron and he needs to heal from his fight with Logan. I lift my head to meet his gaze. His eyes are stark against what's left of the indigo paint on his face.

'Do you have any of those petals left?' I ask.

He reaches into his armour neatly stacked beside the mat and retrieves a leather pouch. I dip my fingers in when he offers it and pull out a deep-purple petal. The fragrance is soothing as I put it to my nose and rest my head on Aaron's chest. I breathe deep and drift to sleep.

THERE'S something distinctive about the smell of Anthemusa. The air is humid and perfumed, with an icy undertone that reminds me of death. I open my eyes and sit up, groaning when I see the white dress I always seem to be wearing when I visit.

'It's past time you got here,' a feminine voice, scolds. I jerk to my feet and spin to face the breathtaking girl behind me. 'I've been waiting hours for you.'

I stare dumbly at her, thinking of how much she resembles Callista. She has the same pouty lips and small nose, with an equally impressive mane of blue-black hair. She regards me with curiosity, before smirking and folding her arms across her chest.

'I don't see what the fuss is about,' she says. 'The only difference between us is that you have blonde hair and green eyes. Neither attribute makes you special here.'

'Who the hell are you?' I scoff.

She holds out a hand. 'Come with me.'

'You insult me then want me to follow you to God-knows-where —Polite decline.'

She drops her hand and purses her lips. 'I'm Mila, your half-sister.' She gestures between us. 'Explains the family resemblance, doesn't it?'

'My half-sister,' I say staring at her.

She walks a slow circle around me. 'Mother told me we look alike but I had no idea. If it weren't for the difference in hair and eye colour, we could pass for twins.'

We study each other when she steps in front of me again. Her black hair and eyes give her a cold edge I don't see when I look in the mirror. Her jaw is sharper than mine, mouth more severe. There's definitely more of Callista in her than there is in me but she's right when she says we share a resemblance.

'Are we going to stare at each other until you wake up, or do you want to discover the reason you've graced us with your presence?' she asks, jewelled bracelets jangling as she thrusts her hand at me again.

I look down at her offered hand, ice rippling down my spine when I finally take it. Sister or not, it's obvious Mila doesn't like me and I need to watch my back. Her skin is as cold as Callista's, one Siren trait I haven't inherited.

'Good choice,' she says and leads me inland.

I cringe as we cross the beach and try not to think about what the sand is made of. Gorge rises in my throat, saliva pooling in my mouth by the time we leave the white grains. I swallow it back and breathe through my nose until the nausea passes.

'You're going to love the gift I have for you,' Mila sings in her resonating voice. 'I collected it myself.'

I frown at the back of her head, wary of how happy she suddenly seems. For someone who blatantly dislikes me, she sure seems thrilled to give me a gift.

Anthemusa is as stunning as its inhabitants. Beyond the pearly beaches stretch enchanting woodland, filled with rainbow blooms. Fairy lights twinkle amid the branches above, drenching the way in a captivating glow. It's like something out of a storybook.

Morpheus Flowers bloom amid the rich flora, the fragrance a reminder that Aaron still holds me in his arms. It gives me the courage to keep following Mila for the thirty-minute walk through the woods. She remains silent, the tension slowly growing between us, as I refuse to be the first to break it.

We finally emerge beneath the clear night sky and I falter at the sight of more Sirens. Some stop to watch us pass through the pristine, garden-like grounds. White marble structures fill the space, like the buildings of ancient Greece, except these, gleam like they were constructed days ago.

Each Siren we pass seems more achingly beautiful than the last, their black eyes tracking me like I'm a mouse in a cage of cats. I edge closer to Mila as the attention increases, more and more appearing as if a celebrity has stepped into their midst. Being surrounded like this is making my throat throb, the fiery ache delicious in a way it's never been before. Maybe because I'm not a threat to them, so I don't need to hold it back.

Mila releases my hand as we reach the steps of the largest building. The ornate, white pillars around the outside remind me of the Parthenon but on a smaller scale. Two Sirens, bathe in a low-lit pool a few feet from the bottom step. I'm drawn to their beauty, their perfect bodies shimmering in the turquoise water.

A third Siren emerges from beneath the water, skin like polished oak. Her midnight eyes sparkle like black diamonds as she meets my gaze. An inviting smile, curves her lips and she crooks a finger, beckoning me to join them. The brunette, splashes her then giggles. Responding laughter ripples through the air, the atmosphere suddenly playful and I find myself edging closer.

'Don't you want this?' Mila asks and I turn my gaze to her, watching her watch the others playing in the water. 'Don't you crave a life here, where you won't be considered a monster?' Her gaze shifts to me. 'You'd be embraced as our sister. Nobody would look at you with distain, for simply being born Siren. Here, you'd never be alone.'

'I'm not like you,' I say.

'You're not like anyone beyond these shores either. At least here, you'd fit in.'

'I'm as different from you and the other Sirens as I am from the demigods on the Guardian Isle,' I agree. 'But, at least with them, I'm free. At least with them, I have something I could never have if I lived here with you.'

'Freedom,' she scoffs. 'Here, you'd be top of the food chain. You'd be safe from those barbarians, playing with their arrows and swords. What could they possibly offer you that we cannot?'

'Love.'

She blinks at my answer then bursts out laughing, the sound like a tinkling bell as she turns and starts climbing the steps. 'I can't comment on things I know nothing about,' she calls down to me then, 'I think it's time I gave you your gift.'

I follow her up the steps then through a set of heavy, wooden doors. The air inside is cooler, the marble black beneath our feet. Mila's hips sway hypnotically as she walks ahead, guiding me to another set of doors. The other Sirens have the same, seductive grace, like they are advertising allure by merely breathing.

The second set of doors open into an oval room with a sunken pool in the centre. Starlight streams in through the glass ceiling, bathing the space in silver. Mila smiles sweetly as she takes my hand and leads me inside. We step around the first pillar lining the edge of the pool and I falter.

Horror threatens to choke me, as I stare at Aaron on his knees. He's blindfolded, wrists bound at his back. His chest and arms are bare, displaying fresh bruises and lacerations and...bite marks? He's slumped forward, the column to which the rope binding his wrists is fastened, the only thing keeping him from face-planting the black marble. A pool of blood grows around his knees as I watch, suggesting he's been here a while.

'Do you like my gift?' Mila asks.

'It's a trick,' I say. 'This isn't real because I'm not really here.'

Aaron's head jerks up, startling me because I thought he was unconscious. 'Inara?'

Mila watches with curious eyes, as I push past her and fall to my knees in front of him. I peel the blindfold from his swollen face and watch recognition register in his gaze. I cup his jaw and he, leans into my touch.

'Why are you smiling,' I ask, voice thick with tears.

'Because I thought you were here but, now I see you aren't.'

I glare at Mila. 'Let him go.'

She smirks. 'No.'

'But he's dying... Please—'

'You have the power to save him,' Callista says stepping into the room behind Mila. Her black hair shines in the starlight, beautiful face like an avenging angel's. 'All you have to do is come home.'

'No,' Aaron snarls. 'Inara, no!'

I cup his face. 'I'll be okay.'

He fights his bonds. 'Don't do this. You can't do this!'

I press my forehead to his and whisper the only thing I know will settle him. 'I have a plan but you need to trust me.'

He calms at my words and I turn to Callista before Aaron sees the guilt in my eyes. I push onto my feet and walk up to her.

'Why?' I demand.

'You wouldn't come by choice and Mila lost track of you in the Gaming Zone. I had to think of something to encourage your compliance. Imagine my delight when I came across your lover.'

Pain wraps tight fingers around my heart as I realise, the only way to save Aaron is to let him go. I close my eyes as a tear slips free. Deep down, I knew it would come to this. I knew I couldn't keep him.

'I have no way of getting here,' I whisper.

'I'm sure you'll find a way,' she whispers back, delight lacing her tone.

I turn to Aaron, heart in my throat as I go kneel in front of him again. I pull him from the brink of unconsciousness with a feather-light touch and force a smile.

'I love you,' he rasps.

I press a kiss to his cracked lips then moan at the sudden strength in his return. His electricity washes through me, warm and fringed in his love. It's tinged with sadness and I realise, he thinks I'm going to leave him here. He's telling me goodbye.

'I'll always love you, Aaron and I'm sorry.' I shove to my feet and turn back to Callista. 'You win.'

'No!' Aaron growls. 'Inara, no!'

I close my eyes and sob as I force myself to wake.

21

I gaze at the dark sky, mind chasing answers that won't come. The stars stare back, glittering like shattered glass on tarmac. Like the night I lost everything in the accident and now it's happening all over again. I scrub tears from my face, then stiffen when I register the arms around me. I'm cradled against a muscular form and relief blasts through me that it was just vivid nightmare.

I press my cheek to Aaron's chest and close my eyes at the sweet sound of his heart. He's alive and holding me like he promised he would be. He stirs against me then stiffens, before gently tugging his arms from around me.

I look up in confusion and meet a pair of dark eyes. 'Hello, Princess.'

Logan is matted with dirt and sweat and through it, I smell his dark musk. I remember the taste from the kiss we shared; deep and delicious, like dark fruits and a hint of chocolate. I stare and he stares back, eyes pure night but not like the Sirens of Anthemusa. His midnight, with a smouldering core like coal plucked from the fire.

I blink against the hypnotic quality of his gaze then shove away. If Aaron isn't here, he's on Anthemusa with those things and time is running out. I look around the room with beds lining the walls then back at the ceiling. This time, I notice the thin, almost-invisible glass separating me from the stars.

I drop my gaze to the rectangular room. It must be the infirmary Aaron spoke of, where the injured competitors go when they yield from the Games. It explains the sharp smell of disinfectant and Logan's presence.

His hand lands on my shoulder and he spins me to face him. My glare falters when I see the usual arrogance missing from his expression. He studies me like he's trying to figure something out but I don't have time for his games. I push around him and start searching the empty bed.

'What are you looking for?' he demands as I claw at the sheets. When I ignore him, he sighs, 'Whatever it is, you won't find it in *my* bed, Princess.'

I turn and find him sitting on the only other unoccupied bed, the Artemis blade in his hands and a pile of gold armour on the floor at his feet.

I hold out my hand. 'Give that to me.'

'I find it funny how you keep ending up in my bed,' he says.

'Give me my weapon, Logan.'

He turns the blade between his fingers. 'First, you will tell me where my brother is.'

'What?'

His dark gaze burns into mine. 'You were the last to see him in the Gaming Zone before several Sirens attacked. Tell me where he is and I'll let you leave here alive.'

'They took him,' I say.

He shoves from the bed. '*They?*'

The shadows gather as if drawn near as he towers over me, eyes burning with black fire. The door crashes open, Talia's tall figure filling the frame. She glances between us and draws her sword.

'Who has Aaron?' Logan snarls.

Delia shoves around Talia and says, 'The Sirens have your brother, Son of Hades.'

'I've already told *you*, Aaron isn't dead,' he growls.

'Not dead,' she agrees. 'They're holding him on their island.'

Logan stares at her, the colour draining from his face and looks suddenly younger: lost, like he doesn't know what to do. I realise, how much he really cares for Aaron and my encounters with him start making sense. Collecting me from the temple in Aaron's stead and soothing me during the storm. He's brash and arrogant and fringed in darkness but, Logan loves his little brother.

He pushes the Artemis blade at me, fire fading from his gaze as he falls to his knees. 'I've failed him,' he rasps. 'They'll kill him as they did our mother and there's nothing I can do to stop them.'

'I will stop them,' I say.

'He can't be trusted,' Delia warns me.

'Why would Logan hurt the one being who can breach Anthemusa to save his brother?' I argue.

He pushes to his feet. 'If you know something, then tell me.'

I take a deep breath then pull the wig from my head. My braid falls over my right shoulder, the ribbon Delia wove through it like ink in the starlight. Logan's face goes slack with shock as he stares at me. His shoulders shake and I get ready to fight but he explodes with laughter instead.

'You mean, instead of killing you, Aaron decided to *court* you?' he guffaws then grins, taking me in. 'He actually did it! He disobeyed his father. Almighty Zeus, King of the Gods!'

I stare at him as he laughs. 'Why aren't you angry?'

'Seventy-two years, I've watched that blue-eyed god of thunder mould Aaron into his image,' he says. 'Ever since he took him, after Mother died. Aaron was desperate to please him, living to his father's rules, the guilt of witnessing our mother die forcing him to obey. Zeus never once told Aaron our mother's death wasn't his fault. I tried everything to get him to listen and shed the false shame but it drove a wedge between us.' His gaze warms. 'Then you come along and set him free. A Siren. A gods-damned Siren!'

'So...you're not going to kill me?'

'Not unless you give me cause.'

Good enough for me. I step around him and start strapping my armour into place, brain fixated on Logan and Aaron's mother dying seventy-two years ago. Aaron said she died when he was nine, which would make him eighty-one.

'If you go to Anthemusa, you'll be bound by the curse,' Delia says coming to stand beside me. 'You won't be able to leave once you've entered the confines of the island, Inara.'

'My mother took Aaron for that reason, Delia. She knows the only way to get me there is to threaten someone I love. If I don't go, she'll kill him.'

'I'm coming with you,' Talia says.

'No, you're not. I'm the only one not affected by Siren song, so only I can go. Everyone wants me dead or trapped on that island anyway, so they'll finally get what they want.'

'He's my brother and I won't leave his female to go rescue him alone,' Logan says.

'*His female*—so archaic,' I mutter.

'I too, offer my sword,' the curly-haired boy from the cliff says from the next bed over.

I frown his way. 'You know who and *what* I am, right?'

He nods. 'You aren't like the creatures on that island. You paid the Ferryman to take Lydia to her eternal rest before that Siren could devour her soul then, you saved my life after. I owe you these debts and will stand with you, Daughter of Apollo.'

'As will I,' Adonia says from the doorway.

Helen smirks from beside her. 'I'd add my services to the list but these guys are more protective of me than you are.'

I stop what I'm doing to give her a hug. 'Are you okay?'

'I'm fine but this isn't your fight alone, Inara. You don't get to choose who joins in, so stop being a control freak.'

'I'm scared.'

'Good, so am I. It's okay to be scared. It's healthy.'

'Try telling them that,' I scoff gesturing to the demigods around us.

'I did,' she says. 'They laughed at me.'

I shake my head at her. 'Of course, you did.'

~

IT'S NEARLY dawn when Anthemusa finally comes into view. The beaches gleam like virgin snow in the fading night, a Venus flytrap awaiting prey. We sit quiet in the small boat, ocean slapping the wooden hull, as Logan and the curly-haired boy-Alexander, row us closer. The water transforms in the wake of the rising sun, turning from midnight to clear crystal and I can see the seabed below.

My spine prickles and I grip Logan's arm. 'Stop!'

'Just a little closer,' he says.

I tighten my grip. 'We've crossed the threshold.'

'Threshold?' Talia asks.

I wait for Alexander to drop anchor before saying, 'This is as far as their song will carry.' I peer over the edge and point to a line of rocks littering the seabed up ahead. 'I think that's what those rocks represent. Stay this side of that point and you'll be safe.'

'How do you know this?' Adonia asks.

I shrug and look away. 'I feel it.'

I see it in their eyes when I look back: I'm different, like the monsters on that island. They're willing to cooperate because they want to save Aaron and this is a no-lose situation for them. When they get Aaron back, I'll be trapped on the island, so they'll be rid of me at the same time.

'Describe where they're keeping him,' Delia says ending the awkward silence.

The others turn fully to face me, forming a circle to listen.

'How do you know where to find him if you've never been here?' Alexander asks.

'I've been here in dreams,' I say. 'It's how I know they have him.'

Logan's fingers are warm as they curl around mine. 'Your dreams are divine visitations. The gods use the ability to communicate with us and each other sometimes. It's a rare talent among demigods.'

I stare at him, wondering if he's really trying to comfort me. It's so out of character that I don't know how to answer. I nod instead then turn to the others.

'Beyond the beaches and rocks, there are trees,' I say.

They inch closer, hanging on my every word as I describe my journey with Mila. It's clear they've never heard an account of what lies beyond the beaches—nobody ever surviving to tell the tale. They'll never see it for themselves though, the only reason they're here, to retrieve Aaron if he's too weak to make it from the shore to the boat. My job then will be to distract the Sirens, while they escape.

While they talk about the secrets I've revealed, I slip off my sandals and check the strapping on my armour. I consider taking it off but Logan told me it's a special alloy designed to float. I don't want to leave it, since Aaron gifted it to me. It will be something to have when he's gone and I'm trapped on that island.

'Wait!' Delia shouts when I climb onto the side of the boat and brace to jump.

I turn back, her hair like fire in the first light of day. Her whiskey eyes shine with tears as she comes to stand before me. She presses Helen's friendship bracelet into my palm.

'Helen asked me to give you this,' she says.

'Thank you,' I rasp and pull the lyre from my tunic. 'Use this to get her home then return it to my father.' I remember the phone and pass it over. 'Tell her I recorded a video message before the battery died.'

'I didn't think Sirens could shed tears,' Alexander murmurs.

I wipe my eyes, hating the way people keep saying that.

'They can't,' Logan says, taking the friendship bracelet and pulling me down beside him. He puts my hand in his lap while he ties the bracelet to my left wrist. 'Inara's Siren side doesn't dominate her like it does with the other Sirens. She can feel and her tears are a manifestation of that emotion.'

Okay, that was nice.

'I don't understand,' Alexander says.

'Only the original three Sirens were full blooded,' Logan explains. 'All other Sirens are half mortal, making them half-bloods like Inara. Except, she isn't half mortal but half god. Her sire is no mortal man, so her Siren half isn't the dominant one.'

'How do you know all this?' Talia asks.

'Aaron isn't the only one who speaks with his father,' Logan says. Right...Hades.

I stare at Logan as he concentrates on tying the bracelet. When he's being kind, it's difficult to think of him as the Son of Hades, Ruler of the Underworld. It's such a foreign concept to try and wrap my brain around especially now, when he looks so much like Aaron. He meets my gaze, dark stare burning with the fire I love so much in his brother. My throat grows tight and I look away. I push to my feet and frown down at the heavy weight around my wrist, finding it wrapped in rope. I look at Logan in confusion to see him securing the other end to the rowlock that holds the oar.

'What the hell are you doing, Logan?'

'Sorry, Princess but we've decided you don't belong on that island.'

I look at the others in the boat for help but they all meet my gaze with determination. My heart sinks when I realise they're all in on this decision. I reach for the Artemis blade but Logan's hand clamps around mine. He pulls me close and tugs it free, before tossing it to Talia. She catches it and secures it to the opposite end of the boat.

'You're not going to die for me,' I snarl.

'We're not planning on dying,' Logan says. 'Besides, Aaron would kill me if I stay in this boat and watch the girl he loves, get imprisoned on Anthemusa.'

'It will be okay,' Talia says. 'We'll be in and out before they even know we're there.'

'You don't get it,' I growl tugging on the rope. 'They don't need to see you to know you're there. They'll *feel* it the second you step foot on the island and will find you the same way.'

Surprise lights each of their faces then they look at each other.

'That's how you knew other teams were coming during the Games,' Talia says.

'Yes!'

Determination replaces their shock and Alexander comes to kneel before me. His amber eyes are earnest as he regards me through the dark hair falling across his face. He takes my hand, studies my fingers then smiles up at me.

'You paid the fare for Charon to take Lydia to the Underworld. Whether I live or die today, I will never be able to repay you for that kindness, Inara.'

'I didn't save your life for you to throw it away like this,' I answer.

He stands then bends to kiss my hand. 'I'll bring Aaron back to you.'

I turn away and stare at the ocean, as they all slip overboard. Delia hesitates at my side. She sighs at my refusal to acknowledge her farewell then follows the others to get slaughtered. Anger, burns inside at their stupidity. They say it isn't my choice to stop them from fighting but they're forcing me to do exactly that.

'Inara,' Logan breathes by my ear, startling me into turning his way. 'I'll bring him back to you,' he promises then cups my jaw, gaze burning into mine. 'I hope my brother knows how lucky he is to have found you.'

He presses a kiss to my lips then turns and jumps into the water. I stare after him as he catches up with the others, the burn of his kiss still scorching through me. They climb onto the beach then sprint across the sand, disappearing from view between the rocks. My heart pounds against my ribcage, knowing the Sirens will have sensed their arrival. The earplugs will only protect them from a distance. If they get close enough to the resonating waves of a Siren's song, they'll be ensnared.

I concentrate on letting my anger bubble to the surface, glad Aaron's the only one I showed Apollo's bow to. The bracelets light up as they heat, biting into my flesh and the golden curve of the bow flashes into my waiting palm. Singed tatters of rope lay scattered around my feet and I stamp on them to put out the smouldering. The bow returns to being a bracelet and I snatch the Artemis blade from where Talia left it, slotting it into its sheath on my thigh.

I jump into the water and start swimming, pace slow but steady. It takes forever to reach where the stones line the seabed, detailing the reach of the Sirens' song. The moment I pass over them, an invisible weight drags me down to the seabed. The air is sucked from my lungs and I fight the burning until I can't anymore. I inhale against my will but instead of drowning, the burning in my lungs, ebbs. My breathing levels out and I blink in shock, hair a cloud of gold around me. I glance to the line of black rocks on the seabed and the situation, registers.

The stones mark the edge the barrier surrounding the island. The heavy weight of it was what pushed me to the ocean floor, sealing me within its confines for the rest of my life. Instead of regret, I feel relief that I stopped the boat from passing it earlier. Had the barrier hit me then, I'd have destroyed everyone else's means of escape.

I walk along the seabed, body seeming naturally weighted to the sand. My movements are easy, like I'm taking a stroll along the beach above. I make it to the beach and break through the surf, lungs switching from water to air. It's a strange sensation yet natural, like I was born to live this way. Powered bone sticks to my feet like sugar as I step onto dry sand.

Callista slinks from between the rocks a moment later and smiles victoriously. 'You didn't have to wait for me. This is your home now and you're free to roam it.'

I falter at her declaration, until it registers that she thinks I'm the one that originally breached the barrier. She thinks I've been waiting for her since, unaware that I've only just made it to the beach. She doesn't know the others are here and has come to roll out my welcome wagon.

I sidestep when she reaches for me and stalk towards the rocks. 'I'm not here by choice, remember.'

'I haven't held you since the day I was forced to give you up,' she says, voice so full of sorrow it stops me in my tracks. She's a picture of despair as she comes to me and touches my hair with gentle fingers.

'Why did you do it?' I ask. 'Why save me from being bound by the curse if you planned on forcing me to return?'

'I didn't relinquish you to save you from the curse, Inara. I did it to save you from the others.'

'I don't understand.'

'Look at your golden hair and emerald eyes,' she says. 'I bet you even bleed red.'

'So what if I do?'

'Sirens have black eyes and blood like the velvet midnight between stars, Inara. If I hadn't birthed you, *I* wouldn't have believed it either. You look too human and the other Sirens would've killed you before you had the chance to mature.'

'But...I was a baby.'

A smile curls her lips. 'What do you think happens to our male offspring?'

'Sirens only have female children.'

She snorts. 'Is that what the gods are telling their half-blood children nowadays? Male children don't inherit Siren song, so they have no purpose. We can't use them for breeding because we're all related in some way and, eventually, the need to kill them grows too strong.'

'You...*eat* your male children?'

Her smile widens at my shock. 'How you've managed to be around the Son of Zeus for so long, without succumbing to the bloodlust, demonstrates immense control, Inara. ' She strokes an icy finger down my burning throat. 'This is the only place you won't be in pain. Here, you can be free to embrace your better half and feel the euphoria it brings. You'll never crave anything more ever again.'

I suddenly realise how crazed she is. 'Apollo told me you loved him,' I argue.

'I do, in a way; I just love this more.' She shrugs. 'You know, he always planned on bringing you back to me, as soon as you transitioned and could prove yourself Siren.'

An uncomfortable feeling, unfurls in my stomach. 'What?'

'He isn't a fool, Inara. Apollo may love you but he knows what you're capable of. His only other option would be to let Zeus destroy you.'

The uncomfortable feeling turns into thick nausea. Apollo wants me imprisoned? The warmth I'd started to feel for him is replaced with sharp betrayal. Then I feel stupid because I've fallen for it again; trusted someone despite the risk of them hurting me. I tuck my hurt away because I don't have the luxury of falling apart yet. Aaron and the others need me to draw attention, so they can get away. Once they're gone, I'll revisit the clawing pain in my middle.

'Aaron won't be allowed to leave here,' Callista says as if reading my mind. 'He's seen too much.'

My eyes narrow at her declaration. 'What?'

'You can be the one to end him, if not your sister has become rather attached—'

'No,' I snarl, voice a resonating purr. My brain sifts quickly through the available options then I cruel smirk. 'She can't have what's mine.'

Callista, scrutinises me, mistrust clear in her gaze. 'You came here because you claim to love him; refused to come any other way and yet you'd kill him so easily?'

'Why would I want to be trapped here when I can be out *there*, feeding on whomever I want. *You*, ruined that for me when you stole my trophy. I've been prepping the Son of Zeus for weeks, his scent driving me insane.' I get in her face and let the cold anger that always sits beneath the surface, show. 'Nobody takes what's mine, not even you.'

Her smile is radiant as she grasps my hand. 'Let me take you to your prize then.'

She guides me from the beach, gaze studying me with inky delight. I keep my rage on the surface, let her feel it in the air between us and her smile grows. If Aaron is my prize, then I'm Callista's. I see the avarice in her gaze each time she looks my way. She speaks about the long wait for my return and the plans she has for our shared future.

We breach the far side of the woods and Callista leads me directly to one of the white marble buildings. I mask my disappointment when she doesn't take me directly to Aaron, feigning nonchalance in case this is another test of my intent. Inside, I'm terrified for us both. I want to get him away from here but don't want him to leave me.

Callista, leads me to a room where Mila and a dozen other Sirens laze around. They perk up when we enter and converge on me, fussing over me like I'm a new pet. They all marvel at my green eyes then, croon about how my loveliness will lure more prey. I'm a shiny new weapon for them to add to their arsenal. My rage pulses higher at their conversation and those around me, purr in response. They comment on how potent it is; how much they crave the feel of it against their skin.

They strip my armour and toss it aside. The Artemis blade clatters against the marble and is kicked away, deemed useless by predators that have no use for such things. I'm naked in minutes and the group surround me, scrutinising my form like they're assessing my worth. Mila takes my hand and guides me to a sweetly-scented pool. The water is cool and fresh and I'm bathed by the group. Grime is washed from my hair and skin, before I'm pulled from the water and dressed in soft fabric.

A sense of belonging washes through me as the hours pass. Sirens adorn me with jewellery, cooing over how it adds to my allure. Being around them is like drinking hot chocolate on a cold day, their resonating tones infusing my flesh and calming me in a way I've never felt. I find myself laughing at their jokes and ignoring the niggling sensation that there's something I need to remember. All I can think about is how much I like everyone. They're all really nice and accepting. There isn't any fear because we're the same and it hasn't been like this since before I discovered I was Siren. Even Aaron feared me at first...

Aaron.

Everything about him comes flooding back, making me wonder how I ever forgot. How could I forget what I came here for? How could I forget *him*?

I shove to my feet, folds of aquamarine fabric tumbling down to my ankles. I stare at the dress, fresh panic spilling through me when I realise, it's the dress from the vision Delia had in the square.

Mila offers me a crystal glass. 'Here, drink this. It will calm you.'

I peer at the luminous contents as Apollo's voice whispers through my mind, '*Don't drink of the Lethe unless you wish to forget.*'

I press it to my lips and tip the glass, pretending to take a healthy swig. Anger, streaks through me at my sister's deception. The dead drink from the Lethe to make them forget the life they left behind and she wants me to forget mine. But I don't want to forget—I can't, not until Aaron is free from this place.

I push the glass into Mila's hand. 'No more stalling, Sister. I want what I came for.'

Instead of denying me, excitement glitters in her gaze and she grins. 'We've taken him outside.'

22

Aaron is pale and motionless, like he's been carved from the same marble as the statues in the garden. He's laid out on his back, hands bound at his chest. His fingers are curled around the hilt of his sword, laid flat against his torso. Like a knight, lain to rest.

I'm too late.

Pain grips my chest, heart seeming to fold in on itself. I try to breathe through the agony of what I'm seeing but the air is too thin. He was my reason for breathing and he's gone. Heavy sorrow presses down on me.

A pixie-like Siren steps up to him with a greedy look in her eyes. She presses a dainty hand to his abdomen then licks his blood from her palm. Inky darkness clouds my vision, rage exploding through me. I find myself in front of her, hand gripping her throat. Her feet dangle above the ground, as my resonating growl rents the air.

'Mine,' I snarl in her face.

I drop her and she scrambles back, panting for breath, staring up at me with wide eyes. I glare down at her then around at the others. They've backed away too, giving me space to look over Aaron. He's been washed since I last saw him but he's covered in bite-marks and blood. They've tortured him and it's all my fault.

My hand trembles as I press my fingers to a crescent-shaped mark on his shoulder. His blood is still warm and I close my eyes at the revelation. His death was recent, likely while I was laughing and joking with the Sirens in that room.

My gaze snaps to a blonde Siren, inching closer. I hiss and she stumbles back. They're like hyena, circling a kill, waiting for a taste.

'He's *mine*,' I hiss at them.

Callista pushes through the gathered predators and grins. She glances between my blood-slicked fingers and Aaron's body, an expectant, look on her face. I hold her gaze as I suck my fingers clean. I'm prepared to hide my disgust but pleasure rakes through me instead. It's dizzying and intense and I groan as it tingles up my spine. Aaron's exotic flavour blooms over my tongue, unleashing a wintry desire for more. I want to taste it, bathe in it, drink it down. I want to intoxicate myself, until I sate the raging ice in my middle.

'The stronger they are, the tastier the flesh,' Callista purrs. 'Aaron is the Son of Zeus, a demigod sired by one of the most powerful of his ilk. Enjoy your prize, Inara for you have chosen well.'

I meet her dark gaze, enticed and horrified. I don't know how I can feel this way about Aaron, when I love him so much. I look down at him, feeling like a true monster for the first time since I discovered what I am. Even now, the thirst for his blood claws at my insides.

'His flesh is mine and I will not share,' I say.

'Not even with your sister?' Mila asks, resting a hand on his arm.

Another resonating snarl rips from me, the venom in my tone like verbal poison, 'No.'

She snatches her hand back, a semblance of fear in her gaze. I smirk as she retreats with the others. My father is a god, so I'm apparently stronger and not beyond using it to get what I want. Their fear pollutes the air as they leave, graceful figures drifting from the gardens to cower beyond view.

'I knew you'd be special,' Callista says. She cups my jaw and wipes blood from my lips. 'I'll leave you to your reward, Daughter.'

I wait for her to slink away then turn to Aaron. The fragile seams holding me together burst, rage shrinking into my core, as tears spike my lashes. I use his sword to cut the bindings around his wrists then drop it to the grass. I trace his face with shaking fingers, feeling like my heart is bleeding. I pray for it to happen; pray that I'll bleed out right here beside him.

I press a kiss to his lips, still warm and fragrant against mine. I'm not ready to admit he's gone and find myself climbing the stone table. I curl around him and rest my head on his chest, like I did last night. There's no steadying heartbeat beneath my ear this time and his arms don't hold me close. He's gone and he's taken my heart with him.

I straddle his waist and look down at his peaceful expression. 'I love you, Aaron.'

I press my lips to his for the last time then sob at the absence of electricity. I yearn for it with every fibre of my soul, liquid fire filling me at the memory of it against my skin. Flames lick the underside of my flesh, growing hotter and more intense. I try to pull away but I'm locked in place. The burning becomes searing agony and I shut my eyes. Maybe I've got a built-in self-destruct and will become Aaron's funeral pyre.

The heat ebbs, retreating into me and releasing its grip. I jerk upright, panting and weak, body shaking as I open my eyes to find the pixie-like Siren staring at me in awe. Dark eyes reflect the golden light still gleaming from my skin and she edges closer, mesmerised. A sound pulls our gazes to Aaron and my eyes widen with fear that I'm dreaming.

'Inara,' he rasps.

'Traitor,' Pixie snarls.

She takes a breath to call the others but her body jerks before a sound can escape her lips. Surprise wipes the scowl from her face and she drops her gaze to a dark stain blooming on her chest. She presses shaking fingers to the tip of a blade, sticking from her ribcage. It withdraws and she looks at the black liquid glossing her fingertips. Her expression is confused; child-like, as if she can't comprehend what's happening.

A large hand clamps over her mouth and nose, holding a bunch of purple petals against her face. Her eyes roll back as she passes out and the hand withdraws, petals fluttering around her in its wake. She slumps to the ground and another pair of black eyes replace hers, smouldering with dark fire.

Logan.

Aaron grasps my face, tilting my gaze back to him. 'What did you do?'

The pain in his voice, echoes the look on Logan's face. They know what my being here means but it isn't the reason I'm crying. The joy of Aaron being alive, is stained with knowing I've got to let him go. I climb from the stone table, knowing we haven't got much time before the Sirens realise what I've done. My knees buckle but Talia appears, catching me. I blink dark spots from my vision and push through the fatigue.

Aaron's weak too, so Alexander helps him climb down. We stare at each other, air between us heavy with pain. He steps towards me but Adonia and Delia crash from between the trees to our right.

'The mother and sister are coming,' Adonia pants.

'Time to go,' Talia says and bends to pick me up.

I push her away. 'I'm fine. Carry Aaron, he's too weak to run.'

It's a lie, I'm not fine but there isn't time to argue. Alexander slings Aaron over his shoulder and Talia grabs my hand, pulling me into a dead run. Aaron watches me from Alexander's shoulder and I try to smile, even though we both know our time together is ending.

The time to help them escape comes and I look away, so Aaron won't see the agony in my gaze. The pathway through the trees narrows, forcing us into single file. Alexander is pushed into the centre of the group and I purposely put myself at the back. Talia releases me from her death-grip and glances back to make sure I'm keeping up. I keep pace with her for a few minutes before slowing to a stop.

The group disappear ahead and my eyes brim with the tears I've been holding in. I turn back as resonating screams drench the air. My spine arches then cracks with the approaching danger and I growl through the pain, furious that it dares assault me in this moment. The Sirens have discovered my betrayal and are coming for me... for Aaron.

Rage-drenched vibrations, crease the atmosphere and shudder along the invisible web threading the island. My insides light up at the sensation, an icy purr shivering through me in response. The Siren in me, loves the rage. Luckily for me, she doesn't care who it's directed at. Cold fury spreads through me and I lift my arm, bow flashing into my palm. I pull back on the bowstring, delivering a shimmering arrow into position and wait.

The first ten Sirens don't know what hit them, my arrows cutting them down, vaporising their bodies before they have chance to hit the floor. They're easy targets, resonating their locations before they even appear between the trees. They're drawn to my rage, like I'm enticed by theirs; mine potent from the divinity coursing through my blood, luring them into my path. I wonder why they vanish after I shoot them, spraying the air with a fine mist of onyx. They don't leave anything for Charon to ferry to the Underworld, like they don't have souls to take. I frown, wondering if the same will happen to me when I die.

I get lost in that thought as I stare into the trees, smeared in black, waiting for the next Siren to find me. I've killed at least thirty but more are coming, including my mother and sister. Maybe I can kill them all; rid the island of their curse before putting myself out of my misery.

Rapid footsteps sound behind me, forcing me to expose my back to the centre of the island. It's difficult to pinpoint which direction they're coming from, since they aren't showing on my radar. My adrenaline spikes as I move my arrow back and forth, searching for a target.

Someone crashes through the trees to my right and I spin in that direction, arrow primed to fire. The leaves settle, revealing my target and I falter, before my bowstring slackens and the arrow disappears.

'No. No, no, no—you're not supposed to be here! You can't be here!'

Relief washes through Aaron's gaze when he sees me. 'She's here,' he calls jogging up to me and grasping my hand.

Logan, Alexander and Talia crash into view behind him. Talia gives me an angry glare, as Aaron swipes a curious finger through the sticky, black layer on my skin.

'It's Siren blood,' I say.

'This way,' Alexander orders as if it's a given that I'll follow, turning back the way they came.

I pull against Aaron's hold. 'You know I can't come with you, Aaron. I'll cover you from here—'

'I'm not leaving you,' he says.

My skin prickles, fresh vibrations lapping my spine. I glance back to the coming danger then to Aaron.

'They're coming. Please, don't make me watch you die.'

'I won't leave you behind,' he growls and scoops me from the ground.

The fight leaves me and I cling to him as he runs, wondering how he even has the strength to carry me. Alexander and Logan drop back to flank him, while Talia takes the rear. I bury my face in Aaron's neck and savour his scent through the blood and sweat. I have to make him leave me behind, no matter how much the idea kills me.

We burst from the woodland and navigate the rocks, onto the hideous sand. Aaron carries me to the water's edge and sets me down. He steps into the surf and waits for me to follow. Everyone is watching, waiting for me to do...something.

I step into the surf and Aaron's expression has me realising what's happening. They think the barrier around the island, encircles the beach. Nobody witnesses Sirens swim out to collect their victims and it's believed they have to wait for them to wash onto the shore. But inside the barrier, I sank to the seabed and could breathe underwater. Nobody sees them collect their victims because they're out of sight when they do it.

Aaron grabs my waist and crushes his lips to mine. 'I love you, Goddess.'

It takes everything to match his smile and push him deeper. 'I love you, too. Now go! All of you go. Their voices don't affect me and I swim slow, so I'll catch up.'

He presses another kiss to my lips then dives into the next wave. I keep the smile on my face as I wade out until the water kisses my shoulders. When the others glance back to check on me, it looks like I'm swimming.

Delia is the first to notice something is wrong. She stands abruptly in the little boat and starts waving at the others. Her voice doesn't carry but her movements are frantic. Adonia joins her efforts then Talia, as soon as she climbs into the boat. The choppy waves must drown out their voices and by the time they reach Aaron, it's too late.

I wade back to the beach and turn as Aaron, Logan and Alexander reach the boat. Talia and Adonia help pull them aboard then Aaron stumbles to his feet and tries to jump back into the water. It takes Logan, Talia and Alexander to stop him. He fights them all, despair so great, a wave of it hits me from across the distance. The air punches from my lungs and my knees wobble. Logan says something that pauses Aaron's fight, drawing his gaze from me. His shoulders slump and the others release him. He turns back to stare at me.

'I love you,' I whisper, heart turning to ash as Alexander and Talia start rowing.

The distant shadow of the Guardian Isle, rises against the horizon. Aaron will be so close, yet forever out of reach. My heartbeat, thick and heavy in my throat, counts the seconds until the hazy heat blinks my love from view.

I reach for the Artemis blade, then remember it was discarded on the floor of one of the white buildings. I can't go back there and can't just stand here, waiting for the Sirens to find me. If they kill me, my mother and sister will draw it out.

I squint up at the sun. 'Don't leave me here!'

Apollo doesn't answer, which is answer enough. There's only one way I'm getting off this island and I'm okay with it. Aaron's gone, my family are gone and there's nothing left for me here, except waiting for death. I won't give Callista or Mila the satisfaction of being the ones to give it to me. I turn my gaze to the rocky summit, rising from the shoreline. I climbed it the first time I visited Anthemusa and recall the sheer drop from the highest point. I won't wait for a prolonged death at the hands of my mother and sister, or anyone else. I'll die on my terms and *finally* get something *I* want.

The sun is low on the horizon by the time I make it to the summit. My hands and feet are bleeding from the climb but I can't seem to register the pain. Deep down, I know it isn't right. I should be hurting more but I can't seem to feel anything beyond the blanket of grief threatening to suffocate me. I stare at the stretch of rock ahead, leading to a sheer drop.

My shoulders cramp when I peer over the edge. The breeze of the approaching dusk, kisses my sweating skin and tugs at my hair. I close my eyes and try to feel something before I leave this world. I take a last look at the distant island, smile tugging at my lips when I think of the friends I made. It slips away when dark clouds gather above the Guardian Isle, flashes of lightning reaching like silver thread to the Earth. The sunset is eclipsed by the rumbling wall of grey, stealing the daylight and wiping the island from view.

I look down and wonder if my body will evaporate into mist when I hit the rocks below. Am I enough like the Sirens I shot earlier, that I won't have a body to mourn or a soul to take? I don't even care anymore. Nobody here will mourn me and those who care will never know.

'Aaron,' I whisper, wanting him to be my final thought.

I spread my arms wide and tilt forward, letting gravity take me. Aaron calls my name, as if he's here in my final moments and I smile. Someone grips the back of my dress and yanks me back onto the edge. I crash into my misguided rescuer and skid with them across the rock, before rolling to a stop. I open my eyes and stare at the being responsible for delaying my death. Blue, eclipses my vision as Aaron stares back.

'It worked,' I say knowing this can't be real. I'm bleeding out on the rocks below and this is some pre-death hallucination. 'I'm dead.'

His lips crash against mine, hot and fierce and stinging with electricity. His flavour bombards my senses, delicious and terrifying when I realise, this is actually happening.

'You're not allowed to kill yourself,' he growls at me.

'They were going to kill me anyway, I was just making it quick.' He looks like he doesn't believe me and I sigh, 'What are you doing here, Aaron? You were free and safe. Why did you come back?'

'We have twenty minutes before my father reactivates the barrier. As long as you're on the other side before it goes back up, you'll be free.'

'Zeus lowered the barrier to get me out?'.

'You saved my life, Inara. Add in Apollo and Hades' arguing for your release and he was swayed.'

My eyes widen. 'I understand Apollo asking for my freedom but Hades?'

'I told you, Logan likes you,' he says and presses another kiss to my lips, like he can't help himself. 'Come on, there isn't much time left.'

We reach the only way down from the summit, when Callista appears in our path. 'I knew he'd return for you.'

Her voice is a velvet resonance in the air. Aaron's hand loosens around mine, glare melting into dream-like acceptance. Callista's beauty is cold magnificence, her voice ringing; dark hair a cloud of onyx around ivory shoulders. She's enthralling, entrancing and the embodiment of a Siren.

Slender fingers latch onto the rock around her feet, more Sirens pulling themselves into our path and Callista laughs. I grab Aaron's hand and back us away, lungs and throat burning. Crippling pain grips my shoulders and spine, and a series of audible cracks have me stifling a scream.

'There's nowhere to go, Inara. Kill him now, or watch him die but be assured, Aaron's life ends tonight.'

'Just...shut up,' I snarl, voice wrinkling the air. It feels so good to let it out, the burn instantly easing from my throat. Aaron jerks in response beside me, face whipping in my direction. He stares at me in confused recognition and I stare back.

'Her voice doesn't work,' Mila sneers. 'She's useless to us.'

'Don't be a fool,' Callista hisses. 'She just woke him from my song.'

'Impossible.'

'Her voice is more powerful than all of ours combined,' Callista says. 'The divinity coursing through her blood, means it reaches farther and can ensnare even gods. That's why they're so afraid of her.'

The gods?

'It didn't work on *him*,' another Siren points out, 'and he's just a demigod.'

'Because she *loves* him,' Callista scoffs like admitting it enrages her. 'Love renders her voice useless against him and offers him protection from ours.' Her crazed eyes meet mine. 'Love is dangerous to our kind, Inara. It makes us vulnerable to attack but we can remove your weakness before it's too late.'

Her gaze shifts to Aaron and I step in front of him. We're trapped, hemmed in by encroaching Sirens, a sheer drop at our backs. My spine cramps and I gasp in agony. Hot, sticky sweat trickles down my back as I cry out.

'You're bleeding,' Aaron says, sliding a finger down my spinal column.

He gasps when a loud crack forces my back to arch. I scream and stumble onto one knee as fresh agony rips down my spine. Heaviness pulls at my shoulders and a new sensation arches out behind me.

'It can't be,' Callista breathes as golden feathers rain down around me. 'Only the Original Three were granted wings.'

The pain ebbs and I look at the Sirens before me, awe painting their faces. I wobble onto my feet, struggling under the weight of the enormous, golden wings now arcing from my shoulders. The feathers are the same shade as my hair and match the one I found in the grass at the top of the cliff that day.

'Wings... I have...wings?'

My mother smiles when I take a shaky step in her direction. She opens her arms to me when I smile back.

'Inara?' Aaron calls but I ignore him, leaving him by the edge where he'll be safe.

I stop a few steps from Callista and say, 'This is probably a really bad idea.'

Her smile falters. 'What?'

I spin away and run at Aaron, gaining as much momentum as possible. I smack into him, throwing us from the edge and cling to him. Fear and exhilaration, war inside me but I'd rather die this way than at the hands of those monsters.

Aaron bands his arms around me as we fall. 'I love you!'

'I love you too,' I shout over the rush of the wind.

Muscles I didn't know I had, shift instinctually in my shoulders and my wings snap wide. They catch the breeze, scooping us from our free-fall to glide parallel with the rocky ground. They adjust again, navigating us over a large cluster of rocks then out, over the ocean. Each movement feels natural, like flexing any other muscle in my body and it's like I've been flying all my life.

I stare ahead, wondering how long we were facing off with Callista on the summit. If the barrier has been reactivated, I'm about to crash. I move us closer to the ocean and bury my face in Aaron's shoulder, bracing for impact. This way, he won't have far to fall if I hit the barrier.

He laughs a moment later. 'We made it!'

My head snaps up, gaze clashing with his neon irises in the dark. We look back, as a bright flash of lightning illuminates the dome-shape barrier cresting over Anthemusa.

'We did it—I'm free.'

Aaron is grinning when I meet his gaze again. 'You have wings!'

'Yeah,' I say, still in shock then frown. 'What did Callista mean by the Original Three?'

'The original Sirens were the Handmaidens of Persephone. They were supposed to be watching her, the day Hades stole her and took her for his bride. Her mother Demeter, gave them wings to search for Persephone but it was already too late. Anthemusa was their punishment.'

'Oh,' I say.

I can't help but feel sorry for the original Sirens, being punished for something Hades did. I wonder if they were evil like the Sirens today, or if they just grew bitter and twisted over time. What does it mean for me? Constantly hunted for simply being what I am, is taking its toll. Each time something bad happens, it feeds the wintry darkness in my middle, lending it more strength and control. I'm terrified that one day I won't be able to hold it back.

'Erm, how are you at landing?' Aaron asks.

I follow his gaze to a small boat carrying Logan and Talia. 'I guess we're about to find out.'

We bank around, losing altitude as we go. Salt paints my tongue as we glide a metre above the water. I stare at the surface, the strangest need to get closer, weaving through me. My wings shift and we hit the water, the weight of my wings dragging me under. I shove Aaron away so he won't be dragged down with me then try to swim up.

The water is dark and cold beyond the barrier, crushing the air from my lungs. I take an automatic breath and icy brine rushes in. I realise too late, that I've lost the ability to breathe underwater. My lungs sting, as my extremities go numb and frosty darkness claims me.

'*Breathe,*' Daniel orders, warmth spreading through my body as if I've been wrapped in a blanket. *Just breathe.*'

'I *am* breathing.'

'*No, look,*' he says pointing behind me.

I turn to find myself on a little boat, bobbing on the ocean. A beautiful blonde with silver eyes and a worried expression, watches a dark-haired boy kneel over something on the floor of the boat. I step closer to see what has her so upset and find the body of another blonde girl. This one is in an aquamarine dress, golden hair like spun sunlight around her face. She's familiar but I can't grasp the memory of how I know her. The dark-haired boy is pumping his hands rhythmically against her chest, while another boy covers her mouth with his.

'What happened to her?' I ask, pressing my fingers to my tingling lips.

'*She drowned and they're trying to save her,*' Daniel says.

'But she's gone. Why not let her rest?'

'*It isn't her time, Nara. You have to help her. You have to breathe.*'

'But I want to stay with you.'

He hugs me. '*I'll always be with you but Mum, Dad and I are okay now. You've got to stop mourning our deaths and get on with your life.*'

'I miss you too much.'

'*We miss you too but they need you now,*' he says gesturing to the trio working on the girl in the boat. '*Aaron needs you.*'

'Aaron?' The name sends a jolt of recognition through me. 'I... know that name.'

'*Close your eyes,*' Daniel says. When I comply, heavy pressure slams against my chest and I cry out. '*It's okay, I'll stay with you until it's over.*'

Pain slams into me over and over, until an answering beat echoes the rhythm back.

The slamming stops and a new voice orders me to, 'Breathe!' Warm lips seal over mine, pushing air into my mouth. 'Dammit, Goddess breathe!'

The world tilts and I'm on my back, body jerking, as icy liquid gushes up my throat. Someone thanks Zeus, as I cough stinging liquid from my mouth and nose. Warm air rushes in, each breath agonising as strong hands hold me steady.

Aaron pulls me close as soon as I'm done purging saltwater from my lungs. 'You scared the hades out of me,' he rasps.

I close my eyes, enjoying the scent of his damp skin. He breathes pretty words in his language as he holds me close.

'I'm sorry,' I croak, throat raw from all the seawater.

He looks down at me, eyes luminous in the starlight and something splashes my face. I look to the sky, thinking it's rain and another splash hits my skin. I look back at Aaron in realisation as another tear then another, drips from his chin.

I cradle his jaw in my hand and say, 'Happy tears?'

He drops his forehead to mine. 'I thought I'd lost you.'

'You did for a moment,' I whisper then flinch at the new-found lightness in my shoulders and breathe, 'They've gone.'

Confusion fills his gaze, until he notices the golden feather I'm staring at in my lap. 'They were gone by the time we pulled you from the water.'

I'm saddened by the loss of something so beautiful but relieved there won't be something else making me different. Those huge wings would've been difficult to hide, especially while being hunted. I suddenly feel a thousand years old at the thought and rest my head on Aaron's shoulder. Fatigue washes through me and shadow creeps around my vision.

'Inara,' he says, pulling me from the brink of sleep. I realise he's scooped me into his arms, when his face eclipses my view of the stars. 'Stay awake with me.'

Daniel appears at my other side and I smile his way. 'You stayed.'

Aaron frowns in Daniel's direction. 'Who are you talking to?'

I'm too tired to keep my eyes open, so close them and cuddle into Aaron. 'Don't worry, he says it isn't my time yet.'

'Who?' Aaron demands seeming far away despite his arms around me. 'Who's here with you, Inara?'

His tone is frightened, so I muster the strength to answer, 'Daniel.'

Aaron hugs me tighter. 'I'll never let you go again.'

23

I blink into the dark, eyes adjusting, as if the place before waking was filled with light. The dream lingers, warm and tempting on the cusp of my mind. All I really remember is the joy it made me feel.

As my senses sharpen, I realise I'm not alone in bed. Aaron's electric touch heats my skin and makes my heart flutter. He's holding me like he promised; chest to my back, body curled around mine. Steady breaths brush my nape, his spicy scent infusing the cool air around us. The frigid air makes me frown because it's too cold to be the Guardian Isle.

I lay awake for a long time, refusing to burst the peaceful bubble until my bladder screams for me to get up. Aaron reaches for me as I slide from the bed and I smile, handing him my pillow. He cuddles it close and buries his face in the fabric, frown easing.

His skin is bleached by the moonlight streaking in through a crack in the curtains. He looks carved from marble and the chilling memory of his lifeless body, wipes the smile from my lips. Aaron died because of me and then I'd been trapped on Anthemusa with those monsters.

Bile, snakes up my throat and I hurry from the room. I find a bathroom further down the hallway and shut myself inside. I use the facilities then sit on the tiled floor and put my head between my knees.

It takes a while to talk myself out of a panic attack. The tightness in my chest eases, as I finger the soft fleece pyjamas I'm wearing. I try piecing things together so I don't feel so disjointed. It's cold here, the facilities modern and I'm surprised at the disappointment of realising, I'm no longer on the Guardian Isle.

After a while, I leave the bathroom to pad along the carpeted hallway and follow a warm glow emanating from a stairway at the end. It shines from a doorway at the bottom and I follow it down, stepping into a Human Realm kitchen.

'Hello, Sunbeam.'

Apollo looks out of place, gleaming skin reflecting off the kitchen appliances. Heat radiates from him, reaching to where I'm standing and I shiver. When he opens his arms, I don't hesitate to let him wrap me in his warmth.

'Aaron said you championed for me to be freed,' I say.

'You doubted I'd fight for your freedom?'

'Callista said you planned to confine me to Anthemusa. Said my voice is the reason the gods fear me, that because you're my father, it's capable of affecting them.'

'You shouldn't take everything Callista tells you as the truth, Inara. I was forbidden to interfere but it doesn't mean I stopped loving you. I will always fight for you, something Callista is bitter about. She hates that I didn't champion for her release like I did yours.'

'Why didn't you?'

'Because she is a monster and you're not.'

'So you *didn't* plan to return me to Anthemusa?'

'If keeping you safe meant going to Anthemusa then I wanted you there. After what happened with your mother though, I don't think it's an option anymore.'

'I can't believe Zeus even listened to you.'

'He was watching when you saved his son—twice, Inara.'

'Why didn't he just save Aaron from the Sirens, though?'

'Because he has to lead by example. How can Zeus expect his sons and daughters to abide by his rules if he doesn't adhere to them? Doesn't mean we don't all...bend the rules when we can. We just do it when the rest of Olympus isn't watching.'

'Wait, what do you mean about sons and daughters?'

'The other gods and goddesses, his sons and daughters—'

'Wait,' I say stepping back to study his face. 'If you're Zeus's son and Aaron is Zeus's son, that makes Aaron and I—'

'No,' Apollo says before I can voice the horrifying thought. 'Do you think I'd have allowed you to get romantically involved with Aaron if you were related in that way? Zeus's title as Father of the Gods doesn't mean he is my father and human myth detailing him as such is mere fiction. Not everything the scribe wrote were reality, Inara. Humans have a talent for embellishment.'

'Really?'

'Gods and goddesses don't procreate with each other in the way you're thinking. The titans created offspring from the materials available to them and we have adapted their methods. Yes, Zeus assisted Leto in the manifestation of myself and Artemis but he did not sire us. The children we sire in the way you know are all demigods.'

I sag in relief. 'You don't know how close I was to having a heart attack.'

'Demigods don't suffer heart attacks, Sunbeam.'

'You mean there's an upside to all of this?'

Apollo guffaws and turns to the French doors on the opposite side of the kitchen. 'There's someone I'd like you to meet.'

I follow him outside and bite back a curse at the drop in temperature. I've become accustomed to the heat of the Guardian Isle and thick frost covers the ground here. The grass under my feet looks diamond-encrusted and I shiver as I take in rolling hills and a star-studded sky. If I want proof that I'm no longer on the Guardian Isle, this is it. It's so cold, I can see my breath. Apollo drops a blazingly-hot arm around my shoulders and pulls me against his toasty side.

'Who is that?' I ask when a small figure materialises from the night. It draws closer until I can discern her features. 'Diana?'

She smiles as she stops before me, barely dressed in the freezing night. I leave Apollo's warmth to pull her into a hug. She stiffens before hugging me back then pulls something from a leather strap on her shoulder.

I stare at the Artemis blade. 'But...I left it on Anthemusa.'

'I know,' she chastises. 'You should be more careful. Artemis doesn't gift weapons from her private collection to just anyone.

'Please tell me you didn't go to that island to get this, Diana.'

'I did.'

'Don't ever risk your life for me like that again,' I huff.

'I would've been there with you but I was forbidden to interfere.'

'You shouldn't... Wait, what?'

I glance from her to Apollo then back again. Those are the words he used in relation to not being able to help me. I shield my eyes against a flare of silver light. A tall, beautiful woman appears in its wake, in the place Diana had been standing. She's shimmering and ethereal, with white hair and familiar, kitten-blue eyes.

'Bloody hell, Diana?'

The woman smiles. 'I'm known as Artemis in this form.'

I stare at her, betrayal sliding through me, then turn and head back inside. Diana isn't a Daughters of Okeanos, she's Apollo's twin; my divine aunt. I don't understand why she didn't tell me sooner. The house feels warm now I've been outside. I go to the kitchen table and pull out a chair. The gods follow and sit either side of me at the table, filling the room with their glow.

Artemis sighs when I pointedly ignore them. 'You're in danger, Inara.'

My gaze snaps to her. 'But Zeus—'

'Is no longer the problem,' she says. 'A lot has changed in the two weeks since you escaped Anthemusa.'

'Two... Are you actually telling me I've been unconscious for two weeks?' She nods. 'Fourteen whole days,' I check and she nods again. I drop my face into my hands and ask, 'How is that even possible?'

Apollo winds hot fingers around my wrist and prises a hand from my face so he can meet my gaze. 'It's the price you paid for gifting your life-force to Aaron, Inara. Your body needed time to regenerate.'

'My life-force?'

'The energy you use to heal people is drawn directly from your own life-force. You inherited the ability from me but, unlike me, you're not a god. Your body can't take the strain and when you saved Aaron, you nearly gave all you had.'

I'd accept more than sleeping for a fortnight if it meant saving Aaron.

'If Zeus isn't a problem anymore, why am I still in danger?' I ask.

'Callista and Mila are free,' Artemis says.

'But I saw them on the summit when the barrier reactivated.'

'We believe a god is helping them,' Apollo says.

'Why?'

'To get to you.'

Me? 'For what?'

'You're no longer in direct danger from Zeus but you're still considered a threat to the gods, Inara. Callista and Mila are immune to your song, which is why we believe they've been tasked with finding you.'

I shove from my chair. 'I'm not some pawn to be used in a celestial power-struggle! How many times do I need to prove I can be trusted to be free from Anthemusa? I won't be dragged into this and end up back there as a result.'

'Inara—'

'That's what happened to the Original Three, isn't it? Hades stole Persephone and they were punished for his crime.'

Apollo rests his hand on mine. 'Inara—'

A crash from upstairs has us looking to the ceiling. We glance to the doorway at the bottom of the stairs when Logan's swearing, sounds through it. It's followed by Aaron's urgent response.

Artemis sighs and heads for the French doors.

'What do you mean she's gone?' Logan bellows, footsteps thundering above. 'You don't just lose an entire girl, Aaron!'

'Shut up and help me find her,' Aaron growls.

I grab Apollo's arm when he heads for the door behind Artemis. 'I know it's selfish to leave right now but I can't... Can you take me with you, just until I process what you've told me?'

He leads me outside without question, icy grass crunching under my feet a step before I'm suddenly knee-deep in snow. He scoops me into his arms then sets me down a moment later, onto warm, dry grass.

'Where are we?' I ask looking down at the patch of warm earth beneath my feet. It's a perfect square in the snowy landscape.

He points to a house in the the valley below. 'We were there.'

'Of course, you can teleport,' I drawl.

He grins but it fades quickly. 'Helen will return your key. Use it if you need a moment alone but please, be careful.'

I sigh, 'I'm sorry I yelled at you.'

'I understand.'

'It's just... It isn't fair. I only want to be left alone, what's so complicated about that?'

'I've existed long enough to understand that life isn't fair, Inara. There will always be those who wish to exploit others and not even *I* contemplated the magnitude of power you'd wield.' His smile returns. 'You're a delightful surprise, my little sunbeam.'

'I wouldn't call myself delightful,' I mutter then, 'Did you know I have wings? You should've seen the look on Callista's face.'

'I knew.'

He holds out a hand at my shocked expression and golden light pools in his palm. When it fades, a tiny, gold feather is left in its wake. I pick it up when he offers it to me and hold it between my thumb and forefinger. It's a smaller, downier version of the feathers that made my wings.

'You gifted that to me at your sixth birthday party,' he says, 'at the Butterfly House.'

I blink in disbelief. 'You were there?'

His gaze softens. 'You were wearing a pink dress with fairy wings glued to the back. You and Helen were discussing how cool it would be to have real wings, when you cried out and they sprung from your back.'

'I don't remember any of that.'

'I administered a *lot* of Lethe water that day,' he chuckles.

'You knew how to get rid of them?'

'I was there when the Original Three were alive,' he says. 'Their wings would disappear when submerged in water.'

'Like in the ocean,' I say remembering the instinct to crash into the sea with Aaron. I'd been thinking about how to get rid of my wings, when I'd felt the draw to submerge.

'Others will try to corrupt you,' Apollo says taking my hands in his. 'You have my light but you also have Callista's darkness.'

'I know,' I say and look away. 'On Anthemusa, when I tasted Aaron's blood... I...liked it.'

'It's your nature,' he says not an iota of disgust or judgement in his tone. 'What matters is that you didn't surrender to it. Instead, you saved his life.'

'Because I love him.'

'Because you aren't like the other Sirens,' he corrects. 'You're not alone, Inara. I'll be with you, like I have been since the day you were born.'

'I haven't been alone since Aaron found me and he hated me back then.'

The approaching dawn turns the sky rose pink and I give Apollo an expectant look. He chuckles like I've asked a stupid question.

'Can't you do more than one thing at once?' he asks. 'Just because I'm here with you, doesn't mean I'm not doing my job.'

I smirk. 'And I thought men couldn't multitask. I'd better let you go, though. I don't want to be blamed if you crash the sun.'

He booms with laughter, making me smile and cups my face. 'I'll take you back first.'

My smile falters. 'I'm not ready yet. I'll see you soon though?'

'All you have to do is call my name,' he says then kisses the top of my head. 'Good morning, Sunbeam.'

He's gone in the next breath, the patch of defrosted ground still warm beneath my feet. I look around at the knee-high snow then down at my bare feet and roll my eyes at my own stupidity. It's at least a mile back to the house and I'm standing up here in fleece pyjamas.

The conversation with Apollo repeats in my head and I concentrate on finding my wings. When they were gone in the boat I'd thought they were gone forever but, as I think of them now, pain shudders through my shoulders. The same pain gripped me each time I was scared and desperate for escape. I had another option of getting away all along, I just didn't remember having it.

Pain slices across my shoulders and down my spine, forcing me onto one knee. The back of my pyjama top rips open, the weight of my wings arcing out behind me. A shower of golden feathers glitter to the floor as I find my balance and stand.

I take a while to get used to the sight and weight of my newest appendages. I practice flexing them, then fold them around my body to explore the long, silky feathers. They're downier closest to my shoulders, like the one Apollo kept from my childhood. They turn sleeker and sharper as they travel down the length of each wing, reaching to the backs of my knees.

The cold bites at my bare back as I tie the remains of my top as best I can to stop it from falling off. I concentrate on trying to fly and realise, I don't know how to take off. Back on Anthemusa, I'd launched from the summit so gravity sorted this issue for me. I glance at a noisy flock of crows above, probably laughing at me down here.

'Wings can be tricky,' Artemis says from beside me.

I scream at her sudden appearance then put a hand to my racing heart and ask, 'How would you know?'

'Goddess of Wild Animals is one of my many titles,' she says. 'Birds are favourites of mine.'

'You can turn into a bird?'

'Any bird and any animal,' she says. 'Think about the lightness of flight and how it felt to be airborne.'

I close my eyes to remember the breeze against my face and in my hair. The weightlessness comes back, the shift in my centre of gravity and the steady thwomp-thwomp beat of my wings.

'I remember the feeling,' I say.

Artemis chuckles, 'Open your eyes, Niece.'

I squeak at the sight of my feet hovering above the ground then laugh. 'I did it!' Artemis grunts when I smack into her, in an attempt at a hug. 'Thank you!'

She gives me a playful shove towards the house. 'They're looking for you.'

'Thank you again!'

'I'll be watching,' she says, smile warm then disappears in a flash of silver.

I beat my wings to gain altitude and bank towards the house. The frigid air needles my skin as I swoop back to Earth. I laugh at the exhilarating sensation of flight, the world so pretty from up here. Frosty grass races beneath me as I pick up speed in my descent. Adrenaline spikes, numbing me to the frigid air. The house looked tiny amid the rolling hills of the countryside but now, I can appreciate how big it really is. My wings arc out, catching the air and my body adjusts to land gracefully on my feet.

I walk towards the French doors but familiar voices make me hesitate. I look at my shredded top then back at my wings. I'm so different to the other demigods and different to the rest of the Sirens. I never fit in as a human for reasons I understand but the old insecurities are still there. I'm sick of being an outsider.

I creep to the edge of the French doors and peek through the condensation fogging the glass. The kitchen is packed, everyone crowded around the island in the middle. My name is mentioned several times and I cringe away from the door. I skirt the house, looking for another way inside. I just need to get rid of my wings and find something else to wear before I face them.

I find an open upstairs window and beat my wings to reach the sill. I flatten my wings to my back and squeeze through the opening, biting back a curse when I get wedged halfway. I grip the frame and push, until it cracks and I land with a thump on the carpet.

I stare at the broken window frame, surprised by my own strength, then scramble to my feet. The room smells like Logan, explaining why the window is open when it's freezing out. The boy loves anything dark and frosty. It isn't until I've squeezed out into the hallway, that I realise the house has gone quiet.

I reach the bathroom door as Talia shouts my name from downstairs. There's a question in her voice, as soft footsteps sound on the staircase. I shove into the bathroom and slam the door behind me, slipping the lock into place as my wings knock products from the vanity. They clatter into the sink and across the floor and I step over them to plug the bathtub and turn on the tap.

The door handle rattles and I stare at it. 'Who is it?'

There's a beat of hesitation before Logan says, 'Inara?'

'Yes?'

'Open the door.'

'I'm taking a bath,' I say staring at the water, willing it to flow faster.

'Where have you been?' he demands.

I rip the remnants of my pyjamas off and step into the frigid water. 'N-n-nowhere,' I hiss.

'I *personally* checked this entire house five times and you weren't in it,' he says.

'I j-just n-need a m-m-minute.'

'What's wrong with you? Why are you talking like that?'

Because the water is bloody freezing! 'G-go aw-way!'

'Open this door right now, or I'll break it down!'

'T-two m-minutes!'

'You've got ten seconds,' he says and starts counting.

I drop into the bath, sloshing water over the side and across the tiled floor. Nothing happens... then my wings...dissolve, my back hitting the bottom of the tub in their absence. I scramble from the tub and snatch a towel from the rail as Logan finishes counting. I slip on the wet floor, landing painfully on my backside when he starts slamming against the door. I hiss in pain but pull the towel over me, just before the door crashes open. He stands panting in the doorway, glaring down at me on the flooded floor, towel covering the parts that count. His glare pans the room then drops back to where I'm shivering on the floor. He scoops me up and I hiss at the heat of his skin on mine.

'P-p-put m-me d-down!'

'You need to get warm so, for once in your life, do as you're damn told.'

He pushes past Talia and Adonia out in the hallway and stalks back to the room I came in through earlier. He kicks the door shut behind him then puts me on the bed and goes to slam the window shut too. He eyes the broken frame then gives me a pointed look and I look away.

He sighs and drapes a blanket around my shoulders. 'Where were you, Inara?'

I stare at the white-knuckled grip I have on my towel. 'W-where's Aaron?'

'Searching for you. It scared the Hades out of him, waking up to find you gone.'

I meet his gaze. 'I'm sorry.'

'Are you going to tell me what that was about in the bathroom?'

'I was taking a bath.'

'In freezing water?'

'It's none of your business, Logan. What were *you* doing, breaking down the door?'

'Aaron warned me about the time you disappeared in the hotel bathroom and again, at Helen's house. I could tell you weren't being truthful and didn't want to risk you disappearing again.'

'I just needed a minute to digest things. I didn't... I didn't mean to make anyone worry.'

His gaze softens and he reaches to pluck something from my hair. When he pulls his hand back, he's holding a golden feather the length of my forearm.

He studies it. 'Do you want to talk about this?'

Hell. 'No.'

He stares at me for a long moment then grabs a pile of clothes from the dresser. 'Here.'

I finger the soft fabric. 'Thank you.'

I$\scriptstyle\rm T$'s surreal to be in jeans and a long-sleeve top, not an inch of leather in sight. It's more...me except, I'm not even sure who *I* really am anymore. I'm not human, or what a Siren should be. I shy away from fighting, where every other demigod I've met can't wait to enter the fray. I carry the light of my father but the darkness of my mother. I don't fit in any of the pigeon holes others keep trying to shove me into.

I don't...belong.

The door crashes open and I push to my feet as Aaron grabs me. He holds me, the warmth of his love sending static shivers through my flesh.

'I'm sorry,' I rasp.

'I knew you weren't far,' he says meeting my gaze and presses my hand to his chest, over his heart. 'Ever since you brought me back to life, I've been able to sense you—Like there's a tether between your heart and mine.'

'Because I gifted it to you, Aaron.'

'Your heart?'

I nod. 'It's yours, so you'd better take care of it. It's...' I sigh. 'It isn't what it used to be and is a little fragile but...I want you to have it.'

He presses a kiss to my lips. 'I'll keep it safe.'

He stares at me, gaze intense and I squirm. 'Why are you looking at me like that?'

'To see you looking back at me,' he says. 'Your body was here while you were unconscious but the part of you I'm tethered to was far away and I didn't like it.'

I think of the bright place I was dreaming of before I woke and flashes of memory flutter around the periphery of my mind. 'I don't remember where I was.'

'I think you were with your brother.'

'Daniel?' Somehow that feels right and warmth blooms through me, like something inside remembers things my mind can't. 'I think you're right.'

'Where did you go when you woke up?'

My smile fades. 'Apollo and Artemis came to see me.'

Aaron stiffens. 'What did they want?'

'A god released my mother and sister from the Flowery Isle to hunt me down.'

'They'll have to get through me,' he snarls.

That's the problem. 'Aaron, I won't let you—'

His kiss cuts me off and the fight in me dies at his electric sting. I kiss him back, mentally postponing the argument for later. He's hungry; I'm hungry and Aaron is my favourite food. The back of my knees hit the bed and he follows me onto the mattress, caging me against it. He stares down at me with eyes of blue fire, then grins and reaches to pluck something from my hair.

'This explains why you flooded the bathroom,' he says brandishing one of my feathers. He frowns when I look away and pushes from me. 'What is it?'

I sit up and stare at my hands in my lap. 'I don't want anyone else seeing my wings.'

He takes my hand and rubs gentle circles into the back. 'Why?'

'I'm different and it makes people wary. I don't want my friends to be wary of me, Aaron.'

He's quiet for a moment then gets up and pulls me with him. 'Come with me.'

'Where are we going?'

'You'll see.'

A delicious smell meets us as we descend the stairs. Familiar voices fill the kitchen, adding to the cacophony of clanking pots and pans. I'm reminded of Sunday lunches with my grandparents, the same home-cooked-food smells drenching the air.

We step into the kitchen and my mouth drops open. Talia and Alexander are mixing something in a large bowl, flour dusting their faces. Delia is rolling dough and Logan is sitting at the table, reading a thick book. All are dressed in human clothing, not a scrap of leather or metal in sight. It's unnerving.

Delia looks up from her pastry and smiles, rolling pin clattering to the counter as she comes to give me a hug. I stand dumbly in her arms, the smell of butter and sugar between us.

'I was so worried about you,' she says.

Talia pulls me from Delia and lifts me into a bear hug. 'I thought you were going to miss it.'

I look up as she puts me down. 'Miss what?'

'Somebody's birthday,' Alexander says around a mouthful of food. 'Helen says it's a big holiday here in the Human Realm and we must adhere to the traditions.'

'That sounds like Helen,' I say, smile tugging at my lips that she has a bunch of demigods doing her bidding.

'She called it the Season of Goodwill.'

'Wait, Christmas? It's Christmas already?'

'That's the one,' Talia says like I'm not internally freaking out at how much time has passed. 'We thought you were going to miss it but here you are.'

The atmosphere wrinkles in the centre of the room before I can comment. Nobody else reacts, until Adonia steps into the room, seemingly from nowhere.

'I like my name,' she says, arms full of packages. She's dressed in jeans, boots and a winter coat, looking like someone peeled her from the pages of a catalogue.

'Jane is easier for my parents to accept,' Helen says appearing behind her. 'You already look like a supermodel and you have an accent—'

'Which would explain my actual name,' Adonia argues.

'Maybe you're right,' Helen huffs as she drops her bag on the table.

'Inara,' Adonia says noticing me as the doorway closes.

Helen turns to stare at me in shock, hair a mess of black curls around her shoulders. She snaps from her surprise and runs at me, knocking me off my feet on impact.

'Ow,' I grunt from under her.

She grins down at me and I grin back, then we both start laughing.

'Do you know how much sleep I've lost waiting for you to wake the hell up?' she says. 'Precious sleep I'll never get back.'

I grin. 'I love you too, Helen.'

'Don't make me cry,' she says and shoves away. 'I swear to God if I smudge my mascara, I won't save you any Chocolate Fudge Brownie.'

I look at the bag she left on the table. 'You didn't,' I whisper and go to the bag to pull out a pint of my favourite ice cream. 'Oh my god, you did!'

She plucks it from my hand and shoves it in the freezer. 'Not until after Christmas dinner.'

'I haven't eaten in over two weeks and have been dreaming of ice cream since I went to that freezer-less, boiling island!'

'She means the Guardian Isle,' Helen tells the rest of them like it isn't obvious. She smirks my way. 'Do you really think we'd let you starve while you were sleeping? It's *my* ice cream and I'll let you have some, if and when, *I* decide to share.'

'You're so damn mean,' I hiss.

'And you love me for it.'

I huff and go sit in the chair beside Logan's. 'Fine.'

He glances up from his book to give me an imperious look. I stick my tongue out at him and his lips twitch, like he's fighting a smile.

IT'S cosy around the table for dinner. My hand is laced with Aaron's, both of us eating with just a fork because we need the connection. Logan is on my other side, scent mingling with Aaron's and surrounding me with a spicy, musky mist. I stuff more potato into my mouth and set a mental reminder to never sit between them again. They're both just so...dominant and it's stifling.

I look at Helen, sandwiched between Alexander and Adonia and wonder if she's having the same problem. Do humans feel the dominance of demigods? Did she ever feel it with me? I notice Alexander looking at her while she pretends not to notice and almost choke on the food in my mouth. Envy pangs through me because the life I had is over, the world moving on without me.

'More tofurky?' Delia asks, drawing my focus.

Logan snorts at the vegan alternative Delia made me in place of the turkey everyone else is eating. None of the demigods understand my vegetarianism, especially Logan. I glare his way then smile at Delia and accept another slice. Helen giggles at something and I glance her way to see Alexander whispering in her ear. Her face is red and when she catches my gaze, guilt flashes in hers.

I push to my feet and everyone stops eating to stare at me, Aaron and Logan shoving from their seats too.

'I'm going to the bathroom and neither of you are coming,' I growl at them.

Aaron hesitates before reluctantly sitting down. Logan glares at me but sits too and I stalk from the room. I shut myself in the bathroom and slide to the floor, back to the door as tears burn my face. Someone has cleaned the mess I made earlier and I stare down at the dry tiles like they hold the answers. I feel like I'm losing myself, don't know where I fit or what's going to happen.

I hear approaching footsteps before Helen's voice sounds through the door. 'Inara, can I come in?'

'No.'

'Come on, Nara. Pity-Party-for-One, isn't really your style.'

'Sod off.'

'I brought the ice cream.'

I make her wait then shove to my feet and rip the door open. 'Don't think a tub of ice cream will—'

She slaps the ice cream against my chest and pushes past me. 'Bathtub meeting, now.'

We sit in the empty bath, legs dangling over the edge, passing the ice cream between us. Bathtub meetings started as a place to paint our nails when we were afraid of getting it on the carpet during sleepovers. It evolved from painting nails, to chatting about boys, drama at school and who Helen was going to rage at each week.

Helen sighs, 'I know I broke the first rule but so did you.'

'I didn't plan on falling in love, Helen. I thought Aaron hated me until.... I'm not exactly clear on when his feelings changed or mine for that matter. Love is surprisingly close to hate.'

'Nobody *plans* on falling in love, Nara. Fair enough, we didn't get each other's approval before making it official with our boyfriends—'

'He *is* your boyfriend then?'

'To be fair to me, *you* were unconscious when Alex and I got together.'

'And *I* was in a different realm when I figured out my feelings for Aaron,' I say.

'Which is what I've been getting at! Neither of us planned to break the first rule, it just happened.'

'Like you would've approved of Aaron, even if you'd been there.'

'He's...growing on me.'

'Because it's convenient to you now.'

'I hit him,' she says.

'What? When?'

'When he got back from Anthemusa without you.'

'Helen,' I whisper.

She stares at the spoon in her hand, a haunted look on her face. 'He left you there and I couldn't... I think he let me do it, even though he seemed really weak from whatever happened to him.'

'He died, while I was being pampered by the other Sirens.' Tears roll down my face at the admission. 'I was so captivated by how they made me feel, that I forgot why I was even there. They killed him while I was laughing and joking in the next room.'

She stares at me, tears glistening on her lashes. 'You brought him back, like you did with me?'

I nod. 'I tricked him into leaving me there because I knew I was already trapped. By the time he figured it out it was too late. The others had to hold him in the boat, to stop him from coming back for me.'

'He really loves you.'

'He petitioned his father for my release, which is the only reason I'm here, Helen.'

'I owe him an apology.'

'Nothing has changed, though,' I say.

She frowns. 'What do you mean?'

'My mother and sister have been released by an unnamed god, to hunt me down. It means everyone I'm around is in danger. I'm not... safe, Helen. You, Aaron, the others—All of you should leave while you can.'

'Are you done?' she huffs.

'Excuse me?'

'No more Inara Thompson Pity Parade, okay?'

'I'm not—'

'You don't seem to realise how good you have it,' she says. 'You know for a *fact* your family are happy in the afterlife. How many people get that, Inara? You have amazing powers and, sure, you don't like all of them but it doesn't make them any less awesome. You walked away from a car crash and can bring people back to life! Who the hell cares if you're a Siren?'

'I do!'

'Try being human for a day, *then* tell me how crappy your life is,' she huffs. 'Nobody that matters, cares what you are, Inara. I'm not saying it has been, or is going to be, sunshine and lollypops but one day you'll realise it has all been worth it. And you got Aaron out of it, didn't you?'

'I... When did you get so wise?'

'I've always been wise, you've just never bothered to listen,' she says and hands me the ice cream. 'Stop whining and eat that. You're getting too thin.'

'Okay, *Mum*,' I drawl.

We grin at each other and my bad mood dissipates.

THE KITCHEN IS empty when we make it back downstairs. I follow Helen to a door in the corner and along a short hallway, to find everyone lounging in what looks like a living room.

'Tell me *again* why we're doing this?' Logan drawls.

'Helen said it was fun,' Adonia says sounding as bored as Logan.

'I've had more fun visiting my father in Hades,' he says looking up to meet Helen's gaze.

She stalks into the room and growls, 'Because you're doing it wrong.'

Aaron pulls me down to sit next to him on the sofa. 'Do you feel better?' I nod and he presses a kiss to my lips.

'Hey, Earth to Inara,' Helen hisses. 'Put Aaron down and come help me show the "Mighty Demigods" how to do this right. No offence,' she tells me.

I smirk. 'None taken.'

She waves me over to the coffee table in the middle of the room and I kneel across from her, a stack of playing cards between us.

'The idea is to play as fast as possible,' Helen says shooting a glare at Logan. 'Not slow like you were doing it. It's a game of fast thinking though, so maybe you should stick to watching.'

God help Logan for casting aspersions on the ancient game of Snap.

'And the point of this tedious game?' he scoffs.

'To give everyone time to digest the huge meal we just ate, Genius. We usually play poker but I don't know if you've got the mental capacity to pick it up.'

'I know how to play poker, *human*.'

''Whatever, you barbarians can go outside and practice fighting as much as you like after the game, so kindly shut up.' She meets my gaze and grins. 'Ready to go down again, Thompson?'

I believe *I* hold the current title,' I say. 'What was it again, forty-three to thirty-five?'

'Pure luck,' she scoffs.

My smile falters because, is it really all this is, luck? I never believed in fate but now? My mother and sister are hunting me for a god, for reasons I can't fathom and I hate the not knowing. I feel like a pawn on a chessboard, ready to be sacrificed.

I look at my new friends, playing the game with me, refusing to cower. They're choosing to face this danger because it's what friends do; what...family do. I meet Aaron's gaze and remember falling with him from the summit that day. I feel the same sensation now; of falling uncontrollably towards a gruesome end. We'd been okay with it back then because we had each other. I smile and he smiles back, still falling but uncaring because, we're doing it together.

I turn back to Helen and pick up my cards. 'Bring it.'

Whatever happens, I'll go out fighting.

End of Part One

SIREN BURN PREVIEW

SIREN BURN

BOOK 2 IN THE SIREN SERIES

Dante

Creatures shine like freckles along the seabed; little stars amid sand and rock. Not that I truly remember stars after so many years. The palace rises into view: pillars of light from the fathomless deep. The shine is brighter than before I left, meaning Father has returned early. I mentally groan at the argument my absence will cause and speed up.

I reach the transparent dome separating the palace grounds from the rest of the ocean and slip through the barrier, taking a breath of air as my skin and hair dry. I dress in the clothes I stashed earlier and run towards the palace.

'There you are,' Milos says meeting me at the top of the marble steps.

The armour he's wearing suggests he's just returned from the surface and I push my envy away at the simple freedoms he takes for granted. I've only been to the surface twice in my whole life and I'll never be allowed to compete in the Guardian Isle Games, like Milos.

'Did you win?' I ask.

His smile fades. 'Nobody won this year, the Games were...interrupted.'

'Interrupted?'

'Your father will know you've been outside the dome, Dante,' he says avoiding my question. 'Even *I* can smell the ocean on you.'

I huff, 'What's the weather like up top?'

'Stormy.'

The weather is affected by my father's temperament. If the weather is bad, Father's mood is still foul. That, or Zeus is angry and that too will lead to Father's anger. Either way, I lose.

'Do you know why he's so angry?'

'If he won't tell his son what's going on, he's hardly going to tell me,' Milos says. 'I'm a distant, distant, distant relative through marriage, Dante. Your father tolerates me at best.'

'He *tolerates* everyone lately,' I say.

Milos grimaces. 'He sent me to find you.'

I take a longing look at the ocean beyond the dome and sigh, 'Let's get this over with then.'

Tremors shake the marble as we approach my father's chambers. I wince at the sound of objects crashing within. An attendant, hurries out, flowing garments rustling as she sprints past us.

The doors blast open when I reach for the handle, Father's roar stilling my feet, 'Where have you been!'

Milo bows his blond head and escapes back down the hallway.

'*Coward*,' I hiss into his mind. He mentally snickers in response, before disappearing around the corner. 'Swimming,' I say aloud.

Father's nostrils flare as he inhales the smell of salt on my skin then snarls, 'Outside of the dome.'

'I didn't go to the surface.'

He hurls his trident across the room, spearing the marble with the glowing tines. 'You're hereby forbidden from leaving the dome, Dante.'

I resist the urge to roll my eyes, since I'm already forbidden to leave the dome. We both know I still do it. Like my father, I'm an aqueous creature. It would be cruel to enforce such a thing and he knows it.

He flings himself into an ornate armchair, too small for his muscular frame and rubs his temples, before reaching for a folded parchment. Gold light glitters from the broken Apollyon seal along the edge, something fluttering from between the pages as he unfolds the missive. I meet his green gaze, curious as to what the sun god wants.

He retrieves the object that fell and holds the long, golden feather up for me to see. My breath hitches because I've seen feathers like it before, only black instead of gold.

'It belongs to a god-sired Siren,' he says confirming my suspicion.

'There's another?'

'Yes.'

I lick my bottom lip before I ask, 'Is he yours?'

'You're the only Siren I've sired, Dante.'

I glance at the missive with the Apollyon seal. 'Apollo's then?' At Father's nod I ask, 'Is he free from Anthemusa too, like me?'

'He is.'

'When can I meet him?'

'Olympus knows the other Halfling inherited Siren abilities on their seventeenth birthday and they've been hunted for it since. I won't risk them discovering you, Dante.'

'This is why you've been so angry,' I say feeling betrayed. 'You've known for a while and haven't told me.'

'For your safety.'

'But this boy and I are the same,' I say plucking the feather from his fingers. Siren energy, prickles my fingers on contact and my insides light with ice. 'He has wings like me,' I say staring at the feather. 'Does he have Siren song like me too? Can he—'

'Apollo's child is his concern, not yours or mine,' Father says.

'But if I could just meet him—'

'No.'

'Father!'

'A god has freed two Sirens to hunt the Halfling, Dante. I won't risk them learning of your existence too.'

'I'll be careful,' I say, desperate. 'Nobody will discover what I am.'

Father's eyes glow neon with anger. 'You are confined to the palace grounds. If you want to swim, use one of the many pools within the dome.'

'But—'

'If I catch you outside the dome, I'll confine you to your rooms.'

The ground trembles against my anger as I match his glare. He glares back and I know he won't yield. The acid of my song, coats my throat and each inhale becomes torture. Darkness hazes my vision and I know it's my cue to leave.

I lock myself in my suite of rooms and take the golden feather from my pocket. Pain slices my shoulders as my wings unfurl, showering jet feathers across the floor. I hold one against the golden feather for comparison and find mine much longer, meaning Apollo's son must be smaller than me.

I try to picture him: seventeen with golden hair the same shade as his wings. His eyes might be black like the Sirens on Anthemusa or maybe, like me, they're the same shade as his father's. Just the thought fills me with desperation to meet him.

I place the feather on my nightstand before dropping into the sunken pool in the centre of my bedroom. I wait for my wings to dissolve in the water then climb out and tear off the remains of my ruined shirt. I pull on fresh clothing, tuck the feather into my pocket then leave to see my mother.

I stand in the little room and stare at my mother's beautiful face. Her expression is serene and inviting, making it difficult to believe she was the monster everyone claims she was. I touch her cheek, cold and unyielding beneath my fingers; forever set in stone by the gorgon's gaze. It seems a cruel way of keeping my existence secret and I spent hours as a child in this room, wondering what she was like when alive.

'You still come here,' Father says from the doorway.

'So do you, it seems.'

'I loved her.'

'I could've loved her too, if you'd let her live long enough for me to know her.'

'She would've killed you,' he says. 'I've told you many times, they lack the capacity to love back, Dante.'

I've lost count of how many times he's warned me of how vicious Sirens are. I was raised with stories of how ruthless my mother had been: of how she'd have killed me the moment I was born, had she been given the chance.

'Are you talking about Sirens, or women in general?' I ask.

'Any female that discovers what you are, will fear you, Dante.' He sighs, 'I know you think me unfeeling but I'm trying to save you pain.'

He believes what he's saying but I've spent my life in a luxurious prison, cut off from the world and its wonders. All because my mother was a monster. Father sired me with her though, so surely there was at least a sliver of good in her.

'Maybe I should just go to Anthemusa,' I say. 'At least there, I'll be surrounded by beautiful females for the rest of my pathetic existence.' I'd be exchanging one prison for another but at least my misery would have company. The beings around me wouldn't fear me for simply being what I am.

'A Siren's beauty is skin deep, Dante. Inside they are all monsters; something I found out the hard way.'

I wonder if he realises, he just called me a monster? It isn't the first time and won't be the last. I'm sure he thinks I'm immune to derogatory comments about Sirens by now and I know he doesn't include me when he says such things but it still needles.

I turn and eye the blue-green silk of his formal tunic. 'You're leaving for Olympus again?'

'I'm leading the ocean-bound search for the escaped Sirens,' he says then gives me a pointed look. 'I've told Milos to keep you company.'

'To babysit me, you mean.'

He rests his hands on my shoulders. 'I love you, Dante.'

I sigh, 'I love you.'

He smiles then disappears in a flare of blue light, and I retrieve the feather from my shirt. I stroke the silky gold between my thumb and forefinger. A ghost of Siren energy remains within, making me shiver as it sinks into my skin like an icy splinter. The need to find the other god-sired Siren, grows.

AUTHOR'S NOTE

Hello there!

I know a lot of you have been waiting for the next book in the Archaic Races series. I promise, it's coming. My to-do list keeps growing and the stories are keeping me up at night. But this is something I needed to do. I loved the Siren books when I first published them—they were my babies but my writing has evolved beyond that first publication. I read *Siren* again last year and it just needed a rewrite. I think this version is way better than the last but I'm biased. I wanted the characters to be more realistic and have more substance. I can't explain it, other than I think they were missing something before and I feel like they've levelled up.

I love the world I've built in this series. I'm going to rewrite the other books too and you won't have too long to wait for those releases, since rewrites aren't as chaotic as drafting new stories (she says hoping life doesn't get in the way). I *have* changed a few things to make them better though.

I hope you like them and thank you for your invaluable support. You've helped make my modest dream a reality.

Hannah

Get release dates first by signing up to my mailing list via my website:
www.hannahwestauthor.co.uk

Or, find me on social media:
Facebook: @HannahWestAuthor
Instagram: @hannahwestauthor
X (Twitter): @Hannah_E_West
TikTok: @hwauthor

For authors wanting to discuss collaborations, email me at:
hannahwestauthor@gmail.com

If you find a mistake in any of my works, please feel free to email me at the above address. It's hard being an indie author and, although my works have been edited and proofed over and over by more than just me, things get missed. Unfortunately, I'm only human—dang it, so appreciate your help. Just state the name of the book, chapter and what the mistake is.

Thank you!